ALSO

Wh

Wh

Rotten

This is a work of fiction. Names, characters, places and incidents are either the product of the author's imagination or are used fictitiously. Any resemblance to actual persons, living or dead, events, or locales is entirely coincidental.

Copyright © 2024 by Aaron Dick

All rights reserved. No part of this book may be reproduced or used in any manner without the written permission of the copyright holder except for the use of quotations in a review.

First Edition

Book Cover Design by oliviaprodesign

ISBN 978-0-473-73172-4 (Paperback)
ISBN 978-0-473-73173-1 (eBook)
ISBN 978-0-473-73174-8 (Kindle)

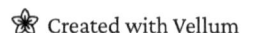

❀ Created with Vellum

THERE IS A STRANGER HERE

AARON DICK

This novel is dedicated to my mother Sue.
An endless well of support and love.

DRAMATIS PERSONÆ

RESIDENTS OF SHEERWALL CASTLE

Lord Iosef Uvaniah – Lord of Castle Sheerwall, keeper of the town of Blackriver and lands nearby.
Lord Alaks Oviosef – Heir to Lord Iosef Uvaniah.
Commander Mikel Ofeli – Captain of the Castle Guard.
Mata Ofeli – Mikel's wife. Lost to Red Lung.
Tuomas Ufmita – Mikel's son with Mata.
Zhon Ufioda – Second-in-command of the Castle Guard.
Zhuud Ovalak – A healer.
Marq Sulumon – An alchemist.
Sir Tadeus Ovyuda – A respected nobleman of Sheerwall.
Symin Ovyolia – Son of Sir Ovyuda.
Louka Ovanany – A friend of Tuomas.

CASTLE GUARDS

Luuk Oveslee – Recruits Master.
Andru Uviulius – Former Recruits Master.
Salom Uvyak0 – One of the Heir's personal childhood guards.
Zhameys Ovyams – One of the Heir's personal childhood guards.
Simeon Uvberil – One of the Heir's current personal guards.
Mari Ovyash – A recent recruit.
Pata Ufsurmin – A recent recruit.
Lefi Ufkloay – A recent recruit.
Miara Ufmari – A recent recruit.
Surman Ufilip – A recent recruit.
Matin Ofyosh – An experienced guard.
Akim Oftafid – An experienced guard.
Zhosh Ovsafi – An experienced guard.
Shorn Ufpita – An experienced guard.
Willam Uvsaara – An experienced guard.
Somin Uvmita – An experienced guard.
Pita Ovkloay – A former guard.
Nikolaas Ovlukus – A former guard.

RESIDENTS OF BLACKRIVER

Dafid Ufyeesab – The current kirkman of Blackriver.
Ulius Ufiames – Owner and bartender of the Gilded Rooster.
Simyn Ofati – A merchant. Uncle of Saara and Filip.

Zhosua Uvuuda – A merchant.
Salo Uvpater – Tuomas's childhood nursemaid.
Zhuda Ovioda – A boy from Mikel's youth.
Yosep Ovyuda – A boy from Mikel's youth.
Yulia Ufmalki – Mikel's maid.
Mattieu Ufiosef – An old man from Blackriver
Safi Ufpita – A young woman from Blackriver
Saara Ofseera – A young woman from a farm south of Blackriver. Filip's sister and Simyn's niece.
Filip Ofseera – A young man from a farm south of Blackriver. Saara's brother and Simyn's niece.

GUERSHAN MERCENARIES

Akub Ufpater – A mercenary. Andreus's brother. Pelep's cousin.
Zhonathin Ofilip – A mercenary.
Andreus Ufpater – A mercenary. Akub's brother. Pelep's cousin.
Pelep Uvanany – A mercenary. Akub and Andreus's Cousin.

RESIDENTS OF HIGHFORT

Lord Niko Ovyolia – A young lord, Safeera's father.
Safeera Ufneek – Niko's daughter.

PRAEMÈDE

It looked human, this thing pulling its legs through the thick, silty mud of the riverbank. Yet its movements were more graceful than a human would ever manage in such a place. The heavy muck slowed the creature's stride no more than a field of grass would have. With each step, thick mud schlucked aside. A thin film of water lay over the mud, darkly reflecting the pinprick stars overhead. The creature wound around rushes that sprouted in bunches from the slimy surface.

As the creature ran, ripples spread out behind it, following its passage and nudging the rushes so that they bobbed gently from side to side. Beyond the rushes, the broad expanse of the river Black drifted lazily, as though the water wished to be as asleep as the rest of the world. The creature kept moving, pulling its feet forward so fast that they left an open space behind them, outrunning the slow ooze of mud falling into the gap.

The creature paused beside a particularly tall clump of rushes. It leaned lower, resting its arms on its thighs, and turned its head from side to side, scanning the quiet landscape around it, searching the darkness for something. Air hissed through its frowning mouth and into its lungs. Insects chirruped from the plants nearby. Eventually, the thing's head ceased moving. It had found something that captured its attention as though a string bound its gaze. Lips parted, like a child that had found its favourite toy.

The creature dove forward and slung out its arms, using them to drag itself across the surface of the mud instead of relying solely upon its legs. It splattered through the water, droplets of dark mud scattering into the night as it moved. It scooped its hands into the silt and pulled, thin muscles standing out on its light frame.

Someone else was trekking through the mud by the river. Their breath wheezed loudly across the mud. They glanced around themselves sometimes, occasionally leaning closer to the river's edge as though searching for something. They struggled to turn as they heard the slap of skin on wet earth but the thing launched itself out of the darkness before they could lift their arms. The creature bore the person down, into the dark mud.

The person shoved against the creature's body, lifting it far enough to see what had attacked them. Their eyes widened in confused recognition before the creature reached out to their throat with one hand. It pulled and tore a handful of flesh and skin away from the person's neck in a single, fluid, sickening motion. The body fell limp into the mud and began to sink under its soft wetness.

The creature hunched over the body and set to work, tearing with its fingernails, using its teeth to sever skin from flesh. Blood stained the thin grass red and the movements of the creature flattened the reeds. Blood poured through the layer of water over the mud, curling out into the slow-moving currents of the river like a red cloud. One more shadow on the water, cast by a white moon in the black sky.

Before the blood slowed, the creature was finished with its gruesome task. It raised itself slightly over the body, though it remained hunched, and then set off through the mud and rushes once more. It left the ravaged body behind without another glance. The creature moved slower now, slower than it had while it was hunting.

It headed closer and closer to the river. Closer to the point where the riverbank fell away, and the thick mud vanished into the deep channel of the water. The thing stepped further into that darkness below the gently rippling surface of the river, slipping its body down until only its head remained above the water.

This part of the river Black bent around the massive stone walls of Castle Sheerwall as though trying to hold the castle in place. As though the stone edifice was something terrible that had to be restrained lest it escape into the world. Lights moved along the battlements far overhead, as the evening guards carried out their patrols. The creature glanced at the imposing walls on the far side of the river and then lifted its eyes up their sides to their heights. Its lip curled in a sneer before it dove beneath the murky water of the river. A bubble grew on the surface and popped. All was still.

CHAPITRE 1

"Cheer up Mikel!" laughed Lord Uvaniah as he lifted a dripping leg of chicken to his mouth and tore off a chunk. "There have been no truly worrying stories from the roads in months, and there is little you can do from here. I think you should enjoy your meal and be happy!" The old man's eyes sparkled between wrinkled corners. He scrubbed shiny grease from his lips and chin with the back of his hand.

Mikel Ofeli, Commander of the Castle Guard, sighed and shook his head. "Your son is out there too," he replied as he poked at the roasted potatoes on the plate in front of him. The warm buttery smell filled his nose. "Your heir. Surely some amount of concern is reasonable."

Lord Uvaniah laughed again, soft chuckles that bent him closer to his plate. Mikel could see the effort strained his friend. The hubbub of people talking in the great hall lowered momentarily as various nobles and important townsfolk paused to check on the condition of their lord. When they saw him straighten and smile at Mikel, they turned back to their conversations.

Mikel admired that the old man was able to continue in his duties, despite his advancing years. The Lord of Castle Sheerwall spent his days out in the town, in the lands he controlled. Always busy meeting the people who he had responsibility for, despite the weariness in his limbs. Mikel was younger than him, but still desired a sheltered corner where he could slouch against the wall during the day. If he was honest, he would prefer to simply return to his rooms and rest but he was conscious of the poor example that might set for his castle guards. Mercy's Shield relied upon everyone sticking to their duties.

"Yes, some concern is perhaps reasonable. But you go too far! I fear you will die of worry some day."

"So you say my lord, so you have always said." Mikel took a sip of his ale. The drink warmed him from the inside out. "But it is my job and my duty to keep the peace in the castle and Blackriver. I must keep Mercy's shield strong. Before you judge my temperament, do recall that you said I worry too much three years ago and then the Eastern Road became thoroughly unusable. I believe there were at least six merchants who braved the road and died that year."

"Oh Mikel." Lord Uvaniah rolled his green eyes and winked at his friend. The lord's chin was stubbled white and his fingers as thin as the chicken bones that he was returning to a plate in front of him. "There are always tragedies in the countryside. Why, we may hear tomorrow that the Far Off King declared war against any number of other countries! But as I eat this delicious dinner, he hasn't yet. And neither have any of your other ever-present concerns come to pass." Uvaniah licked one finger and then ran a tongue over his thin lips.

"In the meantime, the harvest has been excellent this year!

The flocks have bred well, more craftsmen have moved into Blackriver, new houses are being built all the time." He lifted a silver goblet that was filled with wine so dark and red that it looked like velvet had been squeezed into a liquid and poured into his cup. "The summer was beautiful, with birds flocking to the castle roofs. The morning chorus was delightful. Flowers bloomed along the paths that we walked this year." He looked directly into Mikel's eyes. "There is always tragedy somewhere, if we are so determined to seek it out. But don't forget that there is always beauty as well!"

Conversation buzzed around the two men. The great hall was filled for the evening meal, and Lord Uvaniah's extended family were seated throughout, among and between the various people who worked and lived inside the castle's gigantic walls. Mikel leaned back in his chair and looked around. The hall was huge. Its arched roof was held many metres overhead by a series of large stone columns. Torches set around the walls illuminated the huge chamber, as there were no windows, but the real source of light was found in three massive chandeliers hanging from stout black chains from the ceiling. The thick dark beams of wood holding them up looked as solid as the stone walls.

Heat radiated from the candles on those chandeliers, dripping their slow white wax, and combined with the heat from the large number of bodies squeezing together along the long wooden tables to eat. The effect was a room that was exceptionally warm. Many of Mikel's dining companions were wiping sweat from their brows and removing jackets and coats that had been needed to walk through the chill of autumn outside. The smell of molten wax and smoke filled the air.

The old man is right, Mikel thought. *There has been plenty to be happy about this last year.* A pain stabbed at his chest, and he frowned.

"I suppose I will simply be happier once Tuomas has made it home," he finally said, rubbing the back of his neck and sighing as he did. Lord Uvaniah nodded and reached out with a ladle to scoop three large soft buttery potatoes into a bowl in front of him.

"Of course, you worry for your son in such times. But be proud my boy! Tuomas has taken great care of my heir Alaks from all accounts, and they cannot be far from home now. They will be safely back in our presence before you know it."

The lord's words were meant as encouragement, Mikel knew. But still, after he said polite farewells to the lord of the Castle and retreated to his bedchamber, thoughts of bandits and wild animals and flooded rivers plagued his mind. He attempted to read for a short time, but gave up after he realised that he had read the same page three times in a row and still had no idea what was contained in its words. He climbed into his bed, blew out his candle, and sought sleep.

CHAPITRE 11

A memory of Tuomas grew in Mikel's drowsing mind. He dreamed of a day when he had taken Tuomas out on the river in a boat, when Tuomas had been only a small child. Tuomas had shrieked from his seat near the prow as the dinghy had pushed out into the current. The small child's soft cheeks had been pierced by a wide grin, and his eyes were bright stars. Mikel had laughed as the boat rocked slightly, bobbing into the river, each movement drawing new yells from his son.

"It's alright Tuomas, nothing is going to happen."

"Dad, the boat is sinking!" cried Tuomas, scandalised by Mikel's lack of concern. The small boy reached out as wide as he could to grab both sides of the boat at once. Mikel laughed. His sleeping body felt warm and safe as he recalled ruffling his son's hair and soothing the boy's nerves.

Mikel had rowed the boat further out into the middle of the Black. The shadow of Castle Sheerwall had fallen over them as they were carried downriver by the current, and Mikel shivered. It was so cold in the shadows that fell behind the castle.

Tuomas had stared up at walls that seemed to stretch higher than the sky.

"They make the whole world disappear." The child's voice was little more than a breath.

Mikel turned to look at the castle and agreed with his son. The walls were imposing and dark and reached so high that they filled up his entire vision. The sun was low behind the castle, so the walls were even darker than usual. Light seeped away from the walls, and Mikel felt colder and colder. He leaned back, trying not to let the edges of the walls move beyond his vision, and the boat tipped sideways beneath him.

There was a splash and he tore his gaze away from the castle to see Tuomas struggling in the water next to the boat. The small boy thrashed in the water, fighting to keep above the surface, but quickly sank down. His tiny hand stretched up, searching for something to hold on to. Mikel nearly fell into the water himself as he launched over to the edge of the boat and reached down.

"Swim Tuomas!" he yelled into the river. Tuomas' face was blurred by the water, pale below the shimmering surface. Mikel wondered if his son could see or hear him. "Swim! You have practised many times! Swim now!"

In the dream, Mikel watched from the edge of the dinghy as his son sank further down into the river, slowly vanishing into the murky water. He could feel his body twisting and turning in his bed at the same time, caught up in the blanket that had trapped his legs.

Mikel pushed himself upright in his bed. The room was dark and the air was still and stifling, though the sweat on his forehead was icicle cold. He groaned and pulled the blankets off in a rush, then climbed off his bed and stood with his head clutched in his hands.

What a nightmare, he thought. *Where did that come from?* He rubbed his face and moved over to the narrow window that looked out over a courtyard in the middle of the castle. *Tuomas is fine. Tuomas has always been fine.* Tuomas had been able to swim out into the deep water and back to the riverbank without trouble. He would splash through the water and then stand laughing and covered in mud. No expert, but certainly not a child that would slip beneath the surface as he had in Mikel's dream. Mikel wondered if the nightmare had been caused by some noise out in the castle grounds, something that had set him ill at ease.

Mikel moved to his window and looked out into the empty courtyard. Beyond his slim window, the castle was still and calm. A wide moon illuminated the grounds as clearly as daylight. Stars flickered in a quiet sky.

Mikel had spent a long time teaching Tuomas how to swim in the shallows of the river and there had never been a moment that Tuomas had fallen overboard like he did in that nightmare. Or had there been? Mikel grimaced and pressed a hand to his stomach. There was a burning sensation there that was rising towards his throat. Perhaps Tuomas had fallen into the river, and Mikel had simply blocked out the unpleasant memory? He shook his head. He couldn't remember for sure. Tuomas had grown so quickly. Those days were an ancient past in Mikel's mind.

But Tuomas was older now, a man, and he was alive and well. He was travelling with Alaks, the heir to Lord Uvaniah, and he had an important role in the heir's personal entourage. Mikel could be proud of his son, and confident in his well-being.

Mikel decided that he didn't feel like returning to bed. The chance of the nightmare returning to him and keeping his sleep from being restful was too strong. Perhaps some small night gods had crept in beneath Mercy's Shield and were driving sleep from him. Instead, he decided to move into his anteroom. Perhaps the cool air there would soothe his mind and he would be able to return to sleep before long. In recent months Mikel had spent more time than he had ever expected sitting in his well-cushioned chair in this anteroom.

He settled into its soft padding and stared at his low bookshelves. He picked at the velvety material that covered the arm of the chair. One foot bounced on the rug. For some reason, the normally comfortable room was making him restless. He felt the desire to get up and head out into the halls of the castle, as though he needed to go on patrol.

He remained in his chair as he considered. It had been a very long time since Mikel Ofeli, Commander of the Castle Guard, had patrolled the halls and yards of the castle. Realistically, he knew that he was too old now. His joints had stiffened with age, and he often had to massage cramps out of his hips if he was standing in one place for too long. His shoulder-length hair was no longer the deep orange of autumn leaves. Now the soft waves of his hair were spun with grey, and the short beard he wore held only a few speckled remnants of the colour he had been so proud of as a youth. What good would a man whose joints ached before a rainstorm be in the case of trouble within the castle? As he grew older, Mikel had realised that there was no way he could continue to chase the desperate men that the Castle Guards might find themselves up against.

CHAPITRE III

Mikel stared unseeing into the dusty ashes of his fireplace, a few tiny sparks still weakly glowing in the last few chunks of firewood. His memory provided images and sounds of chases past, of times he had clambered onto tiled roofs within the castle walls and leapt over the dizzying heights between buildings. He recalled the sound of his own breath panting from his lungs as he pushed himself further, faster, chasing some brigand who had dared enter the Castle. In his room, the older man he was now smiled as he remembered catching some of those men, and the punishment he had been able to mete out before dragging them away to await judgement from the lord of Sheerwall.

Iosef Uvaniah's father had been Lord of Sheerwall when Mikel was a child, and the boy had thought that man was hewn from granite, with blood as cold as ice. One of Mikel's earliest memories was of a man who had been caught after deliberately trying to unbalance Mercy's Shield over Blackriver by invoking malicious gods inside the village. As a child Mikel had been unable to comprehend why someone would deliberately invite such possible disaster. As he grew older he realised that the man had hoped to profit from the disaster he instigated, supported by the gods he had called upon. He understood the man's aims more clearly now, and was even more angry that anyone would do such a thing than he had been in the past.

Of course, the kirk could not tolerate such an imbalance and had taken the evidence to the lord of the castle. Lord Ufyona, the current lord's father, had agreed that such a betrayal of the whole town must be dealt with swiftly and with certainty.

The young Mikel had joined the crowd that made their way into the great hall to hear the Lord's judgement. The crowd was tightly packed, each person pressed shoulder to shoulder with those beside them. Mikel climbed up the wall, using the holds that elaborate decorations provided, and sharing grins with other children who'd had the same idea.

Opposite the main doors a huge seat had been prepared for Lord Ufyona, and he sat staring down at the man kneeling in chains before him. It was a strange thing, that chair. It was not the normal chair that the Lord sat in during meals in the great hall. Mikel remembered thinking that it must have been brought out just for this occasion of judgement.

Lord Ufyona described how the man had put the community in grave danger with his actions. He had unbalanced Mercy's shield by forcing the boundaries to cave in, rather than keeping danger far from the people of Blackriver. Just as the Kirkman explained during Sermon, disharmony amongst the people of the town forced Mercy to defend the people from each other instead of threats from outside. This man had raised even more serious and dangerous threats within the community, weakening the shield so much more.

But then the crowd had gasped as Lord Ufyona outlined

the deeds the man had summoned the gods to perform. Theft and mischief were expected, but the violence he had meted out against those he considered his rivals was terrible. Gods of anger, gods of stone and fire, gods of disease had all been escorted deep into Mercy's Shield and allowed to wreak their havoc. Mikel felt a chill in his bones when the Lord explained that one victim was likely to die from the injuries he had suffered.

There was quiet restrained anger in the lord's words, and patient revenge. Mikel's stomach turned to a ball of ice when the Lord pronounced that the man was to be hanged, and then the sound of the crowd's cheers had lifted around him and their emotions barrelled his own aside.

After Mikel had become part of the castle guard, and made his way into the upper echelons of the castle community, he had found that chair of judgement once. Tucked into a small storage room near the hall, covered in dust. Lord Uvnaiah had told him that it was cleaned and brought out only for the most dire circumstances, when the Lord had to put on a full show of his authority. Mikel had only seen it used two other times in his life.

Though Mikel had become friends with the new Lord of Sheerwall, and he knew that Lord Uvaniah was warm and friendly man, there was a pillar of stone inside the Lord as well. When needed Lord Uvaniah could be just as strong as his father.

CHAPITRE IV

Mikel sighed and pulled his heavy dressing gown closer around his shoulders. The vision of Tuomas slipping away from his hands was still hovering behind his eyes, and he couldn't quite shift it.

"It's no good," he growled to himself. "I can't just sit here all night. I have to do something."

He stood up out of the chair and hung his dressing gown back onto the stand in the corner of the room, then lifted a long blue coat from the rack. He ran a thumb across the hardy material and smiled, then spun it around his shoulders and dug his arms into the sleeves. The coat settled over his figure like a second skin, and Mikel shivered slightly. Mata had given him this coat years ago, when he had first been lifted to the position of Commander of the Castle Guard.

They had come back to their rooms after the ceremony in the great hall, his hand settled on the small of her back. Mata stepped forward and turned to face him, her back to the door to their room.

"Hold on a moment," she smiled.

"What's this?"

"I have a surprise for you, just wait." She reached behind her and opened the door, before slipping through and leaving him standing outside in the hallway.

Before Mikel could think too long about what might be going on, the door opened again. Salo, the young maid who they had asked to watch baby Tuomas, stepped out and smiled at Mikel.

"Do you know what she's up to?"

The maid nodded.

"It's a lovely gesture. Have a good night my lord." Salo bobbed a curtsey and hurried off back to her own rooms. The door behind her was still open, and so Mikel stepped forward and peeked through.

Mata was standing by the coat stand, lifting one sleeve of the blue coat. He walked over to her.

"What is this?"

"It's a present. You're an important person in the castle now, and you will be rubbing elbows with other important people. You won't be able to just wear any old thing."

She lifted the coat off the stand and helped him put it on. She stepped back to his front and smoothed the material over his shoulders and leaned up to kiss him.

"I'm so proud of you," she said. "You might even become close with Lord Uvaniah." Her eyes shone as she looked up into his face.

Mikel closed his eyes as he re-lived the memory. Then he opened them and forced himself to leave the memory behind and return to the waking world, the night he was living in now, where he stood by his coat-rack, alone. He patted at his clothes. He had been so tired when he got to his rooms that he had burrowed into his bed still wearing the pale shirt and trousers that he had been wearing during the day. With his coat on and his feet slipped into his boots, he was dressed enough for an evening walk. He crossed his room, opened the door, and stepped out into the corridors.

The cold of the night air slapped into his cheeks as he strode through dark hallways away from the warmth of his room. The air smelt of stone and dirt, with a hint os something metallic behind it. He walked without thinking of any particular destination. After turning at a few intersections, he realised that his feet had settled into the old familiarity of patrol. His body knew its routines, even though it had been so long since he had spent his nights following the duties of a guard, walking through the narrow hallways of the castle in darkness and silence of the night.

The courtyards always looked so empty during night patrol. Mikel remembered the way he would walk past the kitchens, looking eagerly for the soft glowing sign of their lanterns that would let him know dawn was only a few hours away. He would listen to the clatter of bakers and cooks beginning their work. On good nights, he might be given a warm but misshapen roll to chew on as he continued in his patrol.

After he was made commander, Mikel's life had turned into a series of meetings with other men in the Castle. He was responsible for organising more than just who was to walk through which halls, or stand before which doors. He had to ensure that all the new recruits were skilled enough to protect the inhabitants of Sheerwall and so he watched from high windows as they were drilled in the guards' yard, put through their paces and introduced to their wooden practice swords.

CHAPITRE V

Overlooking the yard in recent years, Mikel had become disconnected from the process. He hadn't grown to know the new recruits as he once would have, working alongside them and getting a feel for which guards he could count on when blades were drawn, or which were simply good for conversation during a long night's post.

He chuckled at his thoughts as he continued his late-night stroll. It had been nearly a year since he had even observed any training at all. He had left the duties of commander in the hands of his second, Zhon. He had realised that he was watching without observing. Mikel thought about the conversation where he had informed Zhon of his decision. The man had saluted as he came into Mikel's office in the guard rooms.

"Yes sir? You wanted to see me?"

"Yes, I did." Mikel had placed his quill down and leaned back in the chair behind his writing table. "Zhon, I don't know if you have noticed, but I..." His throat was dry and he coughed. He picked up a mug with water in it and took a slow sip. "I haven't felt like myself recently."

"Yes sir."

"What do you mean?" Mikel frowned. *Did Zhon think I haven't been performing my duties correctly?*

"I just meant that I understand sir. You've had a rough time recently. It must be very difficult."

Mikel brushed the comment aside and continued.

"It has, yes. But I cannot deny that I have not been completing my duties to the standard that I would like recently."

Zhon stood silently with his hands behind his back.

"I think that..." He sighed. "I think that I will need to take a step back from my duties, just for a while."

"I think that is a good idea sir."

Mikel forced himself to not to let his frustration show on his face. Zhon wasn't saying anything that didn't make sense, or was inappropriate, but Mikel resented him for it. *He doesn't have to be so keen to replace me,* Mikel thought. *No, that is uncharitable. He isn't forcing me out. This is my own decision.*

"Only for a little while, as I get my head in order."

Zhon nodded.

"I need the work, as a distraction. But I can't endanger the castle. The guards must maintain order, so that Mercy is free to Shield the people of Sheerwall and Blackriver."

"I understand sir. I will make sure to follow the example you have set."

I didn't even tell him that he was going to take over for me, complained Mikel to himself. *He might be Second Officer of the Guard, but maybe I had some other plan? Surely he shouldn't assume!*

Mikel stood and walked around his table, reaching out to shake Zhon's hand. *It doesn't really matter, Zhon will only be in charge for a few weeks, maybe two months at the most.* Then Mikel would feel back to normal, and would return to his duties as Commander of the Castle Guard.

That had been his plan, anyway. As he pulled his blue jacket tighter, Mikel realised that the conversation had occurred roughly a year ago. *And if it has been that long since Zhon took over commander's duties, then that meant that it has been nearly a year since-*

Mikel sniffed heavily and coughed to clear his throat.

His patrol had led him outside the protection of the castle's halls. He walked out into one of the many open spaces between the buildings that huddled inside the castle's walls for protection. The night breeze slid down the back of his coat. He shivered. Far over his head the sky was full of bright stars, but as he watched he saw thin fingers of cloud, hiding the stars as they grew. Thicker piles of cloud were beginning to form.

Mikel climbed the narrow stairs from the yard up to the heights of the battlements on the south wall. From here he was able to lean on the rough stone and look out over the town of Blackriver, nestled alongside the castle and spreading up the river like a dog curled around its master's legs before the fireplace. The town slumbered peacefully, safe and quiet beside the might of Sheerwall.

The town stretched away to the south of the castle like a cloak trailing behind a nobleman. A chill was creeping through his old bones now, and he had to keep flexing and clenching his fingers to keep the feeling in them. Even so, Mikel realised that it was warmer than usual for this time of year. When he had been unable to sleep earlier in the night, he had been quite comfortable while sitting in his chair. At this time of year he should have required gloves and a scarf to walk outside at night, if not more thick layers.

Memories tumbled through his head as he leaned over the

stone and stared out across the land. He had hoped that the walk would calm them down, and allow him to focus on something else. But they had gone nowhere, and now the empty night was drawing them out. His search had brought him to the tops of the battlements and he deliberately squeezed his palm against the sharp edge of the stones so that it would scrape across his skin, bringing his thoughts back to the present.

Across the farming fields that surrounded Blackriver, he saw the reason for the pressure in the sky, the unsettled feeling that must have given him those nightmares and kept him wandering through the castle. Thick black clouds spun and whorled towards the town. They rolled softly across each other like young pups playing before a fireplace. Mikel knew that it was a deception of the distance. By the looks of them the storm would be fierce.

Blackriver was a sprawling mass of pointed roofs strewn beneath him, thick beams supporting tiles and slate atop white plastered walls. The storm-threatened night had driven any townsfolk lingering in the streets this late back inside and only a few windows glowed with the fitful light of candles or fires. Mikel sighed and shook his head, wishing that a few candles in his room would settle his own thoughts at night. *Mercy save them,* he told himself as he studied the town. *Maybe Mercy actually will save us all.*

CHAPITRE VI

A lightning flash arced from the sky to a distant hilltop and was quickly followed by a long peal of thunder. Mikel lifted a hand to squeeze the bridge of his nose. *You're getting too old to be out on nights such as this old man,* he reminded himself. He shifted his feet in his thick leather boots. As he turned to go back to his rooms, his memories sought out warmer, happier times.

When Mikel had first joined the Guards of Castle Sheerwall, he had thought that his life could never get any better. He had done it out of a desire to impress a pretty young woman from Blackriver named Safi. Safi was the most beautiful person that Mikel had ever seen. She had large blue eyes that sparkled like the surface of the river on a summer's day. Just like the river, those shining lights hid the mischief and depth that lay beneath. Her high cheeks and small mouth had made the younger Mikel think that perhaps she was half-goddess, descended from the gods of flower and fruit and tree that old folk said lived in the forests outside Mercy's protection.

After he saw her laughing with her father when she delivered him a midday meal, Mikel had put that idea to bed quickly. Her father was a blacksmith and no man as craggy as the broken edges of the castle walls, or with hands as scarred by burns as her father's were, could be a god. To Mikel's young mind it had been even more unlikely that such a man could have ever had the fortune to fall in love with a goddess either. One of the man's eyebrows barely existed anymore. So Safi must have been as mortal as Mikel himself.

He had grown up in the same street as Safi and her family. He had watched her as she walked out to the market with her mother in the morning to pick up goods for the day. Sometimes he caught glimpses of her helping her mother take care of the small rooms that were theirs, sweeping or cooking, and he relished the brief moments when her bright eyes were looking out of a window.

Mikel hadn't been quite so helpful to his own parents when he was young. He spent his days running through the dusty streets of Blackriver with a gaggle of other small boys from the alleys, filching fruit from the market stalls until one or the other of them was caught and dragged by the scruff of their neck back to their parents, who would deliver them a sharp reminder of how young boys were supposed to behave. Mikel had in fact been particularly good at tapping the leg of the apple-trader's stall just enough that an apple would fall to the ground, all the easier for him to scoop it up and run away laughing and chewing the fruit's sweet crunchy flesh as he went.

As he had grown older he had seen Safi grow also. He had begun to notice the way she walked so smoothly and yet with curving grace while she strolled alongside her mother through town on their errands. He had got into scuffles with some of the other boys, arguing over who should get to talk to her. Unfortunately, he had never won any of those fights. He remembered sitting on the stoop of an unfamiliar building, nursing a bloody nose and watching as Zhuda handed Safi the bright yellow flower that Mikel had picked from the fields outside town.

As he touched his swollen nose and winced at the pain, Mikel noticed a member of the Castle Guard walking through the street. The man stood tall and straight-backed. His black and silver uniform looked clean and tidy. Everyone from the street paused as the man walked past, and Mikel saw more than one woman smile and tuck her hair back into place as the guard passed by. It was right then that Mikel decided he would have to find another way to impress Safi, something that no one else would dare to do. And from that day, he had tried to join the Castle Guard.

At first Mikel was simply laughed away from the gate to the Castle when he tried to join the guards. The two men who stood at either side of the large wooden doors looked so fine in their shining armour and long sharp spears. Mikel was a little surprised to see how coarse their faces were when he came close enough to see. For some reason he had expected them to look smooth and wise. Instead one bore an ugly red scar that jagged sideways along his cheek and the other's beard was short, rough, and spiky. With some trepidation he coughed until he had their attention.

"Excuse me, how do I become a Guard?" he said, wincing at the tremor of nerves he could hear in his voice.

The scarred man grinned, an action that twisted the scar into a new terrible configuration. His dark eyes had slowly travelled down Mikel's body, clearly amused by what he saw.

"You, lad?" He nodded at his partner at the other side of the drawbridge. "Hey Pita, look at this half grown rodent. He wants to know how to be a Guard!"

The man named Pita had laughed.

"I'll tell you how you can become a guard," said the first man, leaning forward on his spear. Mikel leaned away. "You can find yourself a wizard and wish to be one!" Both men roared with laughter at this joke. Mikel's cheeks glowed red as he turned and walked back into town.

Over the next weeks and months, he came back to ask again and again. At first the different men on duty had continued to joke at him, sometimes going so far as to prod him with the butt of their spears and comment on his small frame. But soon he began to glean advice between the humour. He began spending less time racing through the streets with his fellows and more time helping his father work the fields. Over time his muscles started to grow and harden. By working the fields, he earned a worker's meal too, filling out his frame further. It had meant that he saw less and less of Safi, but he had the pleasure of seeing her smile in his direction the few times they passed. Mikel was confident that his plan was working.

CHAPITRE VII

Finally a day came where Mikel asked how to become a guard and one of the men on duty responded with a frown instead of mockery.

"Well, I suppose we do have a bit of room in the bunkhouse right now. And we are expecting a few merchants over the autumn." Mikel knew that the merchants often brought guards of their own, mercenaries and bodyguards. These strangers could find ways to cause plenty of drunken violence before the Lord's men were able to deal with them. "Come on then boy, we'll see what Andru thinks." And within the day, Mikel was a recruit.

He had spent the first afternoon shifting his few possessions into the guard's bunkhouse within the castle walls, and dreaming of how his new position would help him win the heart of Safi. He began imagining visions of himself arriving in her father's smithy decked out in his official armour, bearing his official sword, and declaring his intentions towards her. She would swoon with the delightful heroism of it all and her father would grunt some form of approval. After all, nothing could be manlier than being a guard, charged with protection of the innocent.

Unfortunately, he soon discovered that there was more to being a member of the castle guard than walking around town with your chest puffed out, wearing your shiny armour. Instead there were days upon days of drills, performing the same repetitive sword movements over and over while standing in a line with the other twenty new guards and being watched over by old man Andru, the man responsible for them. And his armour would not stay shiny, no matter how long he spent scrubbing and buffing it. Mikel ended each day covered in sweat and grime, and choking from the rank smell of himself.

After a few months of tedium Mikel realised that he hadn't thought of Safi, let alone had a chance to talk to her, for weeks. The life of a guard was far too busy for such things.

Andru marched up and down in front of them, hands clasped behind his back while his shaggy grey moustache puffed against his lips as he bellowed commands. Mikel had been sure that the old man never actually looked at the recruits, a belief heightened by the scar that curled beneath Andru's left eye socket, leaving the instructor half blind. Yet any time one of them stumbled or failed to follow through with his blade the old man would leap sideways and swipe his meaty fist across the back of the poor youth's head. Mikel flinched at the memory. He had suffered that blow many times in the first year.

When the recruits weren't being trained to defend the castle and town, they found themselves performing the lowliest tasks that Andru could find. They would spend hours scrubbing the flagstones and steps of their quarters with heavy wooden brushes until they were clean enough to eat from, and then they would clean them all from the start again.

Mikel developed an intimate understanding of the elaborate system of pipes and tunnels that allowed Lord Uvaniah to wash and for waste to be carried away from his presence. Some of the tunnels were too small for him to squeeze into and crawl through, pushing piles of built up waste before him, but far too many of the recruits were just the right size. The putrid smell that leaked from the pipes made Mikel throw up many times, which just meant he had fresh filth to clean. But those too-small tunnels were always large enough for the rats and it was the rats that he spent his nights combatting.

It somehow fell to Mikel to clear the castle of the black and scraggle-furred rodents, setting traps and poisoned bait amongst the foul smelling stones of the waste tunnels. While nights spent chasing pests and clearing traps of the dead remains of their brethren left him exhausted, the new friends he had made amongst the recruits complained of worse jobs. Taking care of the pigs, including mucking out their dung-filled pens and providing the latest old rotten food from the great kitchens. Polishing the armoury's equipment to the satisfaction of Andru, a task which never reached its end, for the old man's one good eye was able to detect rust and specks of dirt that even an alchemist would have trouble confirming. Each had to be laboriously scoured away before the next item could be picked up, giving time for decay to build up on the other pieces and ensuring that they would take weeks to clean as well.

For months Mikel wondered if he had made the right choice. He couldn't understand why anyone would continue in the position of Castle Guard unless they were forced to. But everyone in the town knew that Lord Uvaniah was a fair man and would hold no servants in his castle who wanted to be released. A winter earlier there had been a man who suddenly developed a strong desire to go on a pilgrimage to a distant katedraal, though Mikel didn't understand why. They had a perfectly reasonable kirk in the town, a tall pointed stone building with bright colourful windows. Surely there could be no better sight elsewhere? But the man could not be dissuaded, despite being informed of the sure chance he would encounter bandits on the road. He had packed a sack with hard bread and cheese offered by Lord Uvaniah, set his face to the west and then strode off at dawn one morning. Mikel hoped the man had made it to the katedraal that he so desired to see.

CHAPITRE VIII

Lightning flared again, illuminating the clouds overhead from within so that the sky looked pale, bruised and smeared all at once. The endless rumble that followed within a breath indicated the storm must be almost on top of Blackriver. Mikel sighed and shut away his memories. *You were very young once upon a time,* he told himself, smiling again. *But not any more.* The sight of Blackriver laid out below him, sleeping through the oncoming storm, made him feel tense. His time was passing, but who would take over for him, who would protect these people?

Mikel lifted the collar of his coat against the rain as it began to fall, spattering heavily on the stones. The walkway that followed the battlements around the height of the walls was narrow and Mikel dared not run to get out of the rain in case he stumbled and dropped to the distant cobbled courtyards below. He remembered Nikolaas, a guard who had lost his life in just that manner, chasing a fool of a thief away from the lord's personal rooms.

Nikolaas had cried out from his patrol, rousing Mikel and

others from their bunks in the guardhall. They had rushed outside just in time to see their fellow guard fall, with only a single shocked shriek, before he struck the ground. The crack had been heard from all corners of the castle. Mikel had been first to Nikolaas's side, as other guards had continued chasing after the thief.

Mikel frowned. He couldn't remember whether the others' had caught the lad, though whether they did or not hardly mattered to him any more. Perhaps they returned some golden cup or pearl necklace, perhaps the boy got away with enough to trade for a few glasses of ale at a tavern. Maybe even a warm bed for a night or two if he had taken off with something especially valuable from some lord's bedchamber. But regardless of what happened to the thief that night, Mikel was left with the clear memory of Nikolaas lying on the cobbles with blood all around, his eyes staring up at the darkening sky, limbs twisted in unnatural directions. Mikel had been the one to reach out and close his friend's eyes. Later, Mikel had been the one who had to find Nikolaas's parents in town and let them know what had happened.

They had known already, of course. Blackriver was not so big a town as to allow gossip of that kind to pass unheard. But still someone had to do it officially. So he had stood at the tiny door that led into their home as Nikolaas's mother had cried into her hands and his father had awkwardly placed a hand on her shoulder. Mikel hadn't been able to think of much else to say, so he had said nothing. The funeral had been small, attended only by the guards and Nikolaas's parents. The Kirkman had mouthed kind words about Mercy's embrace and Nikolaas's good deeds. Mikel had thought of evenings spent dicing in the great hall with Nikolaas. Then it was over.

Mercy shelter me, Mikel frowned to himself from his spot on the walls of Sheerwall, looking down on Blackriver. *I am certainly in a black mood this evening!* He hurried as fast as he dared towards the nearest door that would lead him away from the rain. Ponderous drops grew heavier and the wind rose to a howl across the wall. Just as he grasped the handle to pull open the door to warmth and safety, Mikel heard a scream.

CHAPITRE IX

The scream slid out of the night air as quickly as it had arrived, but Mikel's instincts spun him instantly, searching for the source of the sound. His hand clutched at his side for the sword he seldom carried any more. Instead, the rising wind was all he could hear, strain though he might. Mikel waited, rain blinding him and dripping down his face and neck. He stood still as long moments passed, counting slow careful breaths as he did, before he told himself that it had just been his imagination.

Deep in his mind, the sound had reminded him of his son Tuomas. In the darkness of the night, his mind had mixed the memory of Nikolaas with Tuomas, and filled his thoughts with glimpses of his son's face, plunging through the empty air beside the walkway, plummeting towards the hard unforgiving stone below.

Of course it couldn't be Tuomas. Everyone would know when the travellers returned. Tuomas was part of the personal guard of the lord's heir, and they would not be permitted to sneak into the castle without full pageantry and celebration.

On top of that, Tuomas was no fool. There was no way he would have been on the roof in such a storm as this!

The scream came again, distant and faint this time.

Mikel grabbed the rough edge of battlements and leaned over the wall carefully, holding tight as the wind tugged at his shoulders. He stared down towards the river Black, lazily curling around the feet of the castle walls. A flash of lightning came to his aid and he saw two tiny figures standing at the edge of the water on the far side of the river. Clearly the scream must have come from one of them.

"I'm coming!" Mikel yelled, forcing his lungs to launch his voice against the storm, hoping that the two would hear it. He avoided thoughts of what might have caused them to scream, as there was little chance he would reach them soon. Despite his fears, he pushed himself to run along the battlements until he reached a door that led into the halls. He flung it open and raced inside in search of a flight of stairs.

Mikel caught glimpses of shocked faces as he pounded through the castle halls towards the gates. They were the faces of servants in the castle, still awake as they completed the work from the day before, or rising before midnight in order to get a start on their duties for tomorrow. A pang of guilt flashed through him as he thundered by and forced them to squeeze against the walls. But years of guard duties had been ingrained in his muscles, and he was responding in the only way he could, the only way that was right.

The only way to get to the figures by the water was to get to the Castle's gate, cross the drawbridge and then run back along the riverbank on the far side. He knew that it would be a long time before he reached them, and there was a good chance that he would not arrive in time to help.

As he ran towards the closed gates, he looked for the guards who would be on duty. He spotted one standing by the entrance to the gatehouse, and two more standing on the battlements overlooking the drawbridge. Their faces were familiar to him, but he could not remember their names. He used to know the names of everyone who worked for him.

The guard inside the walls recognised him and saluted, and then pulled aside the heavy wooden bar bolting shut a smaller door set into the huge gates, shoving it open for the commander just in time for him to sprint through. He heard one of the guards above call down to him "Sir? What's happening?" but there was no time to explain.

He left the warm glow of the torches that were lit around the castle grounds and pounded across the wooden bridge. *Thank the gods of sleep that the bridge is down,* he thought as he ran. A heavy curtain of rain fell across his vision. *The river will be rising,* he thought as rain washed down his face. He turned at the end of the drawbridge to follow the edge of the river in search of the figures he had seen from the walls.

The muddy banks were more waterlogged than usual. Heavy reeds slapped his face as he trudged through the thick silt. One of his old boots was still lost somewhere near here, sunk below the dark surface of the riverbank, after he had failed to tie its laces securely.

Grass whipped at his leggings, as he had known they would. He was thankful for the warmth the leggings provided, though they were already soaking up rain and river water. It was harder and harder to lift his legs high enough to step forward. *Mercy keep the gods of mud from pulling me down,* thought Mikel.

There was a clatter on the drawbridge behind him. Some of the other guards must have seen him racing through the hallways and decided to join him. *Good work my guards,* he thought proudly at first. *So long as none of the gatewatch left their posts,* he thought next. One of the people behind him called out.

"Commander! What happened?" Their voice struggled against the wind and rain. Blackness swamped the riverbank, leading Mikel to wonder if his companion would be able to follow safely. He kept running anyway.

"I saw someone on the riverbank," he hollered over his shoulder, not waiting to find out if his reply made it through the rain to the guard's ears.

Without warning Mikel nearly splashed into a deep channel of the river. The soft earth under his feet finally surrendered to the dark shifting water. Mikel floundered backwards to more stable footing and then stared up at the walls of the castle across the river. He was trying to remember where he had been standing when he heard the scream. He recognised the south tower, lifting higher than the walls at its sides in a squat rounded bulk, with a single light in one of its narrow windows like a guiding star above him. He had raced down that tower's stairs, so whoever had screamed must be around here somewhere.

The other guard caught up to him, sloshing through the muck to stand beside Mikel. The commander nodded shortly at him, taking in his face, before moving left alongside the river. *I should have guessed it would be Surman,* he thought to himself, pleased that he recognised the youth despite the rain and darkness. The lad was keen and good hearted, a fresh recruit, who had barely been with the guards for a year.

CHAPITRE X

In the mud at the river's edge, beneath the storm, Mikel moved slowly as he searched between the reeds and rain for any sign of the figures he had seen from the top of the castle walls. The rain was dripping from his nose and chin when he found a dark shape low in the reeds nearby. His gut twisted. Then the shape moved.

What river god is this, panicked Mikel at first. A moment more, and he realised that he was mistaken. The spatter of rain made it hard to hear, but Mikel was sure that the shape was crying. He stepped forward and saw a second shape lying in the mud. The first figure hunched over it, in a pitiable attempt to protect it from the rain.

"We are the Castle Guard! Who is there?" Mikel called out. The hunched figure turned towards him. A young woman's face met his eyes, her face slick with water and her eyes dark with tears.

Mikel waved Surman forward and instructed him to help the woman to her feet. The young man put an arm across her shoulders and leaned in to talk softly to her. Though she was still sobbing fitfully and erupted in wails sporadically, Surman began to soothe her nerves. *Good job lad,* thought Mikel. *Don't forget to find out why she is out here though.*

He turned to look at the shape the young woman had been covering with her body. His guts clenched and nausea rose in the back of his throat as he looked down. The shape was a body. Whoever they were, it was clear that they had been ravaged. *Did this woman know the victim,* wondered Mikel. He swallowed heavily and crouched down to examine the corpse closer. *Given how horrifying this is, maybe she didn't. Maybe it's just the sight of the blood that has upset her.*

The body had sunk deep in the mud, feet first, as though the person had stood still as the riverbank swallowed them. Wet earth held them tightly to their waist and from there the corpse bent backwards onto the wet surface, twisted further than any living skeleton would allow. Mikel's shoulder ached in sympathy, though the poor figure was clearly beyond the reaches of pain now.

He thought that the figure was male, a cursory judgement based on the remains of clothes hanging off their body. A tattered vest and shirt clung damply to spongy flesh, just the sort of thing that a hunter or woodsman might wear, durable leathers and cloth. *But if they are meant to be so durable, then how have they ended up looking like...* Mikel tried to think of anything he had seen in such a decrepit rotten state before, but failed.

There were surprisingly few large wounds on the body, which made its swollen flesh all the more disgusting. The body had soaked up water from the marshy bank, swelling up like a pale fungus. Mould had begun to grow, blackening its white skin, and small creatures had taken the opportunity to feast on as much exposed meat as possible. Runnels and tears crisscrossed the bulging surface. But it was the face and hands that turned Mikel's stomach.

The skin had been taken from both, stripped entirely to expose red and white muscles beneath, though the red had leached out of them in the damp, leaving just thin shining white ropes of tendon. No eyes remained in the skull, just cavernous holes that looked blacker than tar in the stormy night. Rain ran in waterfalls across the intact dome of the skull, layered as it was in strips of pink stringy flesh, the jaw barely connected and hanging lop-sided below the nasal hole. Teeth tilted in the jaw, no longer held in place. Mikel held his breath and leaned in. As he had thought, there were claw marks gouged into the exposed bone. Edges of skin hung torn and ragged from the corpse's wrists and neck, thin and fluttering like silken handkerchiefs. Mikel wondered what sort of monster could have done this.

He turned to Surman and the woman, grateful to be able to distract himself from the nightmarish scene.

"Are you alright?" he asked the drenched and still sobbing woman. She looked young and Mikel's throat tightened in sympathy for her pain. Her eyes were red.

"'No," she began, before bowing her head, unable to continue. Mikel shook his own then looked at Surman.

"Were you able to get anything from her?"

"Her name is Saara. She lives with her parents on a farm to the south of Blackriver. I don't know what she's doing here."

Mikel looked around the riverbank as he thought about what he had found.

The storm was upon the three of them fully now. Wind whipped their clothes tight against their bodies, sleeves sliding up and down their arms, and the rain pressed against them as though it were a person, trying to shove them down into the mud and rising water. Lightning splintered the sky every few minutes. The lights from the castle were difficult to see.

Mikel glanced at the body wedged in the mud and shuddered. Even though it looked as though the body had been lying on the bank for a long time, he found himself wondering if whoever or whatever had killed the poor man was still nearby. Was the noise he had heard simply Saara's cry of discovery? He had thought he saw more than one figure moving. The idea made his blood run cold, colder than the wind.

"You take the girl inside to the great hall," Mikel told Surman. "Get her set up in front of the fire so that she can dry out. And send someone to get whatever warm food they can from the kitchens. Once she's calmed down a little we'll ask her some questions. In the morning, once the storm passes, we'll get her back to her parents." Surman nodded and then paused, turning his eyes to the body.

"I'll stay here and make sure nothing else happens to it. Send some guards to come and help me carry it inside. See if Marq will allow us to store it in his rooms."

CHAPITRE XI

Marq was the castle's alchemist, and he had the privilege to occupy a large network of rooms, much more than anyone else in the castle. Not only did he require rooms to eat and sleep in, but he commanded half a dozen young apprentices as well, who also needed lodgings.

Then there were his workrooms, filled with strange glass bowls and bottles that bubbled in unnatural colours and gave off beguiling scents. Mikel was sure that somewhere within that confusing warren of workrooms there would be a spare bench to store the corpse on. He just hoped Marq would not make too much complaint at the imposition.

Mikel hunched his shoulders beneath the rain and huffed warm air out of his mouth. Thankfully the guards Surman had sent out arrived before the cold and damp leached too deeply into his old joints. One brought word that Marq had acquiesced to Mikel's message and that his apprentices were preparing a space in the alchemist's rooms for the body. Mikel's shoulder ached and he desperately wanted to go inside. He needed a fire, to dry and warm his old body. However, duty had other jobs he must complete before he could tend to his own needs.

Mikel supervised the moving of the body and watched while one of the young guards, a skinny youth with a sharp nose that must have been broken earlier in his life, threw up into the river. The youth wiped his mouth with the back of his sleeve and looked sheepishly up at his commander. The rain plastered his long soft blonde hair down against his skull. "Sorry sir," he began before Mikel waved his apology aside.

"I understand boy, I do. Now let's get this thing inside. I want to try and figure out who it was. Some family in Blackriver deserves to know what's happened to their boy."

The assembled guards tied ropes under the corpse's armpits, and then stood to either side and hauled, in an attempt to pull it from where its legs were rooted in its squelchy prison. Another of the guards began gagging when the corpse's flesh gave way exactly like a chunk of wet bread. Mikel covered his mouth as the young men handed out shovels that they used to lever the legs up, gouging into the soft muscle of the body as it began to rise to the surface. They slung their ropes into a sling and covered the body with a blanket that they had brought for this purpose. Then, they carried it inside. Mikel followed the disquieting procession, making sure that no horrific pieces of flesh fell to the ground and might be left to terrify the occupants of the castle.

In the alchemist's rooms Mikel was joined by Marq at one side of a broad table inside his labyrinthine chambers. This room of Marq's was one of the most easily accessible to the rest of the castle. It faced out into a courtyard near the great hall, but was usually kept clearly separated from the rest of the castle by bolted and barred wooden doors. A series of windows were built into the wall high over the door, in order to allow light into the room.

Morning had arrived somehow, without Mikel's permission, and now the sun's illumination was trying to push through the remaining storm clouds that hung overhead. A greyness was all that entered the chamber, and the two men looked at the body that lay before them with the aid of tall thin white candles.

Somehow the dead body looked less threatening now, laid flat on a wooden tabletop, with cold light slowly filling the chamber. Last night, in the wind and rain, with an hysterical young woman panicking beside him, Mikel had known that the thing was a bad omen. The blackness of the night had clustered tightly behind his shoulders and his nerves had frayed almost to the point of breaking. He had expected the body to sit up and point a bloody hand accusingly at him, or for some beast to launch itself from the shadows, all teeth and claws and pain.

But now, in the morning, he was just looking down at the results of another accident, something he had done many times before. Each time, he felt deep sorrow for the family that would be left behind. He knew this poor boy here had suffered something terrible, but at least his suffering was over as travelled beyond Mercy's crossroads.

The body's flesh sunk down towards the table it lay on, as though it was melting off the skeleton. The rain had washed away a lot of the brighter blood. The gaping eye sockets that stared up to the ceiling from the tattered skull's face still twisted Mikel's stomach though. A dead body was supposed to have its eyes closed. They were supposed to finally be allowed to rest, safe in the embrace of Mercy's Shield. Was this boy still expected to carry the burden of expectations and duty that life piled upon people? Did no one ever get a chance to put life's woe aside?

"How long do you suppose it had been there, half buried right under our walls?" Marq's voice was high and thin, just like the alchemist himself. He had one hand clutched at the front of his robes and his eyes were wide but not scared. Mikel knew that the alchemist had seen the nightmarish results of alchemical experiments amongst his apprentices from time to time. The ruined figure on the table was not far outside his experience.

"I don't know. It looks like it has soaked up a lot of water, so I would have thought it had been rotting there for quite a while. I can't imagine how no one had stumbled across it earlier. Do you have any thoughts?"

The alchemist pursed his lips. "I would agree, but I can't guess how long it would have needed to be stuck there to decompose so thoroughly. You say the blood was redder than this until the rain washed it away?"

Mikel nodded, but then grunted and shrugged. "I think so. But it was night, in a rainstorm, and the sight of the poor boy gave me quite a shock. I don't know if I was seeing what was truly in front of me."

Marq reached forward and pressed one finger against the corpse's side. The flesh left a dent that did not fill in again. "I'm going to say it must have been there for at least a month. I don't think we can be sure of that, but it seems reasonable." He wiped his finger on his dark green robes unconsciously. "How long will you need to leave it in my rooms?"

"Just until we can find the family and arrange for them to come and pick up the body."

"And if you can't?" The alchemist raised an eyebrow. Mikel turned aside from the question, scratching at the grey beard under his chin.

"I guess if that happens then we'll just have to ask the Kirkman to bury the poor soul anyway." The empty eye sockets stared at Mikel. He left Marq standing by the table and strode out of the room. The other tables in the room were lined with alchemical equipment. The smell of sulphur swirled around him, pinpricks of light twisted and flaring in the glass baubles that lined every surface. Mikel's head cleared as he stepped out into the grey drizzle.

CHAPITRE XII

Mikel avoided thoughts of the kirk as he walked through the soft morning rain towards warmer rooms. But funeral memories clambered forward anyway, uncaring of the way his stomach twisted or the pain that seized his chest.

Mikel had stood outside the kirk in Blackriver for hours after Mata had died. The Kirkman had come to see him when he arrived, but their conversation was brief. Mikel had told the Kirkman of his loss, and that Mata would want to be brought to the kirk for her contemplation before burial. The Kirkman had nodded sadly. He had stretched out a comforting hand to lay on Mikel's shoulder. He had expressed his sympathies and enquired as to whether Tuomas was bearing up well after the news. And then he had sighed and told Mikel that he would not be able to allow Mata's body into the Kirk.

"What?"

"My responsibility is to the people of Blackriver Mikel," The Kirkman had said, meeting his eyes with his own sorrowful gaze. "I must ensure that Mercy over Blackriver is not strained and stretched too thin. You of all people should know how difficult it is for Mercy when the troubles of people grow too large, when we do not take our responsibility for each other seriously."

"I don't-" Mikel's voice caught in his throat. He was stunned. Would the Kirkman really refuse Mata? "But she was devout, she came to Sermon every Resting Day."

"Yes Mikel, I know" soothed the Kirkman. "She knew the rituals as well as I do. I am sure that she would agree with me. After all, she knew what condition she would be in after she passed on."

Mikel could not bring himself to respond. The Kirkman had said something else, some pleasantry, but he didn't remember what it was. He had stood still in the street outside the kirk, trying to process what he had heard.

The Kirkman, the man whose who life was centred around the well-being and protection of the people in Blackriver, who ensured that Mercy's Shield was not distracted by the petty quarrels of the people, that man had declared that he would not accept Mata into the kirk. And why not? Because Mata had suffered and died, leaving behind an imperfect body? Somehow this imperfection would offend Mercy, would cause its Shield to be withdrawn?

Mikel's anger blossomed and grew inside him as he stood in the street, looking up at the spire on top of the kirk. He let it stretch itself out inside him, tingling down his shoulders and arms and right out to the tips of his fingers. Then he stood until the anger faded away before he turned and walked back to the castle. He had learned something important about the kirk, and it was a lesson he would hold on to firmly.

For instance, if the family of this poor boy could not be

found, Mikel would need to ensure the boy would lay in the kirk for Contemplation and then burial. He might need to lie to the Kirkman about the condition of the boy's body in order to achieve that. It was much more damaged than Mata's had been. But if that was what was necessary to do, then he would. If Mercy could not welcome such a person's soul to strengthen its shield, then maybe Mercy was not as valuable as the kirk had always taught.

The great hall was mostly empty at this hour of the morning, but a few people had risen for their morning meals already and a fire had been lit in the grand fireplace. The fireplace took up a huge pit in the centre of the hall and the beaten bronze hood above it was like another pillar, reflecting light from the torches around the room's distant walls. The smell of cold ash lingered.

The hum of conversation lessened as Mikel entered the room, and his skin tingled as he imagined every eye fixed upon him while he crossed the floor to where Surman sat with Saara.

Surman had done well, finding a bowl of some sort of stew for the girl, and he was now lifting a spoonful of the hot meal one mouthful at a time to her. Her eyes had lost focus and she was staring across the huge room at nothing on the opposite wall. Her skin looked pale and Mikel wondered if she was going to faint. He pulled up a chair to sit next to the two young people and leaned closer to catch the girl's eyes with his. Around them conversation was slowly restarting, echoing hollowly at first in the cavernous hall before building to a faint murmur.

"Hello miss. My man here said your name is Saara, is that right? How are you feeling now?" The girl barely moved. Her eyes were looking at him, but he thought that might be more due to the fact that he sat in line with them than any deliberate action on her part. Mikel sucked on his lower lip for a second then turned to Surman. "Have you managed to get any more out of her?"

"Not really sir," answered the young guard, placing the spoon back into the bowl in his lap. "She fell asleep as soon as I found a bed for her, and she only just woke up a little while ago. One of the kitchen girls shared her mattress last night. I thought it was best to let her recover."

Surman's face grew tense and Mikel realised that the young man wasn't sure if he had acted rightly. He nodded and gestured to show that he agreed with Surman's actions, but that he wanted to hear more.

"I'm letting her warm up and then I thought I'd put her back in the bed until we are ready to speak with her. She hasn't spoken since we came inside though. I think the sight of... it... really shook her up." They both looked back at the girl, wondering if mention of the body would spark some sort of reaction in her. Nothing.

"That's alright," Mikel leaned back and knuckled the small of his back. "I was heading to bed before all this happened and now I've been awake for the whole night. I'm going to try and get some sleep now, before anyone sees me and decides they have something important for me to do. She may as well try and do the same. But if anything happens relating to Saara or what we found, send for me straight away, alright?"

"Yes sir."

Mikel rose and smoothed down his shirt. His back was aching and his right knee had a twinge in it every time he placed weight upon it. He knew that he needed some sleep to allow his bones a chance to rest, before he added new pains to them. But at the same time, he was more alive this morning in this hall than he had been in nearly a year. His thoughts turned to his son Tuomas, on his way across the country with the Lord's heir.

The few early risers in the hall saw his forehead crease, and his lips slid down into a frown. They could see that he was not happy about something, and they looked at the young woman with wet hair hanging down her face and they gossiped.

CHAPITRE XIII

After a long sleep, the afternoon sky that greeted Mikel when he woke was bright and blue. Only the faintest streaks of pale clouds far overhead interrupted the endless azure expanse. The last trails of the storm had passed as he slept. Mikel dressed and thought about the events of the prior evening. His head was still bleary and he rubbed his cheeks frequently, trying to wake himself. *Clearly you can't expect to remain awake so long, through so much excitement, without suffering the consequences anymore old man,* he told himself.

He stood at his window, looking out at the drawbridge and across the river to the town of Blackriver. Tiny figures crossed the streets and waved to one another, ducking into shops and houses. The occasional squawk of their chatter managed to reach him, even high and distant as he was in the castle. Then, trying not to search the horizon for a sign of his son returning, he set off to the hall for some food.

The hall was full of people now. Workers were coming in from the end of their day's work, and those who would be working through the night were beginning to prepare themselves. Mikel saw some of the young guards who had helped him in the night, and he could see by their bleary eyes that they must have slept through the day as he had. Some servants were taking the chance to grab a bread roll and some cheese from the tables before heading back out into the halls to continue their chores.

Mikel found a seat near Lord Uvaniah's high table and gathered a handful of small sausages from a platter nearby. He bit a piece off one and chewed, savouring the flavour. It was strong and spicy and he sighed as he ate. He hadn't had any food since dinner the night before, seated at this same table. His stomach growled at this recognition, and he grabbed a few more of the sausages.

As he chewed, Mikel searched the crowd for Surman or Marq, wondering what news the day had in store for him. Thankfully, he didn't have to wait long before he saw Surman walk in, guiding Saara to a space at a table with some of the laundry workers. They all leaned over to fuss over the young woman, but Mikel did notice that she was answering their questions now. *Perhaps a quiet day with Surman to watch over her has done her good*, he thought. Surman looked around the room and Mikel waved, beckoning the guard over.

"So, what news?" he asked Surman, offering a plate of cheese as the boy sat down next to him.

"Only a little, though it is tragic," answered Surman, taking a piece of crumbly yellow cheese and biting off a large hunk. "It seems she was out searching for her younger brother. She is fairly sure that the body we found was his."

Mikel clucked his tongue and shook his head. "I feel for her. No wonder she was so grief-stricken when we got to her. But from our perspective that is good news. At least now we know where he came from. Perhaps we can piece together what has happened here."

"That's just it, there's something strange about her story. She says that her brother is named Filip and he had been away for just about a year. He had set off with an uncle of theirs, a merchant, to try and learn something of the world, perhaps pick up some skills. He came home a few months ago. Ever since then he's been hanging out with some of the rougher men in town. He's been offering to carry gear for some of the mercenaries as they pass through; she even thinks he's begun an initiation into the Guershan."

Mikel frowned. The Guershan were a group of mercenaries that he had tried to remove from Blackriver for years, without any luck. Lord Uvaniah found them simply too useful in times of trouble, when bandits grew more determined or word of war began to spread. At times like that, being able to employ a group of hardened men who were familiar with their swords was worth all the gold that could be gathered. But in the meantime there were always at least a dozen of them living around the town, drinking their gold away and scaring many of the townsfolk with their leers and rough habits.

If Mikel had thought that the Guershan were more impressive than the Castle Guards when he was a boy, he supposed he might have attempted to impress Safi by joining up with them instead. He thanked Mercy that he had gone to the castle. Looking back, he had come to recognise that the Guershan had given him signs that they would have welcomed another body in their force when he was a boy. A few nights, not long before the Guards had finally allowed him to join, one or another of the Guershan had seen Mikel at a tavern and bought him a drink. The Guershan had listened to his boyish talk and innocent jokes, laughing as though he were one of them. *To be honest,* Mikel thought as he sat with Surman at the lord's table in the castle hall, *I absolutely would have joined them if the guards hadn't let me in. Maybe that's why the guards had finally relented?* He would do the same now. Better to have a guard who was not perfect, than one more of those thugs wandering around Blackriver.

Mikel scratched his chin. "Don't the Guershan mark anyone who's joined up with them?" He recalled that some of his boyhood friends had ended up with a tattoo and left Blackriver amongst that band. He realised he didn't know which of them, if any, had ever come back. The life of a mercenary could be very swift. The more experienced mercenaries often took enthusiastic boys along with them to carry equipment and to run to the front of any danger. It allowed for those experienced men to remain experienced rather than dead.

Surman nodded. "Yes, they do. They usually get a tattoo of a dog somewhere on their body, I think."

"Well, let's make sure this thing was Saara's brother. Let's go see if it has a tattoo."

CHAPITRE XIV

Mikel and Surman stood from the table and headed out of the great hall through the afternoon crowd. Mikel listened to the rise and fall of conversation around them and wondered what they were talking about. He used to sit with his own friends in this hall, and discuss the news of the day. What would the hall be discussing today? Did anyone here know about the horrible thing that had been recovered from the riverside? Did they look at Saara and wonder why she was given such attention? Did anyone know her?

Another thought crept into his mind as they walked. When had he last taken the time to talk about the day's events with his friends? He looked to the west of the hall, where the long table he used to share with a few others who had entered the Castle Guard around the same time as himself would often sit with a joke for one another, playing cards. The table was empty. *It's just the early afternoon, they're probably all still at their day's tasks. I will try to find them tonight,* he reassured himself.

Mikel saw that he and Surman were about to walk past the

launderer's table at the end of the hall where Saara was sitting. The men and women from the laundry were joking and smiling, and some even reached over to touch her shoulder in a comforting gesture. Though he could see that the young woman met the eyes of her new companions and her mouth did seem to be moving as she spoke with them, Mikel got the impression that she wasn't sure what to say to these people. They were mostly elderly men and women, heavily wrinkled from years working in the steam, with hands as soft as cream.

Mikel turned to approach the table, smiling at the launderers as they burbled pleasant afternoon greetings to him. As they lifted their hands in well-wishing gestures Mikel noticed how red and wrinkled their hands were. He could see the glint in their eyes though, like the eyes of an eagle who has spotted a rabbit cavorting across a field below. These workers had nothing to do while they spent hours with their arms elbow deep in boiling soapy water; nothing to do except talk. Every tale that whispered through the shadowed hallways of the castle seemed to have its origins in those laundries and he didn't want to provide more fuel for their fires than was necessary.

"Excuse me, Miss Saara?" Mikel motioned for her to shift closer to him at the end of the bench. Then he leaned in close enough that the workers wouldn't be able to hear his words. He knew that this secrecy would only cause a different set of rumours to be spun and left drifting on breezes throughout the castle, but it was better than the inhabitants of Castle Cragismesa hearing the truth and panicking. "Do you remember me?"

Saara turned and looked at him. Her eyes widened and she nodded. It made Mikel very aware of how young she must be. Her eyes looked like a child's, ringed by thick lashes and with hazel irises shining damply. The corners of her eyes were still red and bloodshot, and Mikel knew she must have spent much of the day sitting in the corner of the laundry crying. *It was probably the best place to keep her,* he thought. *All that steam should have hidden her distress. Hopefully we can seek out the cause of this gruesomeness in time to forestall panic. Well done Surman.*

"Good. I was wondering if you could just tell me your story? I want to make sure Surman told me everything he could." The girl frowned and swallowed, then looked down her lap. However, before Mikel could carefully repeat his suggestion, she nodded. She lifted her eyes back to him and nodded again, then looked around the great hall. Mikel followed her gaze. The room was becoming busier. Figures now crowded the tables all around them, and the noise was spiky and rising in the air. Voices burst above the tumult and then dove beneath the surface of the cacophony again like fish leaping from a river.

"Could we go somewhere a little quieter," she asked in a soft voice. Mikel nodded and held out a hand to help her up. She started slightly at his movement, but quickly reached out to take his hand and rise from the table. The launderers all called out best wishes and smiled for her, but she barely noticed.

Together Mikel, Surman, and Saara left the hall; following a stream of people who had snuck in for an afternoon meal but still had tasks to do. Plenty of others ate and remained behind in the hall, ready to meet friends and family as they came in over the evening, sitting and spending time in each other's company. There was a swell of noise from behind them as the three left the hall's doors and rounded a corner. Mikel knew that Lord Uvaniah must have shuffled in, with smiles and waves for everyone.

Mikel led Saara through the halls until they found a small empty room that would suit a more private conversation. It held low shelves with folded fabric, and a table to one side bore dusty scissors and pins. A canvas figure with no head and no legs resting in the corner of the room. For a moment Mikel flinched. The torso with its arms extended made him think of bodies he had seen in the past, and he was concerned that Saara might take fright from it. However, it must not have resembled the body in the marshes, as she walked into the room quite calmly.

CHAPITRE XV

There were a few stools and chairs spread around the room. The canvas figure stood as though in the middle of a lecture, looking over the assembled furniture. Dust hung from the ceiling, caught in flimsy strands of spiderweb and lightly covering every surface. A waist-high wooden cabinet stood against the wall on their right. Mikel assumed it would be full of threads and strings and all the other tools necessary for the repair of clothes. He hoped no tiny gods had set up hiding places in this disused room.

Mikel and Surman sat down on two of the low stools while Saara moved to the far wall where she stood by a tall narrow window that illuminated the room. Despite the golden sunset outside, it was dim in here where they waited for the young woman to speak. Mikel assumed that when it was in regular use the room would be lit by plenty of lanterns. It would be nearly impossible to sew in such a shadowy space otherwise. A brief inspection showed that there were plenty of iron hooks set into the wall to carry lanterns and Mikel's pride was satisfied.

"So," Mikel began carefully, not wanting to set off the girl's grief again. "Surman tells me that you were looking for your brother last night." From the way she pulled in a tight breath and then set her shoulders, Mikel could see that Saara was gathering her nerves now. She must have had time to settle her emotions and stomach, helped by the warm geniality of the launderers. He motioned at the chairs, hoping that she would join them.

Saara nodded without turning to face him, but didn't speak. She looked out the window, which outlined her figure in a golden aura. It made her look like something out of a dream, her face touched with bright light and the rest of her figure hidden in gloom, while pinpricks of light drifted around her as dust caught the setting sun. Mikel wondered what she saw beyond the window. As she offered no answer, he decided to press on.

"He also said that the boy had been hanging around with the Guershan. Is that so?"

"Yes. My brother Filip came home with a thirst for adventure." Her voice was stronger now that they were alone, but Mikel could hear how brittle that strength was. The wrong word could shatter her reserve in an instant.

Saara turned from the window and looked at them both. Mikel could see the events of the last evening had worn themselves into her face over the day. Thin lines traced across her forehead and the sides of her mouth. Though she was still young, she would carry a hint of the maturity that had been forced upon her last night forever. Her eyes had the gaze of those who had seen how fragile life truly was, and how little separated the laughter and love of life from the raw blood and emptiness of death. She would likely never forget the sight of the body and its memory would haunt everything she did for the rest of her life.

Thinking of how this horror would affect Saara brought Mikel to mind of his own first encounter with unnatural death, from his time in the Castle Guard. He had been barely twenty, only just considered skilled enough to take a short evening patrol by himself. Some fool had decided to try and sneak into the castle and steal some valuables from a noble's room, and had the misfortune of backing out of the doorway directly into Mikel. The man had spun and his face had blanched with shock before he took off down the hallway. Mikel ran after him, quashing the impulse to yell out while he was still in the halls, alongside the sleeping chambers of the inhabitants of the castle.

The man dashed around corners, always managing to keep a finger's breadth from Mikel's clutches, until he reached a broad empty window and jumped through it. There was a narrow tiled roof not far below the ledge, and Mikel's stomach had plummeted through his body as he dutifully clambered after the thief. Starlight made the jewelled necklace in the thief's hands sparkle.

But before Mikel could give chase, the man stumbled and slipped, and then slid down the tiles, pulling a few off as he grappled for a handhold in order to save himself, finding only a second to scream before his voice was cut off by a sickening thud as his body struck the gravel below.

Mikel had cautiously peered over the edge, keeping his balance as he peered down at the twisted body below. He had muttered a plea to any nearby gods of sky or roof to keep his feet firm and then, with a dry mouth, and his heart racing, he climbed back through the window into the halls and made his way down to the yard.

No other guards had arrived at the thief's body before he got there, and so he retrieved the jewels from where they lay near the thief's outstretched arm. Blood spread out from the cracked body, legs twisted beneath it. Mikel had closed the thief's eyes before seeking out other guards to help him deal with the body, but the memory of those sightless eyes staring up into the night sky, above a human figure twisted like string, haunted the young man's dreams for months. Mikel realised he had become used to such sights in his time as commander.

CHAPITRE XVI

"He had always been such a quiet boy, spending most of his time at the kirk performing Vindication," said Saara, shaking Mikel out of his memories and returning him to the present. "We thought it unnatural for a boy so young, that is why we sent him away with my uncle Simyn." She paused and drew a deep breath. When she didn't say anything else Mikel wondered how long she would be able to speak about her brother. He motioned for her to continue, worried that if he spoke himself that he would break the quiet moment that had allowed her to speak.

"Uncle Simyn has been a merchant for many years, and a good one from the stories he brings us, and the fine clothes he always wears. He agreed to take Filip on one of his trips, so that my brother would learn more about the real world. We decided to give him a present, something to show him how proud we were of the journey he was to go on. My father commissioned a silver locket for him, and we got one of the artists on Long Road to sketch the whole family on a tiny parchment that could be kept inside the locket. He treasured that locket in the weeks before he left." Saara smiled weakly at the memory. "He would open it and reveal the sketch to anyone who made eye contact with him on the street, no matter whether he knew them or not. It didn't leave his neck, not for a moment. But when they came home a few months ago he was like a different boy. " She paused again, clearly remembering the moment.

"He had always been so gentle before, but when he got back he was so angry. He argued with my mother all the time. He threw a mug at her when she asked him to clear up after dinner. When I looked into his eyes, it was like he was someone else."

Saara bowed her head and Mikel could see a tear on her cheek reflecting the dying light from the window. He stood, but she raised a hand in his direction.

"I'll be alright. Thank you for listening, I hope you find out what happened." She turned to look at them both. "Filip went missing about a month ago. He had told me that he was going to meet with someone from the Guershan at the Gilded Rooster and then he never came home." Her eyes were wide as she looked at Mikel. "You will find out what happened to him?"

"I will try my best," answered Mikel. He was uncomfortable at the idea of saying any more than that, though the girl acted as though she took his vague promise well enough. "Do you know the name of the man he was intending to meet?"

"I think his name was Akub."

"Good. Thank you." Mikel stood and motioned for Surman to stand also. "Surman, take this girl home to her parents. Let them know that we will send word if we can discover anything."

Mikel remained in the small dark room after the others had left. He found the cool quiet gave him space to think. He moved to the window and looked through it, wondering what Saara had been looking at. The window faced out over the river, lying below like a black ribbon that had spilled out of its basket. The drawbridge was just visible if he pressed himself closer to the window and peered along the side of the castle. He turned and sat down again, running a hand through the dust that lay atop the drawers.

Mikel understood Filip's family, though he had never met them. His own experiences with Tuomas as a young boy had been similar to the way Saara had described life with Filip. He had been concerned about his own quiet boy who did not know how to talk to others. He had worried that his own boy would not know what to do with himself as he grew older. That was why he had encouraged Tuomas whenever there was a chance that he would make new friends.

Mikel remembered when Tuomas had been not much more than ten, and had come running into their rooms at the end of the day, bubbling with excitement.

CHAPITRE XVII

"Father father, we went into the orchard and we stole some apples!" The boy's face was shining.

"Stealing?" Mikel couldn't have his son stealing from the townsfolk. If any of them found out that the Commander of the Castle Guard was raising a thief, it could be a disaster.

"Only from the orchard," chided Mata. "I am sure Iosef won't begrudge a couple of apples to some growing boys."

Mikel frowned. He didn't like it when his wife used Lord Uvaniah's name so casually.

Mata stepped forward, while brushing her hair. "And who is 'we' my dear?"

Mikel supposed that the orchard was a little better than outright theft. Technically the apples would have been harvested and sold for Lord Uvaniah by one of the local farmers, but all the children in Blackriver would nip over the fence and grab an apple once in a while. It was part of life. Still, it would have been better if Tuomas could hold himself higher than the other children. Mikel realised he had missed part of Tuomas' answer.

"- said we should grab one each and so we did! I jumped all the way over the fence and we didn't stop running until we got back to the drawbridge!"

"How delightful," said Mata . She smiled over their son's head at Mikel. "Don't you think dear?"

"Surely," Mikel replied, unsure what exactly he might be agreeing to. "Who did you say encouraged you to do this?" Mata rolled her eyes at him, but Tuomas didn't notice. The boy turned around and shrugged.

"I think his name was Yosep?"

"Do you think that you will see Yosep again darling?" asked Mata. "Perhaps you two could go exploring the town together?"

"I don't know. He said he couldn't come in the gate, so we didn't plan to meet again, and I don't know where he lives."

Mikel's jaw tightened. One of those disreputable youths that were forbidden from walking through the gates into the castle! Blackriver was full of them, and Mercy knew those sorts of youth were not the sort that Mikel wanted Tuomas learning from.

"Probably for the best," he said.

"Mikel," admonished Mata. "Don't you think that it was nice that our son made a friend, and one who encouraged him to move about outside our rooms, instead of sitting inside away from the sun and reading all day."

Mikel's cheeks grew red. Those were indeed the sorts of concerns that he and Mata often confided in one another regarding their son.

"Yes, well done Tuomas, lovely to see you getting out and about."

Tuomas was clearly trying to not make faces at his father's

comment, but his thoughts shone through clearly to Mikel anyway. Mikel could see that his son didn't believe or trust the encouragement that was intended in those words. Instead, he was judging his father, and finding him wanting. It made Mikel's stomach tighten. What should he have said? Wasn't he just repeating exactly what Mata had said, and yet the boy was clinging to his mother?

Mikel coughed.

"All the same, I wish you'd find some of the castle children to explore with instead. You know that those are the children you will grow up with. They're the ones you will be working alongside once you are adults grown."

"Yes da," sighed Tuomas. Mata frowned at her husband. Mikel shook his head. There was no way to win.

Another time Mikel had looked down from the wall's in the middle of a bright summer afternoon, and caught sight of Tuomas playing alongside the river with another boy. As Mikel watched, the two had waded into the dark water up to their knees and splashed water at each other. Then they had returned to the riverbank to throw mud at one another, before wading back out and washing off the mud.

That night, Mikel had asked Tuomas about his new companion.

"You were watching me?" asked Tuomas, looking down at the plate of food in front of him. The hum of conversation in the great hall meant Mikel had to lean in closer to hear his son.

"Not on purpose. I was doing my rounds and happened to look over the edge of the wall, and I saw you both."

Tuomas just nodded.

"What's the boy's name?"

"Symin."

"What is his family like?" Mikel speared a heavy golden

potato and lifted it to his mouth. Tuomas was still looking down at his plate. "Tuomas?"

His son pointed across the hall. "Over there."

Mikel followed his son's finger and saw a long table near the far side of the hall. He was able to recognise the young boy sitting next to a tall man who Mikel assumed must be the boy's father. The boy's golden hair shone in light of the torches of the hall just as brightly as it had under the sun that afternoon. His cheekbones were fine and high, and he smiled and laughed with the others seated near him.

"Isn't that Sir Ovyuda?"

"I think so."

"My goodness." Mikel kept looking at the man as he chewed on his dinner. Sir Tadeus Ovyuda was a very respected man within the castle community. He advised Lord Uvaniah on trade deals and had helped improve crop yields for the farmers of Blackriver through his studies and careful suggestions. His wisdom was rewarded with wealth, and he was sought after for advice in many fields. "That's a fine companion you have found!" He clapped a hand onto Tuomas' shoulder. "Yes indeed! You should do what you can to stay friends with young Symin."

But Tuomas had barely mentioned the boy again, realised Mikel. What had happened there? Had Tuomas behaved rudely or disrespectfully to Symin? It wasn't likely, but the loss of such a potentially powerful friendship must be part of why Tuomas had failed to find a place in the castle society. If only he had grown into as responsible and decent a young man as Surman had. Mikel remembered when Surman had joined the Castle Guard.

CHAPITRE XVIII

Mikel had watched Surman's inspection in the exercise square, standing by the crowd of recruits lined up before sergeant Luuk. The man marched backwards and forwards in front of them, leaning in closely to stare at first one then the other. Mikel could see their faces sweating even from where he stood at the far side of the square. These young people had been told to stand straight and still as they were inspected, and they were doing their best to remain still, though an early spring sun blazed down from directly overhead. Mikel had been through this himself when he had joined the Castle Guard, and he remembered thinking that it was a waste of time when he stood there. As commander, he knew that it served a purpose now.

Luuk was not cruel. He wouldn't force these recruits to stand longer than they had to, but he also knew that some of the recruits might falter in the heat, and tire of the tension in their muscles. These young people would not be suitable as guards, though they would be told to go home kindly. Luuk knew how to look over someone's muscles and joints the same way a master stablehand knew to look over a horse. He could spot a weak knee that would develop into a limp faster than the recruit's own mother might recognise them as they walked into their home.

"You there, what is your name?" barked Luuk at a tall thin woman with dark hair.

"Mari," she replied, keeping her head straight and her back straight. Her hands were stiff at her sides.

"Very good. Why did you decide to volunteer for the guards?"

"I want to make sure my family is kept safe, sir."

Luuk nodded. "It's the guards' job to protect the castle Mari. We don't always have the time or people to take care of Blackriver."

Mikel smiled slightly. Technically what Luuk was saying was true, and it was a good way to find out how determined a recruit was. Sometimes they sighed, shook their heads and asked to leave when they were told this. Those recruits were always sent on their way as requested.

But the truth was murkier than the craggy old man's statement implied. Lord Uvaniah absolutely expected Mikel to use his people to ensure that the town was kept orderly and safe. After all, if they didn't then Mercy would be fully occupied with Shielding the townsfolk from one another, unable to protect from bandits, envious lords, or hostile gods. The only other power that Lord Uvaniah could control came from the nobles and soldiers that reported to him from other towns outside Blackriver's Mercy. But those people would be concerned with their own homes, too far to help in day to day affairs. Still, Mikel commanded the Castle Guard, and that made some difference to how he could operate.

Mari was determined to join however, and she remained in

line. "I understand that sir. Playing a role in the lord's safety will extend Mercy to the whole town."

Mikel nodded. Stability and protection. Lord Uvaniah showed the way from his hall, and the town followed. The Kirkman helped guide them through their difficulties, and through all this, Mercy maintained peace in Blackriver.

"And you, what is your name?" Luuk asked another of the recruits. This young man was struggling not to let a wide smile break out across his face, and Mikel could tell that he was shivering in excitement, even from far away.

"Sir, my name is Surman sir!" The young man was practically bouncing on his toes.

"And what made you decide to join us?" Luuk asked Surman.

Mikel's second Zhon had whispered next to him, breaking his concentration on the conversation amongst the recruits. "Sir, do you need to stay any longer? Luuk has the inspection in hand, and I'm sure there is a lot of paperwork that will need signing to admit these youngsters."

Mikel sighed. Paperwork. Sometimes he was sure that was all he had to do anymore. "You know that I like to see the new recruits Zhon."

"I do sir, but you have seen them now. What more is to be learned?"

Mikel looked at the twenty or so young people that were lined up on the far side of the square. He drew a long breath and then nodded slowly. "I suppose you're right. There isn't much else to see here."

The two walked away from the square through the hallways back to the Commander's office. Zhon opened the door for him and then sat in the chair that was in front of Mikel's desk. Mikel groaned and shuffled uncomfortably as he settled into his own.

"Alright, what do we need to look at?" Mikel asked his second officer.

"These papers." Zhon moved a stack of sheets over towards Mikel. "The details of each of those recruits, and the oaths that they agreed to. Once you sign the sheet, they will be admitted into the Guard if they pass Luuk's inspection."

Mikel sighed and lifted a quill, dipping it in an inkpot. He had grown up in the alleyways, never thinking that he would need to learn his letters, and now all he did was scratch the quill across sheets, leaving his mark.

Mari, he read as he signed her sheet. She seemed like a promising one. He would be interested to see how she did during training. Pata, a young man from a farm to the north. Miara, the daughter of a tailor in Blackriver. Surman, the enthusiastic boy from the square. Mikel smiled as he signed Surman's sheet.

"What makes you smile sir?"

"That young man, Surman. He was so excited, like a puppy! I wonder if that enthusiasm will serve him well here with us."

"Hopefully so, sir." Zhon waited a moment before speaking again. "And how is your own boy doing?"

"Tuomas? Oh I don't know." Mikel paused, with the quill resting on the edge of the inkpot. "He just doesn't seem to have anything that drives him any more. He stays in our rooms most days, and if I force him to go out he just walks along the river and mopes, throwing stones at frogs."

"Didn't you used to take him to the river often?"

"Yes, when he was small. I had to make sure that he could swim, of course. Growing up by such a river, I would have been a terrible father if I had left him unable to save himself from drowning!"

"Yes," agreed Zhon.

"Anyway, I think it is mostly because of his mother's illness."

"Is she doing any better?"

"No." Mikel's chest felt tight and he swallowed thickly. "She is very weak, and she spends most of her time in bed, resting."

"I'm sure that is for the best." Zhon was trying to put on a sympathetic face, but it only made Mikel's face feel too hot. The commander looked back down at the paper's in front of him.

"I hope so. By Mercy, I hope so."

CHAPITRE XIX

Mikel sighed and pushed a hand through his hair, blinking as he looked around the sewing room. He had more important things to consider right now than to let himself be overwhelmed by memories.

A dead body, and most signs indicated that it was the remains of this boy Filip. But why had it been so horribly disfigured? He considered the Guershan. Rough men certainly, and willing to allow a boy to die in battle if it meant their own skin remained whole, but he hadn't thought they would murder someone who was trying to join their number. Perhaps they might crack someone's jaw in the tavern, or a quarrel might go too far and someone would end up dead, but that was only the typical violence of hired muscle. It was horrible, but it was direct and easy to trace. The violence done to this body he had found was clearly unnatural, stuck deep in the river mud, with its face and hands skinned.

Mikel was glad that the girl had recovered as well as she had. A day in a warm safe space surrounded by friendly faces, even if she felt upset and withdrawn, must have restored her constitution somewhat. He was pleased to know that the people of Sheerwall were behaving in a way that would allow Mercy's Shield to endure. It would help keep people safe until he found out what had happened to Filip.

Mercy knew he had spent enough time tossing and turning during his rest. He kept picturing the empty eye sockets staring up into the rain, bloody water pooling and overflowing from the skinless face. His stomach turned and he swallowed hard. *What has Marq managed to find,* he wondered, forcing himself to ignore his stomach and head into the halls.

Outside the sewing room, Mikel made his way past servants moving through the passages on their own errands. Some carried tools away for storage, others had arms full of dirty linens ready for the laundries. The sight reminded Mikel of his own maid Yulia, who would likely be gathering up the linens from his room for cleaning right now. He smiled to himself and shook his head. Would the Mikel who shivered through dozens of winter nights in the guardhouse bunks have believed he would live in his own rooms one day, or a servant whose only job was to keep those rooms clean?

Yulia was a wonder, and often tucked a bed warmer between his sheets during the winter. It wasn't that the bed got particularly cold but it felt even more empty when he slid into sheets that had not been warmed. Mikel paused in the hallway and frowned, the expression furrowing his already lined forehead, and darkening his eyes. A young serving-boy was carrying a basket of candles towards him. Mikel didn't notice as the boy paled and turned to take a different path to his destination. Mikel shook himself from head to waist. *My bed is nothing to dwell on right now! There are more important things to consider this evening!*

Marq did not answer the door himself but one of the older apprentices welcomed the commander into the workroom where the body had been kept. Mikel was recognised as one of the few outsiders considered trustworthy enough to walk through the workroom unsupervised. Most of the castle's inhabitants would try to run their fingers along the smooth glass surfaces of elaborate devices that were setup across the benches. This seemingly innocent action could apparently completely ruin tasks that might have taken weeks to set up. Mikel found it hard to contemplate both ends of that interaction.

How could someone spend so long preparing these delicate instruments, and preparing such small and unusual samples to be processed through them? What insights could possibly be found here? And yet, looking at the strange coloured liquids that bubbled and hissed through the thin glass pipes winding across the tables, he was equally confused as to why anyone unfamiliar with these things would risk touching them. His nose wrinkled at an unpleasant and unfamiliar smell rising from the alchemist's materials. Mercy knew Mikel wanted to keep a safe distance from it all.

He looked into a clear flask that was full of a bubbling orange liquid, thick globs of the stuff bursting and flinging themselves at the sides of the vessel containing them. Mikel leaned away from the flask. He was glad the substance was well contained. A cluster of apprentices scurried in circles around each table, making notes on large sheets of parchment and staring intently at coloured liquids that bubbled and fizzed. Mikel didn't understand any of it.

Marq was standing next to the corpse on its table when an apprentice guided Mikel over to join him. The alchemist was dressed for sleep, though it was still early in the evening. He wore a long sleeping gown with a thick shawl around his shoulders to stave off the chilly air. Mikel stood next to the tall man, but Marq made no sign that he realised the commander was there until Mikel cleared his throat.

"Goodness!" The alchemist spun and then smiled, pressing his hand to his chest. "I didn't hear you walk up." His robe was green, held around his thickening belly with a bright yellow sash. Marq never let you forget that he came from warmer lands to the south. The locals of Blackriver tended to wear simple woollen clothes spun and knitted from the flocks of sheep in the fields and hills that surrounded the town. In contrast, Marq always made sure to purchase silks and linens from the travelling merchants, sometimes spending more than Mikel could comprehend for a bolt of this or that material. When asked why he didn't just wear the same clothing as the people around him, as it would be easier and cheaper, the stout man would smile and tap the side of his nose. "That is something only a few would understand," was generally his answer. For some reason Mikel didn't think that he meant other alchemists.

"Have you managed to discover anything new?" he asked.

CHAPITRE XX

"Not much. We did find this mark." Marq pulled aside the worn, old cloth he had draped over the body.

Mikel wondered if the cloth was to protect the body from the experiments going on in the chambers, or to hide the body from the sight of passers-by. The cloth was torn on the edges and singed holes peeked through to the darkness underneath. Clearly it was a spare piece of cloth that the alchemist had used to clean up his caustic substances from time to time. Mikel wasn't sure whether it was suitable to cover someone's body. Beneath the cloth were the remains of a person, and it sounded as though that person had been loved in life, and was now missed. The grime of this cloth hiding that body felt disrespectful.

Marq bundled up the cloth in his arms, unveiling the body that the commander had recovered last night. The day had not been kind to the remains. As they dried out, pieces had begun to slip and slough off, falling into chunky piles on the tabletop around the torso and limbs. Mikel's throat clenched and he coughed to try and keep his bile down.

"Here, you see?" said the tall alchemist, pointing with his free hand. High on the body's thigh was a smeary black mark. Mikel bent closer to study it better. It appeared to be a tattoo roughly the shape of a wolf's head in profile, though exposure to the river water and sun had smudged the ink. It was now more like a particularly strange bruise than a tattoo.

While he was looking at the mark on the corpse's thigh, Mikel also checked if the locket that Saara had mentioned was around its neck. It wasn't. *As I thought.* Mikel was sure he would have noticed such a thing while supervising the body being moved. However, he had to check, just in case. *It doesn't tell us much about the identity of this body,* thought Mikel to himself. *The girl did say that he had been acting angrily recently. Perhaps he threw it away, or left it behind. Perhaps it had simply fallen off sometime before we found his body. So much for identifying the boy that way.*

"The girl who found this said her brother went missing about a month ago. And that he was trying to join up with the Guershan. Do you think this could be one of their tattoos?"

Marq nodded. "Yes, that timing makes sense. As I said, the damage to the body makes me think it has been slowly decomposing in the mud for a few weeks now. And I agree that this could be a Guershan mark. But it is quite unclear." He reached out and prodded the mark on the leg. Mikel shuddered and reached out to pull Marq' hand away from the corpse. The other man glanced at him, with eyebrows raised.

"It's just a body now," he said. "This isn't a person any more than the table it lies on is a tree." He slapped his hand against the solid surface of the table to emphasise his point. Mikel shuddered as droplets of clear liquid bounced out of the puddles around the corpse. He shook his head at the alchemist and then refocused his attention on the damaged tattoo.

"There aren't many others who mark their skin like that around here," murmured Mikel as he straightened. "Surely this mark is from the Guershan." The two men looked at each other. Mikel exhaled and broke the silence first.

"I've sent one of my men to tell the boy's family we have his body. They'll have to speak with the Kirkman to arrange for it to be buried decently. Would you make sure to see him sometime soon? I don't want him to think that the body is cursed or anything, you know what a tempermental old fool he can be."

Marq' lips slipped into a slight smile. Mikle could tell that he remembered.

The Kirkman of Blackriver was old and, although his name was thought to be Dafid, no one used it. Instead, everyone called him by his title. He had been trained by the last Kirkman, as was traditional, and he had taken over the weekly sermons after the old Kirkman had died. By all accounts he did a good job of tending to the sick and ministering to the needy and was generally held a good example to all in Blackriver. However, he had a certain view of what was correct behaviour and could become prickly and annoyed, especially when it came to the rituals of the kirk. Some of the younger boys would deliberately inflame his anger by slouching around the back of the kirk during sermons or traipsing mud onto the holy building's clean smooth stone floors. The Kirkman would descend upon them in an aged fury, his thick white beard bristling and his small blue eyes stabbing out above it. His voice still had power to it, and people in far corners of Blackriver would smile to one another as his bellows echoed through the alleyways.

The Kirkman had spoken loudly during sermon about his desire to bar the door to latecomers on Resting Day. Some of the congregation would joke that the bar was intended to keep them inside for the duration of the sermon, winking at each other and making snoring sounds, rather than to keep out latecomers. Either way, closing the door to the chapel at all was an action that no kirkman would take. The door had to remain open to all, at all times. Still, the Kirkman would make his displeasure with late comers clearly known. Mikel and Tuomas had gone to go to a Resting Day sermon only slightly more than a year earlier, and the Kirkman had stormed out of the doors to stop them on the street. He pointed a long gnarled finger at them both.

"You lousy ungrateful children!"

The Kirkman referred to everyone as children. Once when Mikel was himself a youth, he had heard the Kirkman call Old Man Ovandra a child for speaking during the sermon. The grandfather had sat shocked in his chair until the end of the sermon. So it was not surprising that he called Mikel and Tuomas this either. "The kirk is here for your benefit and yet you scorn to treat its rituals with the respect they so deserve, arriving so late yet again! Get out, get out, go away!"

Marq knew about that day. He had sat with Mikel later in the great hall, listening to the commander complain all through dinner and well into the night afterward. Of course, though the Kirkman was certainly a peculiar old man, that barred door had not really been what upset Mikel. He had missed the chance to spend a morning seated with his wife, when his duties so often kept him busy on Resting Day.

There. The thought had reached the front of his mind. His wife. Mikel's eyes grew hot and his throat tightened.

CHAPITRE XXI

"Thank you for your help with all of this. If you will excuse me Marq?" The alchemist nodded and Mikel turned before the concern in his friend's eyes could be voiced. Mikel strode quickly from the room and down the hall, looking for a private space. He climbed the narrow spiral stairs at the end of the corridor until they came out at the top of the South Tower.

From here he could see to the end of the world. Fields unrolled across the gentle hills that surround Blackriver and the Castle Sheerwall. Wind caught at his clothes and against his eyes, forcing him to squint. Tears began to creep out and down his cheeks.

Mikel leaned on a battlement, ignoring the dizzying drop to the earth beyond. His thoughts swirled around a memory of Mata coming to his office to ask him to join her at sermon.

"Are you busy?" she had asked, sticking her head into the commander's office. Mikel frowned and moved the paper he had just signed onto a stack to his right.

"Why, what? Busy?" Mikel picked up a new sheet and

passed his eyes over the first line three times before blinking and lifting his gaze to his wife at the door. "Sorry, what?"

"I was just wondering if you were very busy," repeated Mata. "But it looks like I am disturbing you. I'll leave you to your work."

"Thank you," said Mikel and then he coughed. "No, sorry. What did you need?" He put the papers face down on his desk. "I'm just a little distracted with these patrols, there aren't enough guards to fill each position properly and I'm having to do some juggling."

"I get it." Mata bit her lower lip as she contemplated some thought and then she came to a decision. "I was going to ask if you would join me at the kirk this morning for sermon."

"The kirk? I suppose I could. What time is it?"

"Sermon starts in a little less than an hour."

"So soon!" Mikel's mouth fell open and he made some frustrated groaning noises. "Even walking across town to the kirk will take a while." He gestured at the papers on his desk. "I really need to sort this out though."

"That's okay," smiled Mata. "I'll find you this afternoon."

"I'm sorry sweetheart," said Mikel. Mata blew him a kiss and then left, pulling the door shut behind her.

Mikel turned over the papers and read the list of patrols there. He pulled another piece of paper from a pile and examined the list of names on it. Time passed as he painfully copied the names from one paper to another and then cross checked the new lists with his previous work.

Eventually he leaned back in the chair, pressing a knuckle into his aching lower back.

Surely that will work, he thought to himself. He glanced out the window, trying to judge the time of day by the brightness of the sky. *Can I still join Mata,* he wondered to himself.

"Zhon," he called. His aide walked into the office within moments.

"Yes sir?"

"Could you please check the new patrols for me. I think they will manage for now, and I need to go to sermon and meet my wife."

"I'll let you know if I find any gaps that we might need to address," nodded Zhon.

"Thank you."

Mikel stood and savoured the tingling feeling in his legs as he strode out of the office, through the Guard's quarter and out of the castle. He had been sitting for too long, and his muscles needed the use.

Mikel noted how quiet and beautiful Blackriver was as he walked through the sunny streets. Children chased each other while traders and townsfolk smiled at their shrieks and laughter. The river sparkled under a high bright sun. Mikel found that he was looking forward to sermon. He would walk into the kirk, find Mata and they would sit together, hand in hand, while the kirkman told stories of Mercy and the gods of the land.

When Mikel arrived at the kirk, the large doors were slightly ajar, as usual. However, as soon as he touched one of the doors, pushing it open so that he could walk inside, the hinges squealed like a pig being slaughtered. The rows of pews, filled with devout kirkgoers, all turned to look at him. At the front, standing behind his lectern, the kirkman paused in the middle of his speech and glared at Mikel.

"Well?" asked the kirkman.

Mikel coughed to clear his throat and hurried down the pews, looking for Mata. She was four rows from the front, and he squeezed his way down the long wooden bench seat until he could sit next to her. He mumbled apologies to the men and women who had to try and pull their legs out of the way in order for him to fit through.

The entire kirk was silent, his footsteps and excuses the only sounds to be heard.

He reached over and took his wife's hand, squeezing it.

"I made it in the end," he whispered, just as the kirkman shook his head and resumed sermon.

"Yes, I noticed," said Mata with a small smile.

Sermon continued and Mikel found it as boring as he usually did. The kirkman was talking about Mercy's shield protecting everyone in Blackriver, and how they must all treat each other well so that Mercy was not wasted by shielding them from one another and leaving them vulnerable to the gods of the air and land outside Blackriver. Mikel picked at the crud that had built up under his nails as he nodded along to the speech.

Then the Kirkman told a story about the gods, which Mikel found more interesting. It was about a swarm of water gods in the river, and how they ripped fisherman's nets, broke traps, and even upturned boats. It was a reminder to be cautious and help build up Mercy so that everyone in the town could prosper. Mikel just enjoyed the way the gods in this story were described as little silver fish, but with arms and intelligent eyes.

Finally, sermon was over, and Mikel stood and stretched his shoulders, twisting from one side to the other so that his back made a loud cracking noise. Mata waited until he was finished and then took his hand as they made their way out of the kirk. It took awhile. Lots of older people were taking their time leaving, and they were in the way. The oldfolk spent forever chatting to their friends and walked painfully slowly.

"Patience," whispered Mata to Mikel.

"I didn't say anything," he grumbled in return, but he made an effort to keep his face cheerful as they left.

The streets of Blackriver were still warm and friendly, but Mata leaned into Mikel's shoulder.

"Hmmm, can we take a walk somewhere else?" she asked.

"Of course," answered Mikel, surprised. "Whatever you like."

"You don't have to get back for those schedules?"

"I will do, but we have time."

The fields outside the town were just as busy as the streets had been to Mikel's mind. Crops were growing in most of them, with a few farmers checking on them. Children played out here too, running along the well-trodden lanes. Flocks of sheep and cows were watched over by young men and women. But Mata relaxed as they strolled further and further from town.

"Here, this feels like a good spot," she said when they reached an intersection beneath a large tree, its leafy boughs shading the grass below its trunk. She sat on the grass and leaned back against the wood. "Yes, this is nice."

"Are you alright?" asked Mikel. He didn't sit down yet. Instead he turned to look around the fields.

"Yes. I just feel quite tired after that walk."

"It wasn't very far," muttered Mikel, more to himself than to her. He could still see the buildings of Blackriver clearly back along the path they had followed. He saw a small girl leaning out of a window in one of the buildings and was able to make out her small arm as she waved. He waved back.

"Nevertheless," said Mata.

Mikel leaned down to kiss his wife on the head and then wandered along the grass beside the path. He plucked a few flowers as he walked, small white and yellow ones mostly, with a few purple and red ones mixed in. The bouquet was barely able to be held between his fingers, so thin were the stems, but he brought it back to Mata and knelt down in the grass beside her.

"Here, I got you some flowers," he said.

Mata had her hand to her mouth. Her shoulders shook while she hunched over and then straightened. She moved her hand away from her mouth, looked at it, and then lifted wide eyes to look at Mikel. Red streaks dripped from her lips, and blood was caught in her palm.

CHAPITRE XXII

Mata had died about a year ago. Marq had done what he could, but everyone knew that Red Lung was fatal. She had looked healthy until a few months before she died, but then she had grown rapidly weaker and thinner, coughing frequently and often bringing up blood. Mikel and Tuomas had missed that one sermon when they had been late, but she had never missed any. Her faith that Mercy would welcome her into its sheltering presence had only grown, lending her face a glow that kept her beautiful until the end.

Mikel's mind was filled with sorrow as memories he had sought to ignore came flooding back through him. A month ago Tuomas had left to be a guard to Uvaniah's heir and Mikel had been left alone in the castle, truly alone for the first time. He had managed to avoid thinking about his wife in all that time, keeping the overwhelming fear and grief that crouched menacingly at the back of his mind chained down, so that he could get through his days. And now, when Tuomas must be nearly home, when he would finally be able to feel the comfort of his son's presence, those emotions were breaking free and threatening to crush him. His legs began to shake and he dropped to the ground. He curled up with his back against the battlement wall and dropped his face to his knees. For the first time in months, Mikel sobbed for his lost wife.

Eventually Mikel became aware of time passing again. He sucked in lungfuls of cool evening air through his nose and wiped the tears from his face on the back of his sleeve. He lifted his head from his knees and examined the stars that were beginning to appear in the sky above him. From the position of the moon, he suspected he had sat here for nearly an hour.

When he had regained some measure of composure, Mikel stood and turned to examine the countryside beyond the river far below him. Blackriver sprawled alongside the castle, still filled with golden lights in the resident's windows, finishing their days with their families. Mikel enjoyed watching the town as it settled into a comfortable evening. It made him feel good to know some people's lives were continuing just as they ever had.

As part of a recent habit, Mikel searched the horizon for signs of his son's return.

For the first time in weeks, he saw something.

Far away, silhouetted against the last red glow of the setting sun, he saw a group of dark shapes moving across the ridge of distant hills. Though he couldn't be sure who it was, it certainly looked like a caravan.

Tuomas. Please be safe.

With the hope of his son soon to return to strengthen him, Mikel decided he needed to find the leader of the Guershan in the morning. The corpse from the mud had something to do with that unsavoury mercenary group and he needed to find out what.

He woke the next day and set out into Blackriver. Two story

buildings and market stalls clustered in every street. The thick dark water of the river Black occasionally flooded the fields that surrounded the bucolic town, dumping layers of rich silty earth as they passed, which meant Blackriver was known for luxurious crops. Because of the ease with which farmers grew their crops near Blackriver, they had planted newer, stranger plants alongside the old staples. Though most of the market sold simple grains and flour, alongside varieties of vegetables such as cabbages and onions, recent years had seen the arrival of a small hard green fruit that was being called coan. They grew on low knobbly trees that barely stretched higher than a person might reach. Mikel enjoyed the sweet flavour that cooked coan added to the treats that were served after a meal in the castle.

Mikel considered pausing amongst the stalls to buy some of the fruit or some cakes, but decided that it was more important to get to his destination. If he was right, and the Guershan had something to do with this poor young man that they had found, then there was a chance that they were already covering their tracks. They had a whole day's headstart on him, and he needed to catch up quickly.

Mikel passed from the baker's street towards the west side of the town. Here was where the taverns and guest rooms lay, making their trade from travellers along the west road. Merchants would room here until they had bought or sold what they needed and they would house their guards with them, those who weren't on duty guarding wagons and carts in the empty fields set aside on the edge of town. With such people waiting for their masters to complete their business, the brewers made sure there was plenty of beer on hand to soothe their thirst. The Guershan had their own building slightly to the south of this part of the town, a worn out place made of stone instead of the timber and daub that most of

Blackriver was built from. Mikel strode past by the taverns and headed towards the Guershan lair.

He stood before the building before approaching it, taking the time to examine it closely. The sun was already high above him in the sky, and the heat lifting from the cobbles and gravel beneath his feet was remarkable. The air smelled like a kiln. A bead of sweat formed between his shoulders and then began to slide down to the small of his back. He tugged at his collar, allowing a merciful hint of cool air under his shirt.

He wondered if wearing the formal uniform of the Commander of the Castle Guard was a mistake. He had hoped that his presence in such a notable fashion would impress upon the Guershan how important his questions were, but the clothing was designed for evening meetings in large halls, not trudging across the town under a boiling sun. He tugged at the cuffs of his sleeves and grimaced. *Best just cope with it,* he told himself. *The mercenaries will see this uniform and give you the respect that they should. IT'll be easier to get information out of them this way.*

The lair squatted against the ground like a gigantic lizard, still and resolute but ready for sudden action. None of the neighbouring buildings leaned towards it, which was unusual. Most of the town was built in such a way that the buildings used one another for support, but here they all gave plenty of space to the Guershan.

Although he didn't know how many of the mercenaries were staying in Blackriver at the moment, Mikel knew that they would spring to the defence of their fellows at the first hint of danger. These villains had both quick tempers and quick swords, with their own peculiar brand of loyalty. He would have to speak carefully, and avoid accusing any one of the Guershan unless he was very certain of himself. He stepped forward, lifted the latch, and went inside.

INTERMÈDE

The creature felt unusual. It felt vulnerable, and exposed. Its skin itched where it knew people would be able to see it. It moved through passages, looking for a hiding place, a safe place. It found none, or at least none that it recognised.

The creature twitched its head nervously. It couldn't move as swiftly as it wanted, and this nose was weak. It turned its head from side to side, seeking the scent of its prey. That smell dripped from every stone in this strange black collection of rock. The iron tang of the prey's blood swelled in unfamiliar nostrils. The sour miasma of their sweat stuck at the back of the creature's mouth. But the scent was thick and overwhelmed the creature. There was no way for it to find the prey when the prey was alone, no way to track it through crowds to quiet lonely corners, where the creature could assuage the hunger that drove it.

Sometimes the creature came across its prey, turning a corner by accident and sighting the prey in the distance. But it was never alone. The creature grew more and more frustrated.

The ravenous hole in its stomach opened further and further and it began to move faster, desperation colouring its actions.

The creature was used to hunting in the solitude that followed all things, in the darkness where no one else might see, in the quiet where screams pass by unheard. In those places, the softness of a prey's flesh was sweeter.

But there was never any alone here in this mountain of stones. When it first arrived, the creature had sat in shadows for an entire night, waiting for its prey, but still there had been the feeling of eyes that watched, stabbing out of the deeper night around it. There was no way to blind those eyes, no way that wouldn't allow someone else to see. It hissed with frustration, clenching its hands, stretching the tendons. It had to get closer to its prey. Every coiled muscle begged it to find a way closer, and then it would be able to slake its hunger.

CHAPITRE XXIII

Mikel entered the mercenary's building and was surprised by how cool it was. The room was comfortably shaded after the heat and light outside. He paused for a moment so that his eyes could adjust to the dim space. As he did so, he realised that anyone entering the lair with violent intent would be at a massive disadvantage. The temporary blindness brought on by the contrast between the light outside and the darkness within meant that any unwanted intruder could be stuck with a blade before they drew a breath. He wondered if the Guershan kept the interior brightly lit at night, to achieve a similar effect.

After a few moments rubbing at his eyes and blinking, they began to adjust and he was able to see more clearly. The room was a sort of sitting room, with a few wooden chairs arranged around the walls. He spotted hooks on the walls as well, waiting for the addition of lanterns. He nodded to himself. He was right about the use of light at night here.

There was a window cut into the wall on his right, which he found odd. It was a small portal that led to another room inside the lair, though a heavy curtain hung across it which made it difficult to determine what might lie beyond. Two doors were set in the wall opposite him, and a third in the wall to his left. He stepped up to the window and poked at the dark velvety curtain.

"Hello? Is there anyone here?" Mikel didn't want to walk through the doors unless he had to. He had heard too many stories of jumpy mercenaries striking in an instinctual panic, and then claiming apologetic grief afterwards. A grizzled man not much older than Mikel flicked the curtain aside just far enough to lean through and onto the sill from the next room.

"Afternoon mate. What can we help you with?" he said with a bored expression on his face.

"I have some questions about a young man who may have been planning to join you and your people." Mikel had decided that he needed to explore the situation with the Guershan carefully. If he launched directly into his discovery at the riverbank, they might slam their mouths shut before he could find out anything useful.

The man laughed and scratched the side of his nose. Stubble covered the lower half of his face. "I'll tell you something for free friend, they ain't my people!" Despite this he motioned Mikel to the nearest of the two doors. "Step through there and I'll meet you."

The man stepped away from the window and the curtain immediately swung back to cover his departure. Mikel heard footsteps moving through the room that lay beyond the curtain, and then the creak of door hinges opening. Mikel didn't have much choice. If he wanted to find out as much as he could, he would have to do as the man said. He turned and stepped through the door.

It was pitch black in the next room. *If they like having their guests in a vulnerable position, they really have gone all out,* Mikel thought sourly. He resisted the impulse to grab the hilt of his sword. He briefly considered calling on Mercy to shield him here, or on any small gods of shadow that were nearby. Instead he reached out to either side of the wall he had just passed through and ran his hands across the rough wood. The feeling calmed him a little. He was able to find his bearings easier. There was a movement in the darkness ahead of him, a sound of cloth rustling as it shifted around someone's body.

"What do you want to know, commander?" The voice that slithered out of the darkness was so soft and low that Mikel nearly mistook it for a breeze before he realised that words were carried with it.

"To begin with, I'd like to know who you are?" Mikel began, confused and annoyed by the strange situation he found himself in. "You don't sound like the man who sent me through the door."

The stranger laughed. *Unless that man was exceptionally gifted at altering his voice,* Mikel thought.

"You aren't going to know who I am," the voice continued. "It is safer to be unknown, especially to people outside the Geurshan. We wouldn't want anyone to get any notions of vengeance for acts undertaken at someone else's orders, would we?"

It was a reasonable fear. Running a group of mercenaries certainly could result in a person being hated by some very powerful people. If any of them gathered their resources enough to seek vengeance on the Geurshan the leader would be the first to suffer. *I should have been tracking you all years ago,* thought Mikel. *This organisation, right on our doorstep, is so potentially dangerous, and so unknown to me. What a mistake.*

Despite the concerning revelation he had just reached, Mikel smiled.

You wouldn't want anyone to come claiming a refund for work left unsatisfactorily unfinished either, I expect. He managed not to laugh. Insulting this man would not help him. But also, this voice in shadow made Mikel think that his visit to the lair might be even more dangerous than he had anticipated. He decided that it would be more important to get out quickly than to dig too deeply.

"Very well. I am here because of an incident by the castle that I think you may be able to help with."

The silence stretched on after his words, waiting patiently for him to fill it.

"We found a body on the banks of the Black. It was in an unseemly way. But we are fairly sure it is the body of a young man named Filip, a young man who was interested in the life of a mercenary. We managed to identify a dark mark on his thigh that we think might be a dog tattoo."

"Really." The voice sounded flat.

CHAPITRE XXIV

"I'm not here to accuse anyone. We just want to try and find out what happened so we can make sure it doesn't happen again. Did you, or someone here know the boy?"

Silence stretched long enough for Mikel to swallow and breathe out through his nose, before the voice spoke again.

"What did you say his name was?" asked the soft voice in the dark room.

"Filip."

There was a rustling from across the room. Mikel couldn't say for sure, but it sounded for all the world as though the stranger was rummaging through pieces of paper or shifting a robe drastically. *How can he even see such things in this room?*

"I believe you may be right.' The voice sounded reticent, as though it was unhappy to be revealing even this scant information, and certainly could not be expected to explain itself more fully. "I seem to recall a young boy talking to some of our soldiers at the taverns many nights. If your victim was this same boy, he was very enthusiastic."

"And you are loath to quell a boy's dream to join the Guershan, aren't you?" Mikel's voice was tinged with a hint of disapproval. He was thinking of all the young people who left Blackriver with the Guershan, only to die on battlefields far from home and hearth.

"Far be it from us to tell someone their own mind," the voice snapped like a whip. "Do you send away every child who wants the fancy blue uniform of a Castle Guard?"

Mikel didn't reply. It was true that youngsters tried to join the guards nearly as often as they tried to impress the Guershan. After all, he himself had been caught between the two in his own long gone past. But he reminded himself that it had taken immense determination to convince the Guards to allow him to try out, and they had trained him before allowing him to patrol, so that he had some idea of how to protect himself at least

"When did anyone last see him?"

"I don't know." Footsteps in the shadows moved up next to Mikel. Someone was standing well within his reach. He kept his hands at his sides. Mikel heard the faint clatter of metal moving past metal and smelled the dryness of old leather. Although he knew someone stood right beside him, the voice he had been talking to continued from the other side of the room.

"I do know he hasn't been around in a long time. If his body was the one you found, then that is a true shame. Our condolences to the family. But it has nothing to do with us."

"Wait!" called Mikel. He could tell that the voice was about to send him on his way.

"No commander. There is nothing more to say. You came in here hoping to intimidate us with your fancy blue shirt and jackets, your shinty belt buckle. You hoped that we poor soldiers would grovel before you and apologise for any wrongs you wished to lay at our feet. Instead you will find that we are not afraid of fancy rags. Good day!"

The door behind Mikel opened, yanked by the thick-necked man whose presence Mikel had sensed standing so close to him. Before he could look around the room in the sudden light, Mikel was hustled back through the door. The man from the window in the next room was already leaning through the curtain, nodding towards the front door.

"Best you leave now as I understand it sir. Always a pleasure to see a member of the guard in our neck of the woods. Be a stranger now!"

In a matter of moments, Mikel was standing on the street outside.

The streets in this part of Blackriver were never really empty, but now that Mikel found himself bundled back into them, blinking at the sunlight overhead, they certainly bustled less than they had earlier in the day. He grunted and blinked his eyes, trying to get used to the light. He hadn't realised how much they had adjusted to meet the needs of the dark rooms inside the lair.

I should have realised that I wouldn't get as long as I had hoped. Perhaps having the Commander of the Castle Guard show up to investigate could be taken as a threat. Mikel considered what it would mean if the Guershan had taken offence to his inquiry. *Does that mean they lied to me? Were they trying to cover something up? Or are they truly ignorant of anything to do with Filip? And if they did lie to the Commander of the Guard, does that show they are more confident of their own power in Blackriver than they should be?*

CHAPITRE XXV

Thoughts of the potential danger from the mercenaries mixed with Mikel's concerns about his son. Tuomas had travelled outside Mercy's reach for weeks now, and he had never been the bravest child. A particular occasion rose in his mind as he walked back towards Sheerwall through the warm streets.

"Dad!" he remembered a tiny voice screaming. "Help!"

Mikel's heart had jumped in his chest and his head squeezed tight at the sound of Tuomas's voice. Every limb swung into numb action, driven by fear but aware of no exertion as he raced to his boy. The shouting had come from the stables and Mikel nearly fell as he spun sharply into the wide doors. Rows of narrow wooden stalls swept away from him to his left and right.

"Tuomas!" he yelled, desperately trying to locate his son.

"Here! Hurry dad!"

The voice came from the right. Mikel dashed forward and quickly found the stall with Tuomas inside.

The young boy had climbed up the stall to the height of

Mikel's shoulders, a lofty perch for so small a boy. Beneath him, sitting comfortably in the hay, were two of the castle's hunting hounds. The stall was filled with the smell of the dogs, mingled with hay and horse dung. The dogs sat looking up at Tuomas with long grins, pink tongues lolling out the sides of their mouths. Their tails thumped the ground in the stall.

"Tuomas?" asked Mikel slowly as he took in the scene.

"Dad, oh thank the little gods of noise!" Tuomas' lifted tear streaked cheeks towards his father. "Please help, they won't leave me alone!" He reached out an arm to Mikel.

"What do you mean they won't leave you alone?" Mikel looked down at the dogs and then back to his son. "Did they bite you?" He was confused. The hounds were all well trained animals, they wouldn't harm a beetle unless a hunter had given the order.

"No, they didn't bite me!" Tuomas' voice was strained, as though his throat was about to give out. "They won't leave me alone!" He gestured at the animals, trying to shoo them away. One of the hounds' ears pricked up at the movement and Mikel could tell that the dog was ready to play.

"Come on, you foolish boy. They think that you're playing a game with them. Just climb down from there so that we can leave."

"I can't!" shrieked Tuomas.

"Just do it!" snapped Mikel.

Tuomas began to make his way down the heavy wooden planks of the stall. His hands trembled as he climbed down and he whimpered when the dogs stood and leaned up to sniff at his legs.

"See? They are just curious, no danger at all," Mikel explained as the dogs pushed their tongues towards Tuomas's hands and face. The small boy snuffled and whined, trying to push the dogs away. Mikel reached past the hounds and took hold of his son by the shoulder.

"Come on, let's go and get you cleaned up. Don't tell your mother about this, I'm sure she'd be embarrassed to see you made such a noise over nothing."

Tuomas nodded and the two of them walked out of the stables, with the two hunting animals trotting along behind them.

CHAPITRE XXVI

Mikel walked as he remembered the encounter, eyes looking down to the dirt beneath his feet. Tuomas was so nervous, how was he doing on his own, so far away? Mikel kept to the side of the path so he would avoid others walking through the town, but occasionally he had to turn sharply aside as someone strode past him.

Laughter bubbled through the air nearby. He stopped and looked at the source, a broad building that looked as though its wooden beams were melting with age, sagging down to the ground. Another peal of laughter burst from the building.

"The Gilded Rooster," he murmured, looking at the sign above the door, painted with a yellow bird. The sign's wooden boards were peeling and its chain was rusted solid. Still, the Rooster was a well known spot for the mercenaries in town to entertain themselves, being so near their lair. "Saara said that Filip had been drinking with some of the Guershan here..." murmured Mikel softly as he walked to the door and stepped inside.

Inside, the tavern was surprisingly well lit and clean. Mikel had assumed that the place would stink of sour beer and sweat, with broken cups and chairs covering the floor. He had expected heavy torches in the walls to thicken the air with smoke. Instead he found a well-swept floor, and each table bore a small lantern lit by a thick white candle. The tables were broad and spaced out, so that he was able to walk up to the serving bar with ease. Mikel realised that most of the men in the room were gambling, either playing various elaborate card games or dicing with a small knot of enthusiastic onlookers. *I suppose they need the lights to make sure cheaters are dealt with quickly,* he decided with a small nod.

Behind the bar stood the owner of the tavern, a wide-stomached man wearing a chequered shirt and dark pants. His face was round and welcoming, with a surprisingly red nose. There was something dangerous about the set of his eyes though. The way his eyes glinted as he examined the newcomer to his tavern showed Mikel that this man was not as cheerful and easy going as he presented himself. Any trouble-maker would doubtless find this man had hidden reserves to draw upon.

Mikel walked to the bar and leaned against the counter. The chequered man nodded to him.

"Good afternoon sir, what would you like?"

"Just a pint of ale. May I ask your name?"

"Certainly." The man busied himself with Mikel's drink and served it to him with a half-smile. "My name's Ulius. What sort of thing are you joining us at the Rooster today for then?"

"I'm looking for a man."

"Not here to start trouble I would hope." Ulius's green eyes hardened like small emeralds.

"No no, of course not! We've just had some strange things

going on at the Castle and I'm hoping to find someone who will be able to shed a little light on it all."

"I see. And who is it that you're hoping will have this light to shed?"

"I'm not really sure." Mikel explained about the boy who had been hanging around with the Guershan, repeating the description that Saara had given him. After he mentioned the boy's hair he was sure he saw a light of recognition in Ulius's eyes. The large man turned aside and coughed. "You do know the boy," Mikel declared.

"I wouldn't say I know him, not like a regular or anything" answered the barman gruffly. He groaned and scratched his eyebrow. "I suppose there's no harm telling you. I saw a boy like that hanging around with some of the lads in here from time to time, but I didn't think anything of it. It happens fairly regularly, especially with the weather as it is. Young 'uns dream of setting off across the country and earning gold and glory, and who can blame them. The Guershan don't usually get them into any real trouble."

"It may not have been them this time," Mikel soothed the man. He knew what the barkeep meant by saying that the mercenaries didn't get the boys who followed them around into trouble. He meant that they kept their heads down while they were in Blackriver, and there weren't many fights or accidents between the boys and the soldiers. Mikel kept his anger at the boys who were lost on far battlefields from appearing in his expression. Ulius wouldn't understand.

Although Mikel did find himself wondering, *what if Ulius was wrong? What if it had been one of the mercenaries who had done this? What could have possibly so annoyed a mercenary that he might murder a young boy?* And even then, to have annoyed them so much that they killed the boy in a way as brutal as the remains they had found suggested? The thought was impossible.

Mikel hoped that it hadn't been one of the Guershan. He suddenly became very aware of just how alone he was in this bar. The men around him, laughing and carousing, had no loyalty to him. If he said something to displease them, there was every chance that some similar tragedy might befall him. Oh, Lord Uvaniah would soon clear out the mercenaries if such an accident was to happen to a man with the title and importance that he carried. Perhaps this tavern would even be demolished, just to really scatter any violence to the horizon. But none of those reactions would help him if he was dead.

"I was wondering if you could point out any of the men that he was talking to?"

"You're in luck." This time the man's smile was unmistakably mocking. "They're sitting in the back there." He pointed, cloth still hanging from his fingers.

At the back of the tavern were a series of benches and small alcoves, a perfect place to sit and drink with more privacy for those who had personal business to discuss, matters that would not do well to be discussed out in the open, in the light. He saw there were only three men using the back of the room now, so he made his way through the tables towards them. On the way he managed to avoid causing much commotion, though he did bump one gambler's elbow and found a knife being raised towards him. The knife wielder's friends called him back to his seat with a laugh, clearly finding humour in his sudden violent temper. There was no sign that they thought that their companion threatening the Commander of the Castle Guard was a problem, just that they had no time for their game to be interrupted right then. Mikel frowned and straightened his shirt. He might have to do something about the Guards' reputation outside the castle walls.

The three men at the back of the room lapsed into silence as soon as they realised Mikel was heading in their direction. One of the men glared at him, while the other two looked at each other and narrowed their eyes.

CHAPITRE XXVII

"Who are you?" scowled the first man as soon as Mikel took a seat next to them. He saw their hands drift to their sides, which was concerning. *If they draw any blades, there's no way I'll leave this room again,* thought Mikel. Again, he was surprised that the Guershan were so willing to threaten the Castle Guard Commander. He took a second to truly look at the men he had sat with as he considered his response to the first man's question.

The glaring man was larger than the others, with a thick neck that disappeared into his collar in the same way a rocky spire might plunge into the earth. His hands were fists the size of clubs, resting easily on the table in front of him. The other two were opposite sides of a single coin. Both were weaselly thin, but one had long blonde hair tied back from his face in a ponytail and wore light green clothes patched with thick dark leather and small metal studs. The other had a dark beard covering his jaw and kept his hair cropped close to his skull. He wore a brown heavy tunic. Mikel was sure they would both be carrying knives that were much cleaner than their clothes.

"I'm the Commander of the Castle Guard," he began, hoping that they were simply unaware of his position. *Best to start off by letting them know that trouble can follow me around too.* He was slightly gratified when the two thin men flickered their eyes to one another again and then sat lower in their seats, hands slowly moving away from their pockets and clearly empty. "I'm trying to find out about a young boy named Filip. Do you know him?"

The large man leaned a little closer and scratched his chin, squinting at Mikel. He sniffed. "Maybe. Do you know where he is?" Clearly the big man was the one in charge of this little group.

"I do. And I'll tell you where he is if you help me out first. How do you know him?"

"We've been checking if he has what it takes to join the Geurshan." The big man leaned back in his chair. Mikel noticed the muscles in the man's shoulders took their time to unwind and then settle, like dogs resting before a fire pit after a long hunt, circling each other before finally laying down. The thin men leaned back as well, small smiles crossing their faces. The blonde man had a scar on his chin that pulled at his lower lip, turning his smile into a leer.

"And did he have what it takes in the end?"

"I would imagine so." The big man's face darkened. "What's your name Commander?"

"Mikel. And you?"

"Zhonathin." Zhonathin stretched one huge arm forward with his hand extended and Mikel met it with his own. The two men clasped wrists, each getting a feel for the other. Mikel was made more keenly aware that his power and authority drew from Lord Uvaniah, who was currently sitting safely in the Castle and not alongside him in the Gilded Rooster.

"If you are asking about him, I'm thinking there must have

been some sort of trouble involving the boy." Zhonathin made it a statement rather than a question.

"You could say that."

"Good. Because the boy was trouble for us too, and I'd love to see the guard having to deal with him instead of us."

The comment gave Mikel pause. What sort of trouble could a young boy like Filip provide hardened men like these? Had he stolen something of theirs? Saara had suggested that he was out of sorts since he returned from his travels with his uncle. But surely no youth could trouble these three rogues?

"What did he do?"

Zhonathin grunted and took a hearty swallow of his ale. The blonde man spoke instead.

"It wasn't much," said the blonde man. "My name is Andreus. The boy was just supposed to be helpful, to show that he was likely to be a worthwhile addition."

His dark haired companion snorted into his mug. "Not this boy though."

"No, not this boy. He was terrible straight away," agreed the first.

"What do you mean?" asked Mikel.

"He was a nuisance," growled the one who had laughed. "The boy wouldn't ever leave well enough alone. He showed up and told us he wanted to join, but then getting him to do as he was bidden was like trying to pet an eel! He never stayed put!"

Andreus nodded. "Aye. The boy expressed an interest, same as they all do, and we chatted with him here at the Rooster. We asked him to show up the next day, but he didn't. Then he suddenly appeared under foot when I was just leaving the lair a few days later. It was always like that, unpredictable."

"And yet you thought he would be a good addition?"

"We don't make decisions that quickly. No, it wasn't until

he'd been hanging around for a week or two and seemed likely enough that we sent him to get a keg of ale from Zhosua, you know?"

Mikel did. Zhosua was a merchant who regularly returned to Blackriver, and dealt fine wines and ales from near and far.

"But the little whelp never came back and then Zhosua came in complaining that the boy had been yelling at him, threatening him."

Mikel didn't think the Guershan would have been bothered about any of the townsfolk complaining about the behaviour of their associates.

"And that was enough for you to decide he wouldn't fit in?"

"That wouldn't have done it by itself. We probably would have told the old man to just go back to his store. But he said Filip kept showing up stalking him."

"Stalking?"

"Aye, like a cat. Hiding around corners, walking along rooftops. He said the boy was tracking him like a cat chasing a rat through a garden. The last thing we need is one of our recruits causing trouble in Blackriver."

CHAPITRE XXVIII

Andreus grinned at Mikel as he said that. Mikel could follow the man's thoughts though. The Guershan might sometimes be the cause of trouble in town but they were good at keeping a distance from it. Mikel knew that it was very difficult to connect them to any particular problems. However, something so directly and easily linked to them as a recruit intimidating otherwise respectable members of the town might become a reason to expel the Guershan entirely. Their brawls and indiscretions were usually able to be blamed on individual mercenaries. But if they had been warned that Filip was behaving like this towards someone more influential than the typical hired hands or farm workers, and they didn't stop it, then Mikel would have Lord Uvaniah's blessing to follow that up.

"So you decided to keep him out?" Mikel spoke the question carefully. If these men felt threatened then they might do something he would regret.

"We did. My brother Akub had been meeting with Filip for sword practice, so it was agreed that he would do it."

Mikel turned to the dark haired man.

"How did he take it when you told him?"

The man spluttered a laugh into his ale, then shook his head and wiped his mouth with the back of his sleeve.

"I'm not Akub! My name is Pelep."

"What?" Mikel was confused. The man looked so much like Andreus. They had to be related. "But then-"

"Akub has been missing ever since."

The men sat silently for a moment as the words were absorbed. The gamblers in the middle of the room laughed loudly and continued their game.

"You think that Filip was dangerous? More dangerous than your brother?"

Andreus narrowed his eyes.

"Not more dangerous. But I think he may have caught my brother by surprise."

"The whelp nearly chopped Akub's fingers off during one practice," added Pelep.

Mikel nodded. "I understand. Sometimes a fool with a blade can cause far more damage than someone who knows what they are doing." After all, Filip had grown up with little exercise and had shown no particular interest in violence before declaring he wanted to join the Guershan.

"No, the gods-cursed boy nearly slammed the blade into Akub's hand," interrupted Pelep with a snarl.

Mikel paused before answering, speaking carefully. "Is that not a good sign for a mercenary?"

"It would be," snorted Andreus, "if he could be controlled, or directed. Akub said that fighting the boy was like trying to fight a thunderstorm. He was flailing like the ribbons on a woman's dress, and driving harder than a flood. Coupled with his unpredictable behaviour, we decided he would have fought against us just as hard as he might fight the enemy on any battlefield. It wasn't worth the effort to bring him into line."

"And so Akub went to tell him this, and you haven't seen him since?"

"Exactly. He vanished a week ago."

"And you believe Filip has something to do with the disappearance of your brother?" asked Mikel. The three mercenaries looked at each other and nodded.

"But that doesn't make sense," muttered the commander. "You say Akub only went missing a week ago, is that right?"

"Yes. When he went to talk to the youth and tell him our decision."

"But according to his family, Filip was gone for much longer than that." The body that they had collected bore all the signs that it had been wedged into the mud, hidden amongst the river's reeds, for a month. How could the boy's body have been decaying for so long, when these men claimed to have seen him so much more recently?

Mikel told the men that he had reason to believe that what Filip's family said was true, looking closely at their responses. He watched their faces, studied their expressions closely. Three carefully neutral visages looked back at him, eyes calm and mouths level. It was impossible to be sure how they felt about the situation, or his questions.

The men each paused as they considered their answer. Admitting that a young town boy could have done something to upset a mercenary must be like admitting a weakness for these men. They were supposed to be tough and fearless soldiers. Now that Mikel had pointed out a flaw in what they had told him, would they see that as an attack while they were vulnerable? Eventually the blonde man spoke.

"So you say. But we saw him, and that's where Akub was going the last time I saw him."

"A week ago?"

"Aye." Andreus rubbed the back of his neck and frowned. "He never came back to the Lair after Resting Day."

"Your brother was at sermon?" Mikel's question sounded surprisingly loud, even to himself. The chatter amongst the gamblers in the tavern broke into a sudden silence and Mikel fought the impulse to turn and look at the eyes he knew must be studying him. After a few moments the voices began to converse again, but Mikel was careful to speak quietly when he repeated the question.

Pelep scowled at him and shoved one finger towards his chest. The man's fingernail was cracked and dirt-crusted. "Look at you, with your fine shirts and clean fingers." He sneered, yellowed teeth exposed through the rough dark hair of his beard. "You'd like to think we're a pack of mongrels, mange-ridden, rabid, ready to tear apart the people of this town as soon as look at them. You make me sick. Did you know that the Geurshan go to sermon on Resting Day just like anyone? Of course not. Because you think we're scum." He thumped the table for emphasis. His eyes bore into Mikel with the fire and fury of a blacksmith's forge.

CHAPITRE XXIX

Mikel caught himself before he could let his disbelief show. After managing to get so much detail out of the men, it would be exceptionally stupid of him to provoke them now. Andreus was frowning at him, so he directed his reply to Zhonathin. Despite the fact that he had sat silently while the others explained what had happened, Mikel was still sure that the large man was the leader of the three.

"I'm sorry, I didn't mean to upset you. I admit, I was surprised, but I hadn't really thought about this sort of thing before."

"Yes, that much is clear." Zhonathin's response was dry and sharp. "But as Andreus was saying, his brother Akub was the one who had spent the most time with your boy. At first, he thought the boy would fit well with the Guershan. He had a way of moving, like an animal. We appreciate men with a natural affinity for violence." He smiled, revealing a row of mostly gleaming white teeth, though one was broken in half and ended in a jagged stump. "But after the sword training incident, Akub was convinced the boy was out to get him.

Then, about a week ago, he went to sermon before he was due to tell Filip we weren't interested and never came back."

"That bastard boy," muttered Andreus.

"Much as he may have been a difficult charge for you, I just don't think the boy could have been responsible for Akub going missing-" began Mikel but Pelep interrupted before he could explain any further.

"Of course he was responsible! The boy was clearly a mad man!" The man's jaw was clenched so hard that Mikel was sure he heard teeth grinding. "What other sort of fool would work so hard to join us and then vanish without a trace? He must have known what an insult it would be to us. Only someone with a truly awful secret to hide could have made such a poor decision. Most people know that joining the Guershan is a way to ignore the darkness in your past, but this boy must have had something truly evil that Akub discovered. And then the boy killed him!"

The man's voice had risen with each sentence and Mikel was aware of the silence in the rest of the tavern again. He wondered what expressions would be on the gamblers' faces if he were to turn around. This was turning into a very troubling conversation. He hoped their anger stayed focused on Filip and didn't turn to him when he explained the situation.

"I understand what you're saying," continued Mikel, lifting his hands in a calming gesture. "But you should know that we have found the body of Filip, buried in the riverbank by the castle."

"Good riddance," muttered Pelep.

Andreus lifted his mug to celebrate the death of the boy. "My thanks to the little gods of the rivers and reeds."

Mikel's bile rose at the sight, but managed to hold his tongue.

"I know you feel that way, but there is just one thing you

need to know." Mikel paused until he was sure all three men were paying close attention. "The body is at least three weeks old."

Andreus snorted.

"That's impossible."

"We brought the corpse into the castle and our alchemist examined it closely. He explained that the body has broken down and rotted in the wet earth, and it must have taken at least three weeks to become as ruined as it was when we found it. I'm sorry, Filip can't have had anything to do with your brother's disappearance."

The men leaned back silently. Zhonathin took another draw of his drink then leaned closer to the other two.

"I'd believe him boys, hard as it might be. The sort of man who becomes Commander might be snooty, spending time amongst the other high mucky-mucks, but I can't see him being a liar. At least, I don't think he'd lie about something like this."

Mikel was glad he had earned some sort of grudging trust with one of these mercenaries.

"That's as may be Zhonathin. But then, what really happened to Akub?" Andreus sounded quieter than before, his eyes low.

"Can you tell me anything about what he was doing in the last weeks you saw him? It does sound as though his disappearance could be related to Filip's body being in the marsh. Maybe I can keep searching and let you know if I uncover anything?"

Andreus appeared sceptical. "Wait, are you saying that you think my brother killed that young mongrel?" His eyes flashed in anger.

"No no, that's not what I meant." Although, if Mikel was honest with himself, that was definitely a thread he would have unpicked eventually, and now he knew to be careful around Andreus while he did the picking. "I just mean, they were known to each other, both went missing, and one has been found dead. Mercy knows I wouldn't like to find any bad news about your brother." He wondered if his carefully controlled face would fool the mercenary into believing that Mikel truly cared about Akub.

"And you'd share what you found with us? The dregs that you so assume are simply fleas on the back of this town?"

"I can't let you cause any trouble in the town. Lord Uvaniah expects me to keep the peace. But if I find out anything that I can tell you, then I will."

The men studied him carefully. Then, without speaking, Andreus held out an arm. In turn, the men each clasped Mikel's wrist and shook firmly, first Andreus, then Zhonathin, and then Pelep.

"Thank you." Mikel smiled at the men. Zhonathin allowed a nod of acknowledgement but the other two did not return the smile. "I have a few more questions, if you don't mind, to help me find out as much as I can."

CHAPITRE XXX

From the descriptions the men gave to Mikel, there had been something wrong with the youth who had been following them. They described a manic young man, with wild eyes, who was exceptionally clumsy. He would knock over mugs and chairs and barely even notice. When someone would point it out, he would look at the overturned item and then back at whoever had spoken, shrugging as though he had just stepped on a bug. He never broke anything of value and so no-one had made an issue of it, but now that their man had gone missing the behaviour was more suspicious.

Mikel didn't understand that. He doubted that the men were lying to him, or even bending the truth, but from what Filip's sister Saara had said about him, Mikel had expected to hear about a quiet and careful boy. Where had that small boy who had spent days quietly contemplating life in the kirk gone?

Akub had developed a twitch after the incident with the sword training. Andreus had trouble getting his brother to keep to a promise to meet, and it became difficult to track his movements. Sometimes he would be in the Gilded Rooster with the rest of them, drinking and laughing together, but other nights he was nowhere to be found, in any of the taverns that grew thick as mushrooms on this side of Blackriver. Andreus had spent some time going from tavern to tavern looking for his brother. He had caught up with Akub leaving the Guershan lair and heading towards the castle on more than one occasion. That made Mikel prick his ears up.

"What did you say your brother looked like?"

"I'm pretty sure you would have recognised him. He kept his head shaved bald as a babe, and his dog was tattooed above one ear. He was a loud man, always ready with a curse or a laugh. He stood out, if you mark me." Andreus grinned sadly at the memory of his brother.

"Yes, it sounds like I would have." Mikel struggled to recall if his guards had passed on any word of trouble involving a man such as this. Had there been any intruders, any voluble drunks? Had the Guard tossed any trouble makers out through the gates, or into the damp cells in the bowels of the castle?

Try as he might, Mikel recalled no descriptions that any of the guards had given him in the last year, let alone this particular man recently. The thought worried him. He wasn't sure if they had passed on word of any trouble either. He frowned and bit his lower lip as he tried to remember. Wasn't it his job to listen to the reports, to be the one with a clear view of all the things the Guards were involved with? When was the last time he had paid attention to what was going on in the everyday activities of the Guards? Was it before he lost Mata?

"Regardless, I will ask my men when I return."

Zhonathin nodded before continuing his recount of the days leading to Akub's disappearance.

Akub's twitch had been worse some days than others. He

would sit with a hand on his leg, the fingers bouncing and tapping as though insects were swarming beneath his skin. If no one pointed the movement out, he didn't even seem to be aware that he was doing it.

Mikel spent the remainder of the afternoon with the three Guershan, learning as much as possible about the movements of Filip and Akub in the days before each went missing. Mikel was sure that if he could understand the connection between them, he would be able to find a link between the one's horrific death and the other's strange disappearance.

Eventually Mikel could think of no questions that would draw more information from the three mercenaries, and they showed no more desire to speak with him, so he stood to leave. He had discovered that the body they had found in the riverbank did seem to be the brother of the girl who found it. She had known that her brother was going to meet with someone from the Guershan the night he vanished. He had found the name of the man who Filip was supposed to have met, Akub. But Akub had never returned from that meeting, and no one had seen Filip since then either. Mikel realised that the twitch and the possibility he had been trying to return to the area around the castle may have told him more than the three Guershan expected. His first thought was that Akub had killed the boy and was returning to make sure the body remained hidden.

But in that case, why had no-one noticed him beneath the castle walls? Why hadn't he tipped the body into the river where it would have washed away any evidence connecting him to the boy's death? What had he done with the poor boy's face and hands? And, most strangely, why had he vanished a week ago? He shook his head, thanked the men for the help, and promised one more time to tell them whatever he could of his discoveries.

The walk back to the castle was long. Mikel found it hard to pay attention to his surroundings as he walked. He was lost in his own thoughts, paying no attention to the buildings around him. Instead he relied upon his instincts, developed over years growing up on these same streets, to trace his path through the twists and turns that led back to the castle. As his feet carried him along the familiar streets, his mind was flooded with contrasting images. Some he drew from his own memories, and others that he conjured from the information he had just heard.

He pictured the riverbank in his mind, the same one where he had found the body of Filip. There was no body in the mud as he imagined it. Instead he and Tuomas were crouched in the muck, far enough into the reeds for the water to flow more freely. He remembered looking down into his son's tiny face as he had lowered the reed boat they had made that morning into the river. It had been picked up by the current and sped away from the small boy's hands. Tuomas had whooped with joy as the boat slid along the surface of the river, and away from them. He grinned up at Mikel and Mikel had put a hand on his son's shoulder as they watched the boat sail away.

Mikel's thoughts turned to the riverbank again, empty now, rushes and reeds swaying in a breeze, as he imagined a broad man staggering through the mud. In Mikel's mind Akub was at once walking alongside Filip, or carrying the boy's dead body, or perhaps chasing him. Mikel couldn't decide which was the more likely method the two may have used to make their way to the riverbank. Mikel imagined that there had been a fight once they arrived. Or perhaps the deadweight of Filip's body had caused the mercenary to trip and fall. The boy's body may have plunged into the mud and stuck firmly.

But Mikel shook his head. The vision made no sense. Why

would Akub leave a body there, no matter how it got there? And how was it embedded legs first, as though standing?

Mikel considered the leader of the Guershan, in the black room inside their lair. This business must be why the man was so annoyed by his questions. The leader must have realised that it looked as though his man Akub had killed a member of the townsfolk. That rumour wouldn't do to get out. The Guershan had a poor reputation, but managed to stay on the right side of a distrustful line, giving them a warm and safe place to spend their time between campaigns. If they crossed the line too violently then they would be lanced from the town like an infection and they knew it.

Mikel scratched at his chin as he considered what he had been told about the poor young man whose body they had found. Filip had sounded a lot like Tuomas had been when he was a young boy. Quiet, reclusive. Not interested in the things that young men were usually interested in. Mikel wondered if Filip's family had worried over their son as much as he had worried over Tuomas.

CHAPITRE XXXI

When Tuomas had been young, small enough that his head barely reached Mikel's belt, Mata used to make extra sure the boy was dressed in fine clothes before they went to kirk on Resting Day.

"Stop fussing over the boy," Mikel would say, as he slipped his arms into his jacket. "He can make his own choices I'm sure."

Mata would snort and continue to wipe down Tuomas' face and smooth his hair.

"Ma," the boy would whine, trying to push her away, but she wouldn't back down until she considered him presentable.

"And now you are ready," she pronounced.

"I could do it myself," he muttered, glancing over at his father.

Mata caught the look and raised an eyebrow. "Never mind about your father!" she declared, and strode over to Mikel. She reached out and began straightening his collar, tucking his hair away. "He's just as bad!"

"Mata, please!" protested Mikel. "Not in front of the boy!"

"Don't you try and pretend you're more than you are in front of him," she replied. "He needs to know the real you, so that he grows up with a real person to teach him, not the facade you think is correct."

Mikel spluttered but said nothing else while she tidied his clothes and tucked in his shirt.

"There. I think you are both respectable now." She smiled at Mikel. "Oh relax my love, you always tell us that you want the townsfolk to look up to the Commander of the Guard. We can't have you looking dishevelled in that case, can we?"

Mikel mumbled something that could have been agreement as the family set off.

They walked through the streets of Blackriver, Tuomas huddled in by his mother's legs, wrapping one arm around her. It was as though he was hiding behind her skirts.

"Do you like my shirt Da?"

Mikel nodded briefly. "You look very respectable. Your mother was right, you look like the commander's son in that shirt."

Tuomas stood a little straighter and further from his mother. *Good,* thought Mikel. *He needs to have more confidence in himself. If he keeps hiding and being scared of the world, no one will take him seriously.*

Mata rolled her eyes at Mikel over their son's head. Before he could say something in reply, a scrabble of street children raced past them, narrowly avoiding bumping into them before careening away down an alley.

"Did they take anything?" asked Mikel with a frown. "Those children are nothing but trouble."

"Mikel!" Mata laughed and reached out to take his hand. "You were one of those street children!"

"And that's why I know that they aren't any good!"

"You are good," she said, squeezing his hand. "And I'm sure that plenty of them will grow up to be good too."

They arrived at the kirk while townsfolk were still wandering in through the open doors to the main chapel. Many of the congregation were taking this chance to catch up with their friends, some of whom may not have attended sermon in a while. Others ducked into the kirk to find their seats before the Kirkman began talking loudly about the lack of consideration shown by those who paid no heed to the schedule of others.

Mikel saw no need to chat with anyone he saw outside the doors but he paused to check if Mata had seen anyone. She looked around but then shook her head and the trio entered the kirk.

Mikel frowned. The front rows were already filling up, though a good number of townsfolk were still outside.

"What's wrong Da?" asked Tuomas. Mikle didn't look down at his son. Instead he looked around the chapel, wondering where would be a suitable place to sit, somewhere that he would be able to be seen by as many as possible.

"I'm trying to find us good seats. These others have taken the best ones."

"Do we actually need to sit in the best ones?"

"Of course." Now Mikel looked down. Tuomas' face was serious as he looked up at his father, listening carefully. "It is important that we fit into our place in society, Tuomas. I am the Commander of the Castle Guards. Everyone needs to see me and know that I do my duty to maintain order on behalf of Mercy, so that it can keep its shield strong. I came from the wrong sort of people, and everyone is watching to make sure that I am a suitable person for this role. If people see me sitting in a poor seat, they will begin to wonder whether something is wrong, or whether I am not the best person to be commander after all. Then unease might lead to bad behaviour that diverts Mercy's shield. "

"Oh shush Mikel," Mata interrupted him. She gathered up Tuomas' hand. "You'll scare him. Come on, these seats will be fine." She led the way into a pew halfway down the chapel.

"And try to stop glaring at your neighbours. If you are really serious about being seen in your correct social place, then it might be a good idea not to look like you hate everyone else here."

"I'm not glaring," he grumbled. Mikel leaned back in the pew and forced his cheeks into a broad smile. A few others in the chapel smiled back at him. *See,* he told himself. *They respect the commander.*

CHAPITRE XXXII

The Kirkman told a short version of the kirktale of the Ugly Godling. Mikel had enjoyed listening to kirktales when he was child, on the days when he sought out the kirk. Usually cold days, winter days, days when the Kirk's warm dry chapel was particularly desirable. On occasion, he would step through the always open doors and discover that it was Resting Day, and that sermon was underway.

Mikel remembered the first time he had been in the kirk when the tale of the Ugly Godling had been shared. He had listened with wide eyes and gaping mouth to the old kirkman's description of a strange and awkward creature travelling around an unnamed land and being turned aside by everyone it met. The vision of the godling was enthralling to his small boy's mind. He grinned and imagined his own little monster, fidgeting with his fingers as he decided what it might look like.

"Like so many of the gods outside of Mercy's bounds, the ugly godling was small, and strange," the kirkman said. "The gods of the fields and flowers are barely able to see over the grass that is their home. The gods of eels and streams are small enough to hide beneath the riverbanks. The ugly godling was no taller than a person's knee."

The kirkman stepped out from behind his lectern and held a hand at his own knee height, demonstrating the stature of the godling.

"And it was more unusual than most. While many wild gods have shapes that suit their homes, the ugly godling was indeed ugly. Where a god of the tall trees might see like a shimmering bird, the ugly godling was dark and squat. While a god of rocky hillsides could be short and strong, the ugly godling was frail.

The ugly godling travelled for a long time, looking for a place that it could stay in and grow strong."

The kirkman stood at his simple wooden lectern and explained that the Ugly Godling's travels had troubling effects on Mercy. How whole cities found themselves full of argument and pain due to this strain on Mercy. The Godling was an unwanted thing, small and weak, that had crept through the forests and hills of the world just after existence had begun. With so much indifference, and no small amount of cruelty being shown to the Godling, Mercy's Shield was stretched thin and weak to cover so many. With less in their way, malicious gods of disease and discord snickered as they snuck into the homes of folk who had done no wrong, and these gods made victims of many.

But eventually someone did show compassion to the Ugly Godling, welcoming it in, feeding it. After it had grown into its full powers as a god, it returned to reward those people who had given it shelter and showed it compassion.

"And with that act of kindness, Mercy was able to draw back and reinforce the lands it had protected before, no longer stretched to its limit by the Godling's travels. So may each of you show the same compassion to one another, such that Mercy may shield us from forces larger than hunger and insult."

The story was full of wondrous descriptions of the god and the trials it had suffered, and the lavish rewards it had bestowed. This was what Mikel had loved so much about listening to the story when he was young. On the festival day for the Ugly Godling people gave gifts of fresh bread to strangers and shared fresh sausages or barrels of beer. As a child Mikel had come to associate the story with the chance to stuff his face with anything passers-by had been willing to share.

A woman, whom the child Mikel had imagined must be very old, had once nudged him softly with her elbow. In his adulthood he realised that she was probably still quite young, but small boys are terrible at such estimations. She had smiled and held out a small wrapped cloth to him.

"Here," she whispered. "You look like you could do with a mouthful of something filling."

Mikel, the tiny boy from the street, unwrapped the cloth and found that it held some small hard biscuits, still warm. He took one and munched it happily.

Years later, Mikel and Mata had sat on either side of Tuomas in the wooden pews at the kirk. The kirkman still stood at his lectern, laboriously expounding upon the tale of the Ugly Godling. As an adult Mikel was surprised at how the same old man was able to take one of the most entertaining kirktales and make it into a boring trial. His head nodded backwards over and over again, and he fought to stay awake.

Next to him the small figure of Tuomas shuffled on his wooden seat. The child leaned forward and crossed his arms on the back of the pew in front of him and rested his chin on his arms. Mikel chuckled softly at the sight of his boy, staring up at the Kirkman, listing intently to the tale.

As Tuomas grew older, Mikel encouraged him to get out more, to take part in chores that might build his strength, to spend time with the other children who lived in the castle. If he had a brother to take Tuomas travelling as Filip had, Mikel would have been overjoyed to send Tuomas off to build his character and to find his strength as the Godling had.

But to return and become obsessed with joining the Guershan, the mercenaries who were always somehow connected to any trouble in Blackriver. Well, such a thing would have been troublesome.

CHAPITRE XXXIII

Mikel wished Tuomas was home now. He had gone with the Lord's Heir on a journey to bind Blackriver more closely with a strong ally to the west. They had been gone for such a long time, and they would have had to leave the protection of Mercy in Blackriver. Mikel hoped that they had reached the next of Mercy's shields without incident. He rubbed his hands together. For some reason he was sure that Tuomas would return changed in some unexpected way.

Filip's family had clearly hoped that travelling with his uncle would make the youth braver, more outgoing. And that success had meant that the boy got tangled with dangerous men, and then been killed in one of the most horrific of ways.

Would the travels that Tuomas had been on lead to the same disaster? Would Tuomas return as a braver and stronger man, but one who sought out similar dangers? Mikel closed his eyes and took a slow breath. No, Tuomas was going to be fine. He would be home soon.

The air was cooling as he walked back into the castle, and

the sky was beginning to dim. The sun was glowing a deeper red now than the searing white of noon. Mikel walked across the courtyard beyond the gates and saw people scurrying back and forth. As one man walked briskly past him, Mikel reached out, stopping the man.

"What is going on?"

"Where have you been sir?" Now that he was back among the castlefolk, Mikel's formal clothes were treated with deference. "The heir is nearly here!"

The heir is nearly back. Mikel had been so preoccupied with Filip's death that he hadn't thought of the distant shapes he had seen in the distance at last sunset. The heir is nearly back. That meant that...

Tuomas!

Mikel ran to his rooms, not caring that servants turned and stared, though he knew they wished they could run themselves. Lord Uvaniah doted on his son, and everyone knew that a massive feast must be prepared the instant he arrived. Lord Uvaniah would expect no less. He was not a cruel lord, but his servants would face punishment if they did not jump quickly to ensure his standards were met. Though it was not concern for such consequences that drove them. They enjoyed seeing his smile widen, pressing further wrinkles into his cheeks and foreheads. The lord's joy was contagious.

Mikel changed out of the dusty sweaty clothes he had on and looked for something clean and suitably impressive to wear. It would not do to be too well dressed, but merely dressing for comfort would not be enough either. Eventually he decided on a shirt and long jacket that would emphasise his shoulders and height, without making it seem as though he was going to a ball.

The great hall buzzed with activity and noise. Outside in the courtyard, stablehands were all in their positions, ready to collect horses and safely install them in the stables; brushed, fed and watered. The kitchens were a fiery steam-filled cauldron, from which men and women scuttled like beetles. The doors swung open and closed continuously, as small morsels were delivered to the waiting crowd in order to keep them from growing too ravenous before the heir arrived. Ingredients were still being carried in on people's shoulders, weaving through the slowly filling tables of castlefolk.

Above it all, at his high table, Lord Uvaniah smiled and nodded to the richer townsfolk who sat at the high table with him. Mikel was seated at the low end of that table, as a recognition of his position in the castle, and Marq sat halfway down the far side. Mikel nodded to the alchemist, not bothering to wipe the wide smile off his face.

The hall grew silent, as though every man and woman within had been given a signal. There was a small murmur near the tables on the outer edges, but overall the crowd was quiet enough to hear a single man coughing far to Mikel's left.

The great doors swung open wide.

In poured the group that had travelled with the heir. Guards came first, pretending to search the room for danger, but quickly breaking into smiles as they caught sight of their loved ones amongst the crowd at the tables. Servants and pages swarmed in soon after, running laughing into the crowd and embracing their own friends and family. Mikel searched the sea of faces for a glimpse of his son. His chest was tight. *Surely he has come home safely?*

Then Mikel saw him. Near the back, walking alongside the heir as he strolled into the great hall, one arm raised in greeting, his face shining in happiness. Mikel's smile stretched even further across his cheeks, and a sudden wave of relief spread through his body like fresh water. It was as though his arms and legs were melting. He stood at the table, not caring that one of the richer merchants of Blackriver who sat beside him was staring. All he wanted to do was keep watching as his son returned to him.

Tuomas was not very tall, and his hair absorbed the light, making him easy to lose in a crowd. He kept his hair short, though tufts and spikes grew haphazardly from it. He had grown into a strong and healthy young man, after spending too long as a youth with gangly limbs that were far too long for his size. Eventually his muscles had filled in the space beneath his shoulders, and now Mikel thought he looked good in his Guard uniform. He knew that many of the castle servants agreed. He had overheard appreciative comments as Tuomas strolled through the halls on multiple occasions.

Tuomas had grown up in the castle, which had meant that he received an education beyond anything Mikel ever had the benefit of. Somehow, Tuomas didn't seem to appreciate all that had been provided for him.

CHAPITRE XXXIV

Mikel remembered one morning when he had been strapping a belt around his waist when Tuomas wandered into his father's room. The boy was barely eight years old, with his short black hair still tousled by sleep.

"Morning," he mumbled as he rubbed at his face with one of his hands.

"Good morning Tuomas. Why aren't you ready for the day ahead?"

"What do you mean?" Tuomas' forehead creased as he looked up at his father. He was clearly very confused.

Mikel grunted and frowned. "It is late in the morning. I am already dressed and ready to leave, ready to go out into the castle and fulfil my duties. Whereas you are still slouching around in our rooms. Go and get dressed!"

He snapped the buckle to his belt shut as Tuomas blinked and then turned to leave the room.

"Tuomas," Mikel called before his young son could leave the room.

"What?"

"What are you going to do with yourself today anyway?"

His son paused and pressed his lips together.

"I didn't really have a plan yet, I just woke up." He saw Mikel's frown and lifted his hands apologetically. "I know, I know! But I suppose I would stay with ma and help her fix clothes?"

"Why don't you go and find some of the other castle children?" It frustrated Mikel. Try as he might, he had never convinced Tuomas to take advantage of the position they held, and to interact with the other children who lived in the castle. Tuomas never left to play with the children in Blackriver either, something which Mikel would have disapproved of but at least understood. Instead, the young boy would walk quietly around the castle, finding shadowy spots where he could sit undisturbed for hours at a time. "You should be playing at your age, running after the hounds with the other boys, swimming in the river. You'll never develop good strong muscles from reading all day, nor build connections with the important people of the castle!"

Tuomas had looked directly into his father's eyes. He smiled. "Yes father, I will be active today."

"Glad to hear it," Mikel had sniffed as he turned back to his bedside table. He picked up a pair of gloves and pulled them on. "And don't spend too much time with your mother, she has plenty of her own tasks to-" When Mikel turned back to the doorway, he found that it was empty. "Oh." He didn't know what to say. Tuomas was gone, which was exactly what Mikel had told him to do. He felt awkward, as though there was something else that he wanted to say to the boy, but he couldn't imagine what it might be.

Mata had always known how to encourage the boy. She had found ways to help him, and he had always endeavoured to stay by her side. Since her death, Mikel didn't think he had seen Tuomas smile once.

When the opportunity had arisen to send him as one of the heir's guards, Mikel had jumped at the chance. Tuomas needed something to distract himself from the sad memories that swamped him in Blackriver since his mother's death. Plenty of the Castle Guards had volunteered to be a part of the envoy that was leaving for Highfort, a distant town whose lord had implied certain trade benefits and alliances in exchange for a son-in-law. Mikel chose some of the most stalwart and reliable, the ones who were capable in unforeseen situations, or who had experience travelling beyond the immediate influence of Lord Uvaniah. And amidst those serious faces, he set his son, as the personal guard to the Lord's heir, Alaks.

Mikel didn't know if the daughter awaiting Alaks in Highfort would have tempted the young man, and he knew that all the gossips of the castle were waiting to find out whether his fancy had been tickled. But he didn't care about any of that. The roads from Blackriver to Highfort were long, and bandits were thick in the woods, and Mikel had not admitted to himself how worried he had been every morning.

Tuomas had not been pleased at the idea when Mikel had told him of it. He had claimed that to leave his father in such a time of need was to disrespect his parents. It had been difficult for Mikel to convince him that he was not needed in the castle.

But here he came now, with a broad smile beneath his cheeks. His hair was longer, of course, but his face looked leaner as well. There was something self-assured about the way he moved into the room. He and Uvaniah's son were walking next to each other, each with an arm draped over the other's shoulders. Mikel glanced at the lord seated in the centre of the high table. He was overwhelmed with joy at the sight of his son. *Excellent,* thought Mikel. *To see that Tuomas has taken this task and built such a friendship from it can only lead him to great things. Perhaps he will be able to take over some important function of the castle when he is older.* Mikel even wondered if Tuomas might become Commander of the Guard when the time was right.

Eventually, Tuomas finished working his way through the crowd and held out his hand to his father. Mikel reached out to take his son's wrist and held his other hand over his son's, holding the boy as close as he could. He suddenly had a vision of his son lying in a muddy riverbank, with his hands and face torn away, his eyes missing. The thought made him start and Tuomas frowned.

"What's wrong father?"

"Nothing, it's nothing." Mikel waved aside the question and motioned to the seat next to him. "I am so pleased to see you home safely! Here, there's a place for you." The smile had fallen from his face without meaning to. He sat down and waited for his son to join him, trying to bring it back and ignore the memory of Filip.

Tuomas' mouth hung open for a moment after Mikel invited him to sit in the empty seat. The youth glanced further up the table. "Oh, actually I..." He pursed his lips and frowned, then turned to look back at his father. A small smile tilted his lips. "Actually, I *will* sit here. That would be completely appropriate."

CHAPITRE XXXV

Mikel looked up the table as well, wondering what his son had been looking at. The Heir to Uvaniah was seated beside his father now, talking animatedly to the pretty daughter of the mayor. Perhaps there was some jealousy between the boys, thought Mikel. He hoped that it was a friendly rivalry for the girl's attention, and not something that would cause a rift between the two. Such a promising friendship would have to be nurtured.

Father and son sat together through the rest of the feast, talking about their lives since they had last seen each other. Neither brought up the subject of Mata. They both carefully avoided discussions of bad news, such as diseases that had struck in villages nearby, or storms that had damaged farms. Instead, Mikel spoke mainly of how he was leaving the guards under the tutelage of his second, who appeared to be running things well. They had taken patrols through Blackriver and were considering setting up guard posts around some of the more distant farming villages that sent their produce to Blackriver for the merchants. Tuomas had far more to talk about.

Mikel's son began with the tale of the journey to Highfort. The town lay a good distance away, and the journey had not been without incident. Mikel listened attentively to stories of simple travellers' concerns, a horse who needed shoeing, a broken cartwheel. Occasionally there were nights when the travelling company could really have used more food, but none was to be found or hunted nearby. Tuomas spoke fondly of a farmer who had provided what little he could for the heir and his men, spitting a calf and playing music for the travellers with his sons. The heir had been gracious in the face of such hospitality, leaving behind some very valuable jewellery that the farmer would hopefully be able to sell on. Mikel nodded and smiled. It was the sort of thing Uvaniah himself would have done and Mikel was glad to hear that the son was growing to be as good a man as the father. He asked Tuomas for his thoughts on the heir.

"What do I think of him?" Tuomas first looked up the length of the table, then blinked and stammered before bringing his attention back to the leg of meat he was holding. He coughed and then took a large bite of the juicy flesh. "I think he is a good man. He is generous and kind. He treats all his men and servants as though they are important, even when he has little time for them. That, I think, has some part to play in the failure of our journey."

"Failure?" Mikel was surprised. The travellers had entered the great hall in such high spirits. Naturally, he assumed the journey had been a success.

"Yes. You remember that we were sent to Highfort in order to find a bride for Alaks? Well, she was a young thing named Safeera. It transpired that the girl was not so pleasant as we had been led to believe." Tuomas frowned and leaned closer to his father. "There was one evening when she tripped up a man bringing a plate of quail to the table, and then she laughed as he tumbled to the floor, roasted birds spilling everywhere. When her father Lord Ovyolia asked what had happened, she claimed the poor man had been dallying with one of the serving-girls and not paying attention. This, even though we had all seen what she did. She had not even tried to conceal her actions from us."

"Did no-one speak in the servant's defence?"

"Not from Highfort. Even the man himself simply stood by with his eyes cast down." Tuomas plucked a hard-boiled egg from a nearby plate and cracked it on his own. He continued speaking as he peeled the shell. "Finally Alaks stood and explained that the man had not been careless, though he had tripped. He managed not to mention that it was Safeera who had caused the incident."

"But clearly she was not going to be suitable for him." Mikel could see his son's point clearly.

"Exactly. Alaks made sure to be as polite as possible, and to speak well of the girl to Lord Ovyolia. But a match was not going to be possible." Tuomas took a sip of his wine, glancing up the length of the table towards the lord of the castle and his son again. He smiled. "I will give the girl some excuse, she was quite young."

Mikel smiled himself. "How young could she have been?" His son and the heir were themselves barely men at nineteen. It made his heart laugh at the idea of these two young men shaking their heads and commiserating over the juvenile behaviour of some other youth.

"She was seventeen, I believe."

Mikel's smile broke wider into a chuckle and he lifted his cup to touch the edge of his son's. "Indeed, so young! Here's to children then."

Confused but happy, Tuomas shared the toast with his father.

"It is a shame she behaved that way though," Mikel tutted. "Such behaviour weakens Mercy."

"Yes, it does," agreed Tuomas. "But I am not sure that Highfort relies on Mercy's Shield so strongly as Blackriver."

Mikel blinked.

"Do they have no kirk?" he stammered.

"They do have a kirk, but there are other shrines to local gods set up around the town as well. The people sometimes leave offerings or bring prayers to the shrines."

"Which gods?" Mikel was intrigued. It did make sense that some gods may be more friendly than others, but the kirk in Blackriver had always taught that it was too difficult for humans to recognise them reliably enough for anything more than small favours from common gods. Certainly they would not build a shrine to any of them.

"I didn't recognise any of them. There was one that was said to patrol the streets at night and defend the homes of the people. They described it like a large hound, with thick brown fur."

"Well, I'm sure they know their local gods better than I, but I think I would dislike such shrines if they led to behaviour like that girl's. I know I feel safer when I can see all the people of Blackriver working together to make Mercy's Shield stronger."

"That may be why she behaved that way," agreed Tuomas. "I know for sure that she was one of the people that would leave offerings for the gods."

"How so?"

"Safeera accompanied us for a short distance when we left Highfort. She said she wanted to visit a small shrine deep in the nearby forest, and having us to travel with for at least some of the journey was better than travelling alone. Of course, we agreed to that."

"Did you see the shrine?"

"Yes. We had to turn off the main road and follow a short path to it. It was a narrow way, and not everyone would be able to fit through, but Alaks let me come along. It was a short pillar of rock, uncarved and weather beaten. Moss covered the sides and I could see beetles scurrying across the surface."

"That sounds more run down than I would have thought. Don't gods need shrines that are well taken care of?" Mikel was not familiar with how such things would work, but he thought that it only made sense for the shrines to be well tended.

"All the shrines in Highfort looked to be clean and well-made, so I don't know what was happening with this forest shrine." Tuomas leaned a little closer to Mikel. "The girl was wearing long silk gloves that stretched up past her elbows and a fine veil that was held over her face by a narrow circlet of silver. As we approached the shrine she removed the gloves and veil and placed them on the craggy rock."

"So strange." Mikel shook his head and took a sip of his drink. "Tell me, what else was Highfort like?"

CHAPITRE XXXVI

Tuomas went on to explain that the heir and his men had spent a goodly length of time enjoying the hospitality of Highfort before this journey into the forest shrine. Though a marriage was clearly not going to occur between the two households, it would have been rude to say so before spending some time in each other's presence and making a show of getting to know one another. There had been dances and balls, days spent on the hunt or simply riding through the lands and villages of Highfort. Tuomas appeared to have enjoyed much of the time he spent there and he kept smiling as he spoke of days spent in luxurious pastimes. Mikel was impressed to hear that Alaks had insisted upon Tuomas coming with him for most of the excursions.

"You've done well there my boy! That will be a very fruitful friendship."

Tuomas merely smiled again, his cheeks turning red. He lifted his cup to his lips and took a large mouthful of the dark wine that was being served to celebrate the heir's return. *He's still not got his head for these drinks,* thought Mikel.

Tuomas' story continued. The journey home was unfortunately more dangerous than the journey to Highfort had been. Not a week earlier, while travelling through high passes in the Clouded Valley mountains, the entire group had been waylaid by bandits. Mikel's heart froze in his chest as Tuomas told him of the encounter, even though he knew that his son made it back to Blackriver without harm.

"They rode down out of the hills. It was like nothing you could believe Da. There were so many of them, all riding on tired skinny horses but desperate for anything they could carry off. I saw one grab a pan that had been loosely tied to a cart. He just grabbed it and then spun to ride off. One of the guards put an arrow between his shoulder blades."

Mikel studied his son as the younger man spoke. There was no hint of panic in his voice as he described what he had seen. Mikel was proud that his son was becoming a brave and strong young man. But neither did Tuomas sound empathetic to the poor souls who had become so desperate. Mikel would not brook law breakers, of course, but there was room for pity when dealing with such cases. Did Tuomas not feel that?

Had Tuomas become too familiar with blood and violence in this journey? Mikel hoped that his son was not going to become one of those who lusted after the carnage and confusion of a fight. It was always better to enter a violent confrontation with a desire not to be involved. That way you would minimise the amount of damage on either side.

Nor would he want his boy to have found the fight too traumatic. The boy would have to be involved in some fighting one day, Mikel was sadly sure of it. So it would be no good if he found it triggered nightmares or nausea. Thankfully, his son was simply looking pensive and quiet.

"What are you thinking about?" Mikel asked.

"I was just remembering the way the man lay after the

arrow took him. He came off his horse and lay face down in the long grass. The arrow stuck straight up, like a lord's banner among the waving grass."

"Aye, a fight is a rough place to be." Mikel reached out and placed his hand on Tuomas' shoulder. He was glad that Tuomas had found a moment of pity for the bandits. Tuomas nodded.

"Was there anything that truly turned the tide for you against these bandits?" asked Mikel. "Or did they simply have no chance?"

"From what the other guards said during the return journey, it is unlikely they ever posed a serious threat. They didn't even have any bows of their own, or they could have shot some of our people before they charged in. Simeon, one of Alaks's personal guards, he said that they were hungry from living in the hills for so long without any decent food and they must have been driven half-mad. Alaks agreed with him."

"Did the heir get involved in the fight then? Or was he kept safely under wrap and key." Mikel smiled at his joke as he took a large piece of warm apple pie to his plate. He dolloped a thick spoonful of cream on top of the golden baked pie. The scent made his mouth water, though his stomach protested, already full as it was.

"Actually, Alaks was very impressive. He made sure the rest of us were safe inside the carts first, and then he jumped onto his horse, drew his sword and charged some of the bandits." Tuomas smiled, his eyes reflecting the bright fire of a nearby torch. "He looked incredible. Like a hero from a song. Of course, Simeon and the other personal guards followed him. They couldn't let him get hurt just because he wanted to save the day!"

"What did you do?" Mikel licked a little cream off his lips.

Tuomas blushed and looked down. "I... stayed in the carts with the others."

Mikel nodded and noticed a strange feeling in his stomach. On the one hand, he was glad that his son had avoided the most dangerous circumstance of his journey, which had made it all the more likely that he would make it home safely. But at the same time, there was a sour twist to his gut, as he realised that Tuomas was representing the Castle Guards, and had been sent to provide more protection for Alaks, the heir of Lord Uvnaiah. Instead of fulfilling that duty, his son had hidden away from danger and allowed Alaks's personal guards to bear the brunt of the danger, and the heir himself to be in harm's way. Mikel hid his discomfort by picking up a cup of ale and taking a slow sip.

"You're judging me," said Tuomas. Mikel could hear that his son was sad, but not surprised.

"No," he declared, reaching over to place a hand on his son's. Tuomas looked up slowly. "I'm just so glad that you made it back to me." He smiled sadly. "These castle hallways have been very lonely without you."

CHAPITRE XXXVII

The conversation in the hall was winding down. The night had grown later than any of the crowd had anticipated, and many folk were yawning widely as they draped their arms over one another's shoulders and moved slowly from the great hall. Lord Uvaniah was slumped on his chair and appeared to be asleep, while Alaks was still engaged in loud conversation with the crowd of men around him.

Mikel noticed that the lord looked small tonight. His robe crowded over his shoulders, as though it had been sewn for a larger man. With his face slackened by sleep, his wrinkles deepened as well, exposing his pale, aged skin. Mikel wanted to lift the old man in his arms and carry him to his bed.

Alaks was in fine spirits however, whipping a spoon out of a bowl to press into service as an impromptu sword. Clearly he was reliving some moment from the bandit attack for the people around him. Mikel was glad to hear that the next lord of the castle was going to be a good man, willing to defend his people men as much as ask them to defend himself. In fact, the entire story of what had happened at Highfort sounded very promising. If the lord of Highfort had indeed not been offended by the rejection of his daughter, then perhaps Alaks may have quite a political head on his shoulders.

Tuomas waved slightly to the lord's son and to Mikel's surprise Alaks leaped up immediately from his admirers and strode quickly over to them.

"Tuomas! You can't be leaving so soon?" He tilted his head slightly to one side as he examined Tuomas and Mikel. Mikel was put in mind of a sparrow as he watched the heir's face, like a small bird eyeing up some morsel of food on the ground but at the same time wary of any cat that may be hiding nearby.

"I'm sorry sir, but it is late and my father and-" Tuomas had barely spoken a few words before Alaks reached out to grasp Mikel's wrist tightly and then pull him in close.

"Commander! Of course, we have met briefly in the past, but let me just say what an honour it has been to share the last few months with your son. You should be a very proud man."

Mikel was speechless for a few moments, staring into the heir's deep dark eyes. "I... Thank you... Yes, I am very proud."

"Then come and share a drink with me in your pride!" Alaks smiled, exposing bright teeth and once again putting Mikel off balance. "We shall toast the goodness of your son, and you can regale me with all the stories of the castle that have grown in my absence."

"Thank you, the offer is very kind, but really there have been no such stories..." Mikel's eyelids weighed down and he wondered how he could excuse himself honourably. He turned to Tuomas.

"Nonsense," said Alaks cheerfully. "I've already heard of some sort of murder that took place just outside the walls! I'm sure you must know all about that." Alaks winked at Mikel. "Shall we all be safe in our beds tonight?"

Mikel blinked and opened his mouth to respond but no sound escaped his throat. His son laughed and hugged him.

"You go to bed father. I may just stay to converse with the heir, if that is alright."

"It suits me fine," answered Mikel, relieved. He bowed to the heir who graciously returned the bow and bid the commander a good night's sleep. The last he saw of the two men was Alaks grabbing Tuomas by the shoulders and leading him into the cluster of waiting merchants and rich socialites who had been so caught up in the heir's tales earlier. *I hope this friendship does help him in the society of the town,* thought Mikel. *I hope that he doesn't find himself pulled out of his depth by these new currents.*

These new social connections for his son were a relief to Mikel though. As his son grew up, Mikel had been disappointed by Tuomas' attempts to make friends, always finding the least suitable companions.

Mikel recalled another dinner in the great hall, when he had seen a much younger Tuomas sitting to one side of the hall, across a table from his friend Louka. The two boys held a spread of cards in their hands and were peering intently at them. Mikel walked up behind Tuomas.

"What are you playing, son?"

"Task," murmured Tuomas without turning his head.

"I haven't heard of that one. How does it work?"

"Louka set the goal and now I have to try and stop him or beat him."

"I see."

Louka laid a card down between them and Tuomas groaned.

"Was that bad?" asked Mikel.

"He's going to get the next three hands."

Louka grinned and raised his eyebrows at Mikel. "Once you know the game, it can be easy to predict!" he said.

"Then why play?" asked Mikel. The idea of following through something that was already determined was foolhardy to him.

"Most of the game is in setting the correct task for the hand and then finding out if you chose well," answered Louka. "I think I did good this time!"

"So long as you boys are having a good time," said Mikel. He reached out and squeezed Tuomas' shoulder. "See you later."

The boys mumbled some sort of farewell as Mikel left. He had wished that Tuomas would spend more time with some of the other boys in the castle though. Louka was a nice enough lad, but he spent as much time in corners as Tuomas. The two only encouraged each other to hide away from the rest of the castle, playing their card games or reading. They didn't even go out into the fields around Blackriver and run around together! That would at least be active, even if it still kept them apart from the other children!

But now Tuomas had become a companion of Lord Uvaniah's heir, and Mikel could let such concerns leave his head. He wrapped himself up in the warm blankets of his own bed, deeply aware of the empty space on the other side. Mikel thought about the Guershan he had met in the Gilded Rooster. Talking with them was so very long ago now. No matter. He promised himself that he would ask his Guards about Akub, the mercenary who had gone missing. In the morning. For now, sleep washed over his body with a soothing numbness.

CHAPITRE XXXVIII

Mikel woke late and dressed quickly, just making it to the hall in time to get some cold oatmeal and scoop it it into his mouth as the servants cleared away the breakfast things. He spent some time looking for Tuomas but had no luck. He poked his head through Marq's workshop door and found that Saara's family had collected the body of Filip. The Kirkman had said that he would be happy to perform the funeral for them.

"Did you offer to pay for the service?" asked Mikel, wondering how the family would handle the unexpected expense of a sudden death in the family. He knew it had been hard enough for him.

"I told them that the commander of the castle guard would help them with their expenses. My own pursestrings are much harder to open than yours after all." The smile that split the alchemist's face looked more mocking than usual. Mikel shook off the comment with a snort.

"Good, thank you." And he truly was glad. Mikel hated the thought of a family being put in such a difficult position, when they had just suffered the blow of a violent death for their son and brother. Duty to one another kept Mercy's Shield strong. "You're certain the Kirkman was not upset by the condition of the body?" Mikel was sure that the rules concerning the condition of bodies being given funeral rites was a sign of the old man's fear, not an actual requirement.

"Why should he have?" Marq' forehead creased in puzzlement. "Who would have told him?"

"Marq!" Mikel wanted to laugh and shout at the same time. Trust a foreign alchemist to not give the kirkman such information! Still, at least it meant the family could bury the body and be done with the awful business. He still had to try and find out what had happened so that their minds could be at peace.

After a short conversation about Tuomas' return, during which Marq expressed all the correct emotions at all the correct times; pleasure, shock, concern, delight; Mikel bid the alchemist good day and left.

As he strode away from the alchemist's rooms, Mikel's thoughts returned to the day the kirkman had told him that they would not accept Mata's body. The commander had stood outside the kirk, with his hands in fists and hot tears pricking the corners of his eyes. His breath was hot and tore at his throat as he gathered himself.

"Are you alright Mikel?" asked one of the congregation. The woman smoothed her hair as she stepped closer and then she laid a hand on Mikel's shoulder. "It is a difficult time, I know." Her eyes were overflowing with sympathy.

"Yes, it is," Mikel managed to exclaim before his throat tightened again. He swallowed and grimaced, then turned to more fully address the woman. "But it is not the loss of-" He paused as a wave of emotion spasmed through him. He sniffed. "It is not that which upsets me now."

The woman looked confused and shook her head slightly. "Then what-?"

"The Kirkman tells me that I may not bring Mata to lay in rest within the kirk." Mikel growled through clenched teeth. The woman stepped away from the force of his anger and he lifted a hand in apology. He straightened his clothes in an attempt to divert himself from his own anger.

"Sorry. I'm sorry. Obviously, it's just a very difficult time for me."

"Does that mean that she won't be..." The woman's voice trailed off and she shielded her heart with her palm.

"That's what it seems like to me. Mata spent her whole life devoted to the kirk and sharing Mercy with Blackriver, building Mercy up so that its shield spread as wide as possible, and then now, after Mercy wouldn't protect her from Red Lung-" Mikel hung his head and sniffed. He could feel the sobs trying to fight their way up and out of his chest. He clenched his teeth.

"I'm so sorry Mikel."

The woman had nothing else to say. There was nothing else that she could say. She touched his shoulder and then hurried off into the streets. Mikel clenched his hands into fists and then relaxed them, over and over, wondering what he could possibly do now.

When they gathered to bury Mata, Mikel had resented the sunlight that shone down on him and Tuomas and the friends that Mata had made. Her coffin was made of pale wood and looked much smaller than he thought respectable. They all stood in a circle around it, where it lay on the ground next to the hole that had been dug to inter her. Some of the people he had considered 'their' friends were speaking over the coffin, saying all the right words, crying and comforting one another. He knew that he should speak to them, that they probably wanted to say things that might comfort him. But he just grimaced and wished that the sun would give up and allow the rain to come and shroud the gathering in grey and rushing noise. He needed the rain to fill his ears and eyes so he didn't have to think about any of this any more.

Tuomas walked over to one of the middle aged women who had joined them here, and she opened her arms into a hug. They had cried together for a while and then Tuomas smiled weakly at her before he moved around the circle to the next well-wisher.

Mikel supposed that it was probably an appropriate thing to do. He should probably be doing something of the kind himself, acknowledging these friends and their need to connect with him. But he couldn't even recognise any of them right now. His mind would not allow him to recall their names, or how he knew them. Some of them came to talk to him, and he would nod, but he could bring no words forth. They would sigh and leave.

"It is with a heavy heart that we send Mata's essence to join with Mercy and watch over us all."

Mikel's shoulders had jerked. He had blinked and pulled his lips back from his teeth in a sneer of surprise. He recognised that voice. He turned, not willing to believe that he would see what his senses were trying to tell him was there. But it was true, the kirkman had come to Mata's burial.

Mikel stared. His fingers curled into claws as he watched that cold-hearted old man speak routine words over the coffin. A series of noises that meant nothing. When Mikel had come to the kirkman in need, the old man had cast him out of the kirk with barely a second glance. When Mikel had protested that Mata, sweet Mata, devout Mata, had earned the rituals that would ensure her essence was bound to and accepted by

Mercy, this same bearded fool had raised a hand to cut him off and then told Mikel that he could not accept Mata in the kirk.

And why? Why had his wife been left to the whim of nature unlike anyone else who died in Blackriver? Because the kirkman was offended by her death. He spoke so warmly of Mercy's embrace and how all would find their way to becoming part of Mercy's shield, but he believed that only those who were perfect were worthy of it.

Suddenly all of his sermons had taken on a dark twist. That was why he spent an hour each work exhorting the townsfolk into perfect behaviour and perfect appearance. He wanted them to be perfect enough to join with Mercy.

Mikel's eyes stared at the hole in the ground that Mata's coffin was lowered into. It wasn't fair of the Kirkman. No one was truly perfect. Everyone had their flaws. Most of those flaws weren't visible on the outside, not like Mata's illness had been. When she coughed up blood, that wasn't a sign that she wasn't perfect enough to become part of the Kirkman's precious shield. It was a sign that Mercy had not protected her properly!

Mikel didn't move as the coffin was laid in the grave. He stood motionless as others threw handfuls of dirt onto the box and muttered their farewells to his wife. He barely noticed as Tuomas touched his shoulder and said something Mikel couldn't hear before walking away. Eventually, Mikel stood alone beside the freshly turned mud that covered her grave.

"Goodbye love," he had said quietly. "I wish I could have done better for you."

CHAPITRE XXXIX

As Mikel walked into the guard's hall the morning after Tuomas' return, he was pleased to see that Zhon had kept the hall looking professional while he had been distracted. He had allowed himself to be preoccupied with his grief for too long, and he needed to get back into his duties. This business with Filip was a good way for him to take charge again. This hall was a quiet enclave of order in the centre of the bustling storm of the castle.,

Things were less well organised in the bunkrooms. He caught the guards there by surprise, and they jumped to stuff their belongings into their small trunks. *You're lucky the lord is getting old too, old man,* he told himself. *If Lord Uvaniah asked for a reckoning of these men, you wouldn't have had a thing to say for the last year. You've let yourself mope for too long. That's no way to honour her memory.* He reached the end of the bunkroom and turned.

Behind him, standing next to their beds at attention, firm backs held stiffly straight and eyes staring directly in front of themselves, were about twenty guards. Half the bunks contained lumps that were bodies huddled beneath their blankets, snores echoing out softly. The guards who had been on night patrol. Mikel nodded, once, sharply, dismissing the guards. They quickly turned back to their tasks, tucking blankets beneath thin mattresses and locking their trunks. Mikel was pleased with his men. They knew how to behave. He turned and opened the door to the commander's office.

It had been a long time since he had actually gone into his own office. The room held three chairs and a fireplace, all set beneath a massive window with a small stained glass image set in the centre. The fireplace was not lit, which Mikel was glad of. The weather had held remarkably warm for the time of year. The stained glass held an image of a young man in armour, lifting his sword against a black monster made up of smoke and shadows. It represented the need of the castle guards to be ever vigilant against any foe, realising that danger could come from anywhere and unexpectedly. Mikel had spent many years thinking about the image in that window. It had been the first thing he saw when he had been brought to see the commander when he was young. Between Mercy's Shield and the castle guard, no harm should ever come to the inhabitants of Blackriver or Sheerwall. He took a moment to enjoy the window now, each coloured pane afire with light from the morning sun still low over the horizon.

"Good morning sir," said Zhon, rising from the commander's seat behind a wide table, covered in papers. "Are you feeling well?"

"I'm fine, I'm fine. Tell me, how are the Guard going?" Mikel pulled a chair over to join his second at the table. He glanced at the papers that lay spread across its surface, feeling a shudder run up his back. He had been avoiding all this work for so long. He hoped Zhon was keeping ahead of it all.

For a time the other man spoke to Mikel of supplies and

training schedules and organising the shifts of the watch. He pulled some sheets out of the piles as he spoke, referring to letters of recommendation from well regarded members of Blackriver society, or important reports of strange disturbances during the night patrols. All the tedious work that was required whenever a large group of people was to be organised, boring but vital.

If they didn't ensure that supplies were provided for at least simple meals, or enough arms and armour to equip everyone, then the Guard would be hungry and ill-prepared for the tasks that befell them. If Zhon wasn't checking that the Guard's equipment had been maintained, then armour might give way, or weapons break. Put a young man on the night patrol for three days and then give him a double length day patrol without thinking, and watch him slumber while thieves ducked in and out the smaller gates.

Mikel listened to Zhon's report as attentively as he could. Despite his best efforts, his gaze kept drifting aside to the blankness of the room's wall. Although he wanted to get back into his own seat and perform his duties properly, he was glad to have someone else taking care of all this business. Zhon certainly appeared to have it all in hand.

"Thank you for dealing with all this for me, Zhon. I'm sorry you've been left with such a lot of duties."

"It's no worry of mine," smiled Zhon. Clearly the man was enjoying his role. Mikel hoped that he wouldn't cause trouble as Mikel settled himself back into this room and behind that desk. From what he remembered of the man, there shouldn't be any challenge there.

"Good, I'm glad. Thank you again." Mikel shifted his chair closer. "I have a second purpose in coming here today though."

Zhon raised an eyebrow and crossed his arms, leaning against the tall back of the commander's chair. Mikel was keenly aware that he sat on the wrong side of his own desk, in one of the uncarved chairs left for visitors to the office.

"You know that body we found two days ago in the riverbank?"

The younger man nodded.

"Well, I've done some asking around. It seems the boy whose body we found was planning to become one of the Guershan."

"Really? That seems unfortunate on multiple counts then." Zhon uncrossed his arms and sniffed. "Why would they want to mess up some arrow fodder before it had even signed up?"

"That's exactly what I thought at first. But it gets a bit more complicated than that. The boy, Filip, had been supposed to meet with one of the mercenaries in particular, a man named Akub. But his companions say Akub told them Filip never showed up."

"So say the Guershan I wager. Surely they are simply trying to avoid any suspicion."

"I would have agreed with you," began Mikel. "But Akub went missing himself only a week or so ago. And his companions said they had seen him moving around town near the castle shortly beforehand."

Zhon scowled. "I hope they aren't planning to make any sort of move against the castle. I know mercenaries can be scum, but they aren't usually so lawless as to attack one of the few things that protects them."

CHAPITRE XL

Mikel considered what would happen to a band like the Guershan if they weren't living a semi-legitimate existence on the fringes of Blackriver. They would be considered bandits very quickly, and the local villages and merchants would work together to find someone who could deal with them. By setting up near Sheerwall they were indicating that they followed the rules enough to be trusted for limited work.

"Exactly. Unless perhaps he ran to avoid being caught for the murder of the boy."

Zhon nodded. "Good point. Is there much we can do about that?"

Mikel shook his head. "Not really. The only description of this Akub I have came from the man's brother, and the brother is one of the Guershan himself. If they are covering up for a murderer, then they would have given a false description as well."

"So then why are you here? I can't assume you think we

need to step up our guards after this? There doesn't seem to be much more threat to consider."

"No no, nothing like that." Mikel waved a hand to dismiss the idea, brushing it aside like a faint cobweb in an unused hallway. He didn't want to give the impression that Zhon was doing anything wrong. "I wanted to ask the men if any of them had seen anything. Just in case the Guershan are telling the truth. If their man was hanging around the Castle and did go missing, maybe someone saw something that could give us more information. If they were planning something themselves, I can't imagine that they would have set us on alert by mentioning that he was near the Castle, which is why I am inclined to think that he was there. I don't like the idea that whoever or whatever it was that took the hands off that boy may have killed that mercenary also and is still roaming around us."

Zhon agreed, and the two of them made their way out into the guardhall.

It took the whole day to speak with all the guards. The first step was simple enough, walking through the bunkroom and speaking to the guards there. They woke the men who were sleeping through until their night shift on the walls, taking the time to sit with them until their eyes grew less foggy and their memories returned fully. Then they moved through to the women's quarters, knocking on the door and calling the woman out into the hall for a brief conversation, one at a time.

Each of the guards did their best, despite the lack of sleep, but Mikel was disappointed. None of them knew anything about Akub. They didn't even recognise his description.

He and Zhon spoke to the other guards as well, calling back those who were about to head out for their own duty, or on whatever personal errands they may have had. None of them could tell the two men anything they didn't already know themselves. Eventually they had spoken to everyone at the guard hall.

Mikel was sure it would have been one of the night watch who saw something. Zhon said that one of the guards who had been on the last night duty didn't seem to be in the bunks, so as soon as they had finished speaking to those still in the garrison, he and Mikel set out to find those who were still on duty.

Mikel felt a sensation of satisfaction and comfort as he walked with Zhon through the narrow dark pathways that led to the guard posts around the castle. In order to keep the guards from being easily attacked by traitors or invaders, their pathways overlooked each other and were difficult to navigate quickly. They allowed a force of around forty guards to completely observe every approach to the castle, as well as many of the more important buildings and passages. Mikel hadn't walked them in years, relying on his sergeants to ensure the troop were well-trained and knew how to mount a watch. Now he ducked under the overhanging remains of an ancient archway in shadow; there he twisted his back in order to slip around a tight corner easier. He found himself smiling as he sweated beneath his tunic. It was good to be back in these tiny spaces.

Zhon was following along behind him, cursing softly under his breath, and occasionally cursing not so quietly.

"It's been awhile since I've walked these paths," Mikel commented.

"Aye, and with Mercy's blessings, I'll not be walking them again any time soon," huffed Zhon.

Mikel's smile grew broader.

One by one, they spoke to the guards on duty. At first they made just as little progress as they had in the bunkroom, but then they came across a man named Akim. He claimed that he had seen a man matching Akub's description, and that he had seen that figure near the castle.

"Now, whoever he was, he didn't do anything aggressive," insisted Akim. "The man was just wandering around the streets nearby. I think he started walking towards the gates one time, but he changed his mind and wandered off again."

"Why would he have changed his mind? Was this during the evening?" The common townsfolk had limited permission to enter the Castle. So long as Akub had behaved, he would have been allowed to enter and see if he could find someone who could help him, depending on what it was he claimed to need. However, if it was late enough in the evening that the gates were being closed for the night, then he would have been turned away unless some Castle noble had requested otherwise. Mikel realised he could no longer remember what time the night watch began their shifts. Were the gates closed by the time they found their posts? Was this man even working the night watch when he had seen Akub?

"Clearly he had some sort of mischief in mind," added Mikel as he considered the situation.

"I suppose." Akim looked worried.

"Don't worry, I doubt he looked particularly troubling. You had no call to report him to anyone." Mikel's reassurance calmed the man.

"Where did you see him go? How often did he come by?" asked Zhon.

I must admit, he does have a knack for getting to the heart of the matter, thought Mikel.

"I can't be sure. I think he was staying in one of the taverns on Long Road. He drifted back towards that place most of the time."

Mikel laughed out loud. "One of the Guershan wouldn't be able to afford to stay on Long Road! And no-one there would want him to either." He shook his head. "You must have been mistaken."

Akim bristled. "No sir! I saw him walk off in that direction, and he certainly moved into the lee of one of the buildings. Now, I won't say he definitely went inside the place, but I didn't see him leave for a very long time. And there were others walking into the building the whole evening."

CHAPITRE XLI

Mikel bit his lower lip. "What building was it? Could you show us?"

"I could, though my shift isn't over for a few hours." Mikel nodded. It would take time to find a replacement and send them out to take Akim's place. Zhon had been explaining in the office that they had no room to replace guards in the roster as it was, not without exhausting the recruits they had.

"Why don't you go ask Lefi?" continued the young guard in front of Mikel.

"Who is Lefi? Why would he know which building our man was lingering near?"

"I saw him walking to the same building on a few nights. In fact, he might even have got a closer look at the man you are after, they were there at the same time at least once."

Mikel turned to stare at Zhon. "This is troubling news."

"Indeed." Zhon blinked in thought, his lips moving slightly as though he were speaking to himself below the hearing of anyone else. "Lefi would have been on the night shift about a week ago. That was when you say this man went missing, isn't it?" The second-in-command directed his question at Mikel, who was glad for the cautious words Zhon had used. The last thing he needed was a curious young guard like Akim taking a rumour and setting it free through the castle.

"Yes, according to his brother. So, if Lefi was on duty, perhaps he saw something?"

"Let's find him. The sooner the better. And his name is important for another reason. Why have I heard his name recently?" Zhon's brow furrowed as he racked his brain for some information that did not seem to materialise.

The two men asked Akim if he knew where Lefi was now. The guard did not, but suggested they try a tavern that was near the riverbank to the east of the Castle. It was near enough that the castle folk could get there quickly when they were in need of a drink or two, but far enough from Long Road to ensure the well-to-do merchants and craftsmen were not bothered. Mikel and Zhon took their leave of Akim and moved back through the narrow covered paths that wound towards the main hallways of the castle.

As they went, Mikel took the chance to admire the view that Akim was watching over on behalf of the entire Castle Guard. Beyond the windows wide fields of farmland spread out towards the South Forest, lifting in small hillocks here and there, but largely unbroken until one found the spires of a distant kirk rising above the trees, surrounded by wisps of smoke from its village chimneys. Further still one could just see the larger hills of the Water Ranges, a thickly forested range of hills that edged the ocean. Mikel had never seen the ocean.

He and Mata had often spoken of making the journey one year, when everything was settled and their son was old enough to stay in the Castle by himself. Now they never would. Mikel sniffed and focused himself on the beauty of the land again. Blackriver was a lucky town, set among such fertile and comforting surroundings.

"If this Lefi was somehow meeting with the missing man, then we could have a more dangerous scenario than you expected on your hands," Mikel said to Zhon , before remembering that he was supposed to be the one in charge. His cheeks began to redden.

"Indeed sir, we will have to consider doubling the watch." Zhon didn't notice Mikel's misstatement and strode on without looking at the commander. "Or perhaps we shall figure out what their goal is and put guards in those areas."

"That would be better. That way we will have more men rested and ready in case something does happen." They walked on in silent thought for a few more moments before Mikel continued. "So, let us recap. This man who seems to have killed Filip now appears to have been spending some evenings hanging around Long Road near the Castle. He wanted to come inside but changed his mind and left. One of our guards may have been in the same building as him for at least one of those nights."

"But the Guershan told us they had seen him around the castle. That doesn't make sense? Why would they give him away?" Zhon sounded angry, as though the mercenaries' actions had been taken to deliberately goad him.

"I think they spoke the truth to me. I think they don't have any idea what he was up to. If his actions were linked to them in some way, then they would have directed me away from him. Perhaps they would have claimed he had left town. Even if he was acting alone, if they knew he planned something they surely would have directed me away anyway. Simply through being one of their own they would have known we would connect him to them."

Zhonnodded, grudgingly.

"And if I am right and he is acting alone, then it is possible that our man Lefi was meeting him because he had noticed him and that he managed to stop him, one way or another."

"You think Lefi may have discovered some plot and killed the mercenary in order to halt it?" Zhon turned his head, eyes wide with shock at the thought.

"Why not?" Mikel was genuinely confused. "Are our men not capable of such a thing?"

"I suppose that it is possible..." Zhon's voice trailed off. He rubbed a hand over his mouth as they continued walking. "I just would have expected him to make a report of any incident of that sort. Especially if it had happened on Long Road! You know the people that frequent those places. They would have kept a close eye on any of our guards that stepped into one of the fine establishments there, and you know it. If there had been any sniff of violence between a guard and a mercenary, of all things, they would have stormed my- your office."

Mikel allowed Zhon's slip of the tongue to pass unmentioned and focused on the substance of the man's statement. Lefi would have certainly been noticed if he had caused any incidents on Long Road. So what had he been doing there, and why didn't the commander of the Castle Guard and his second know about it?

The two men turned a corner and began walking towards the main courtyard of Sheerwall. Mikel wondered which of his guards were watching over them now, positioned high in their narrow hidden paths along the walls, ready to warn one another of anything untoward, to react with the speed of a wolf.

"I suppose you're right," Mikel sighed. "Which leaves us having to wonder if Lefi has a more traitorous role to play in this."

"It would appear. And why is his name so familiar?"

INTERMÈDE

The creature felt a sense of satisfaction as it followed new prey through strange passageways. The sweat and blood of this one smelt right to the creature, a feeling that flooded its nostrils and soothed the tension in the creature's limbs. But this prey found secret ways, ways that the creature could not follow, not without being seen by others, or facing undue attention. The creature's skin burned when other's eyes lingered on it. It wanted to be hidden, to be a shadow behind its prey.

This new prey walked through doors that remained barred and secured against the creature, accessed rooms with other warm blooded prey. The frustration that drove it was different now. Before it was searching with no direction, unsure whether the right prey was to be found. It had been exposed and lost. Now it knew where it needed to be, and though it did not have a way to get there yet, it knew how to be patient. The creature smiled to itself as it followed the new one. This one was perfect.

No more days and nights spent circling the hallways and

common rooms of this giant stone structure, exposed, seen, vulnerable. The creature had loathed its position, the coverings it had claimed from its prey were growing less and less effective, and so the creature was driven to change them. It had spent far too long following the entrancing scent of its true prey, the one that smelt of gold and sweat. The new one would help the creature get closer to the true prey. It was a stone sticking out of a sheer wall, a new path, a grip that would allow the creature to pull itself ever closer.

The new one would need to be alone, and somewhere the creature could approach it. This was a simple thing to arrange. The creature was good at waiting.

It licked unfamiliar lips and squeezed its hands into fists as it walked through narrow spaces. These nails dug into its palms, and the creature savoured the bright pain of them. Soon there would be other feelings to savour; warmth, and joy, and blood.

CHAPITRE XLII

The tavern Akim had directed Mikel and Zhon to was named The Ugly Godling. It was a brightly lit building to the rear of a larger, more respectable building. The tavern bore witness to the story of the Ugly Godling with an image of a strange creature on the board hanging above its door. Mikel examined it as he walked inside. The creature had one eye and at least five arms, with tufts of hair and warts sprouting from all over its deformed body. A halo blazed out from behind it, depicted in crude shafts of yellow paint, to show the godly nature of the beast. The tavern was built into the lower story of a crafter's guildhouse, and Mikel guessed the woodworkers that kept lodgings above and shared workshops at the front must greatly enjoy the extra money that the tavern bought in.

Because of the guildhouse keeping rooms only for the woodworkers who were members of their organisation, the tavern could offer no lodging, which meant the grass outside the Ugly Godling was trampled with the comings and goings of townspeople.

This tavern was much more cramped than the Gilded Rooster, which surprised Mikel. Candles stood tall in their candelabras, their light pressing the walls away. They must be swapped out long before they sputtered into low piles of wax, in an attempt to keep the space feeling spacious. A line of broad windows faced the river, and mirrors had been placed to help spread more light around the room. A young boy and young girl were both sweeping the floor as the two men walked in, though it looked clean to Mikel. A throng of people sat around the tables, enjoying their midday meal; including three or four clusters of richly dressed men and women from within Blackriver town, who were leaning in to speak confidentially to one another, clearly making various deals over the tall clean glasses that held their drinks.

There was no sign of anyone matching Lefi's description in the tavern, which frustrated Mikel. He had to remind himself that it had been unlikely that he and Zhon would run into the missing guard so quickly. However they recognised most of the people sitting, drinking and laughing in quiet conversations.

Almost everyone in the tavern was from the castle. There a group of parlour servants sat quietly laughing amongst themselves as they doubtless discussed the gossip of the ladies whose chambers they cleaned and whose linens they changed. There was a huntsman, supping a small mug of something that looked slick and strong, his grizzled weather-beaten face stern as he kept to himself. It made Mikel begin to think of the small tavern as a blanket over a bed, warm and close and comfortable for those inside.

Two guards sat near the door, and they stood to salute both Zhon and Mikel when the older men entered the tavern. After only a few questions, it became clear that these two were exactly the people Mikel needed to speak to.

"Lefi going down Long Road? Yeah, I saw him do that the

other night." The guard they were speaking to was stocky, with a shaved head and thin streak of beard on his chin. He introduced himself as Zhosh. He took a long drink from his beer. "I wondered what he was doing. I figured he must have been sent on an errand of something."

"How is it that you saw him?" asked Mikel.

"I was on night watch at the same time, I was even overlooking the path that led to his post."

"And you say you saw him leave his post and head down Long Road?"

"Yup. Saw the building he went into and everything." The man looked from the commander of the Castle Guard to the man who had been running them for the last year. He swallowed and licked his lips nervously. "Why? Is that wrong?"

"Of course it's wrong," growled Zhon. "Leaving your post is always wrong! Why didn't you report his behaviour?"

Suddenly the stocky man's eyes widened. His cheeks grew redder, and Mikel wondered if it was due to embarrassment or anger.

"What do you mean? I did report it!" Zhosh looked affronted. "I wrote it down for the sergeant and never heard about it again."

"Oh Mercy," muttered Zhon. He was running both hands down his face, as though wiping away something that had splashed over him.

"What's wrong?" Mikel asked.

"I did get that report." Zhon tilted his head back and stared at the none-too-distant ceiling. "About a week ago, is that right?"

The bald guard nodded.

"There's too much to keep up with, and this didn't sound that important." Zhon sighed. "So, Lefi left his post during the night watch about a week ago and went to a building on Long

Road." Zhon leaned an elbow on the table and turned to look meaningfully at Mikel.

"Exactly. He wandered into one of the buildings. I could show you if you like sir, I saw which one, I know where the doorways are."

"I think it's vitally important that we see this building."

"Sure," answered the guard. "I'll show you now." He stood up from the round table they were sitting at and picked up his mug. With one mighty draw he finished his drink and wiped his mouth with the back of his wrist. The other guard bowed from his seat and picked up his beer, sipping at it as his attention shifted across the room to some parlour maids whose giggles could still be heard. Mikel shook his head and smiled as the guard they were speaking with swept an arm towards the door.

"This way."

The three of them left the Ugly Godling and Zhosh led them through some streets and alleys to Long Road. The journey was not far, and soon Mikel was looking up the road at Sheerwall. The road stretched in a straight line toward the castle. From here it squatted against the earth like a massive cow. The sun was beginning to slide down the sky, and already a deep shadow was growing from the base of the castle walls. Its hide was broken by a few points of light, windows where torches had already been lit.

Between the three of them and the castle, the river Black looped around the town, thick and dark. Mikel was glad that the riverbank was far down the street. It was more firm at the end of Long Road as well. His stomach was nauseous at the thought of the thick mud and reeds that swamped the edges of the river on the far side of the drawbridge. The memory of Filip's sightless eyes still haunted him.

CHAPITRE XLIII

As they walked, the guard nodded respectfully towards Mikel.

"It's good to meet the commander of the guard in person sir, you've always been an inspiration to me."

Mikel snorted in surprise. "An inspiration?" He raised an eyebrow.

"Well, maybe that's a bit of an overstatement sir, but you've done well by me these last couple of years." Zhosh smiled.

Mikel searched his memories for when Zhosh had joined the castle guard. If the man had been with them for a few years, then Mikel would have been doing a better job of running things at the time. He used to spend a portion of each day walking past the training courtyard, checking the progress of the latest recruits. He would speak with Andru about their strengths and weaknesses, find out a bit of the history that went behind each of their names. There had been a time when he had been able to recall the name of every guard who worked for him. Now he couldn't bring to mind the face of either the mysterious Lefi, who may have had something to do with the disappearance of a mercenary, or any memories of this man who was helping them find out where it had happened. He was ashamed by his failure.

Long Road was surprisingly empty for this early in the afternoon, but the few people who were walking from shop to shop were clearly unimpressed by the three guards. Mikel looked down at his clothes.

He was wearing thick black leather boots that he had worn for years, crisscrossed with cracks and patches that had worn so badly that they appeared pale brown. His leggings were heavy and a respectable dark grey, but already mud and dust spiralled up from the ends. His tunic was clean, but now that he really looked at it, there were frayed ends and patches over most of it. Since Mata had died he had not worried about fixing its holes, and so its holes had not been fixed. When Mata was around she would have sorted it for him, whether by telling him off for leaving it to reach such a state, or sighing and snatching the tunic from him in the evening in order to repair it herself.

He still remembered the sight of her in the corner of their room beneath the tall candelabra, bent close over his clothing with needle and thread. He remembered the first night she had begun to cough in that position. They had thought it was nothing at first.

Zhosh walked them to a relatively small house towards the castle end of the road. As with most of the houses on Long Road, the front of the building was a craftsman's shop, in this case a weaver of fine rugs. Mikel looked down an extremely narrow side-alley beside the shop. Squeezed into the dark space, a thin flight of stairs led up the outside wall of the building to a door upstairs.

"The craftsman must live downstairs, in rooms behind the shop," Mikel told the others.

"Why do you say that sir?" asked Zhosh.

"Because if he lived upstairs, then the stairs would be built inside so he doesn't have to come outside to go home during bad weather."

"Good reasoning." They all looked at the stairs.

"I get the feeling that these stairs are where our men Lefi went." Zhon's voice sounded grim. He feared the worst. He and Mikel looked at Zhosh. The bald guard sniffed and rubbed his chin.

"I'm pretty sure this is the building I saw Lefi going to," he said slowly. He turned around and shaded his eyes. Behind them the Castle was ringed in light, the sunset pouring around the mass of stones. It was difficult to make out particular parts of the castle, but the outline was clear.

"Yeah, I had a watch on the rooktower." Zhosh sounded more sure of himself with every word. He pointed back towards the castle but Mikel's older eyes could barely make out individual towers rising from the dark mass. "I can see the tower from here." He turned back to meet the eyes of the two older men with him. "I saw Lefi leave his post and come out here, wandering along the road, and then over to this building." He frowned and his forehead wrinkled as he wracked his memory. "I don't think he went to the front door, which only leaves these stairs."

They all looked at the stairs in the cramped shadows again.

"I'll go first," Zhon said finally, drawing his sword from the scabbard at his side. Mikel did the same, wincing as the uncared for metal scraped noisily as it left its sheath. Zhosh didn't have a weapon larger than a knife on him, so looked around the alley until he found an old broken piece of wood that he hefted in his hands. He swung it from side to side. "It's got a good weight," he said with a grin.

Together, with Zhon at the front and Mikel at the back, they began to move slowly up the narrow stairs.

As he climbed the stairs, Mikel noticed the cracked and peeling paint on the side of the building. The stairs themselves were made of unpainted wood, beginning to warp from exposure to the elements. Mikel exchanged a glance with Zhon, who shrugged. There was no alternative, but to climb the thin staircase and hope for the best. The planks twisted and groaned under their feet at each step. The men paused to glance at one another, then grimaced and moved on.

They gathered on the small landing at the top of the stairs, where there was a door to the upstairs room. Zhosh stepped forward to lift the latch on the door, moving it as slowly as a tree's branches grow. Mikel held his breath. Zhosh looked back at the others and nodded once then twice and then, emphasising the final nod with widened eyes and a sudden lurch, he threw open the door and the trio leapt inside.

CHAPITRE XLIV

A wall of stench hit them first, and forced Mikel backwards, lifting his arm to cover his nose. He managed to keep his sword held out in front of him, but his eyes were watering. He hoped no gods of decay had overrun this place. The room was dark, so it was difficult to see what was causing the smell for a few moments. Then Zhosh yelped and swung his makeshift club towards the ground.

"Rats! It's dead rats!" They all looked down, feeling safe enough to lower their weapons a little now that they had not been attacked straight away.

The floor was covered in the rotting corpses of rats, each torn into pieces and left strewn across the wooden planks. Blood spattered every surface, and some darker fluids had coagulated into thick piles. Mikel crouched and used the point of his sword to turn one of the bodies over. As soon as he did, the body began to roll and shift, a sickening pile of maggots exposed on its underside. So many of the bulbous white creatures roiled over one another that the rat looked as though it was crawling along the ground as the maggots sought shelter from the faint light. Mikel retched in his throat.

"Is that... I think... That looks like a bite to me." Zhon's voice was thick, as though his throat was closing up protectively against the miasma in the air. He gestured to one of the rats near him with his sword, and Mikel agreed. The gouge taken out of the vermin's back certainly had the shape of a bite, with the flesh ripped out.

"But what sort of animal would only half eat this many vermin and then just leave their bodies here?" Zhosh sounded more than confused. The large man's voice had the ring of a small boy who had woken from a nightmare and just wanted the warmth and reassurance of his mother.

"If you are right, one of our men was in this room a week ago," said Mikel. They examined the rats. Many were little more than old fur and bones. They had clearly been here for longer than a week.

The furniture in the room was sparse. A table stood beside the only window, a tiny square of glass that overlooked the alley behind the building. A single chair was placed next to the table at an angle. There was a fireplace with a mantelpiece, but there was no wood or ash in the fireplace. The stones looked cold, as though they hadn't been used in months. Together the three men explored what was left of the rooms, finding a washhouse that was completely bare and much drier than any normal washhouse, and a bedroom that consisted of an old mattress on the floor. The mattress had been torn open and the feathers that filled it had been piled up on top in a sinister imitation of a nest, a rough circular pile with a hollow in the middle and bits of rat stuck to some of the feathers. But no-one else was in the rooms.

Mikel rubbed the heels of his palms into his eyes, trying to wipe away the sensation of the rats. He was more tired than he ever had been before. The smell was sinking into his skin, making him feel unclean. He rubbed his hands down his forearms, as though he could scrub the smell off himself.

"What do we do now? What is all this?" Zhosh's eyes were darting across the room, unable to stop and focus on any single one of the horrible sights around them.

"I suppose we could wait a while? Perhaps Lefi will come back? Or maybe that mercenary who was wandering these streets will actually not be dead and turn up?" Zhon turned to Mikel to ask the question.

"Dead Mercenary?" Zhosh's voice rose in pitch. Mikel frowned at the young man. Perhaps he had not been with the Guards long enough to harden him to some of these circumstances. Was the training changing? He had been out of his office for far too long.

"Calm down man, you'll be fine." Mikel thought for a moment. "Yes, we'll wait until the sun has set. If someone comes in, we'll try to capture them and ask them about what has been going on. If no-one arrives then we'll return to the castle while there is a hint of light in the sky and then send some men to watch the area. For all we know, Lefi is back at the guardrooms now anyway. We'll have to be careful not to scare him off." Mikel could only assume that Lefi was more involved in Akub's disappearance than he had thought. He was not only a possible witness, not if he had been in these rooms and reported nothing.

"Scare him!?" Zhosh began to chuckle. "Mercy cover me, he's scaring me, and I don't even really know him!"

As Zhon took the young guard aside and spoke quietly with him to try and settle him, Mikel took another look around the room. On the mantelpiece he found a small locket, slightly hidden beneath a bundle of fur and bone. The locket was silver, on a simple leather thong that had begun to mildew. Mikel lifted it with one finger. The latch was broken and it swung open. Inside he could just make out a fine sketch of a young girl, with two older people standing beside her. Though it was smudged and lined with rat blood, he knew that the girl must be Saara. *This is the locket she spoke to me of,* he told himself. *Filip wore this.*

The wait passed slowly. The smell was terrible, but eventually one's nose began to become accustomed to the reek. Their eyes became acclimated to the darkness and soon they ran out of whispered conversation. Instead they stood, watching each other's eyes reflect tiny splinters of light, listening to the rise and fall of each other's lungs. Then, like a landslide in a silent snow-filled valley, there was a long groan of twisting wood from the stairs outside.

CHAPITRE XLV

Mikel shuffled his hand tighter on the handle of his sword. He felt sweat break out on his brow and trickle down the side of his face. His breath sounded like a storm, thundering in and out of his mouth and nose. *Just like old times,* he thought.

Footsteps climbed the stairs outside. They paused outside the door. They paused for a long time. Mikel wondered if he and his companions had left something outside the door. Was there a scratch in the wood where there hadn't been one before? Was the latch not returned precisely as it had been before they entered? Then the door opened.

Mikel blinked rapidly. He had seen the man who was now standing in the doorway before, not two days earlier. Shaggy blonde hair stood out from his head like the fluff on a dandelion. The man's face held a long pointed nose with the kink in the middle, where it may have once been broken. His thin limbs and narrow chest were easily recognisable. It was the guardsman who had helped move Filip into the castle, the one who had thrown up and carried the body into the alchemist's workrooms. Why was he here now?

There was something wrong with the way the man stood. His back arched higher than most men, his head pulled away from the trio confronting him. Zhon gave a bellow and leaped forward, his sword flashing through the air. Zhosh followed close behind with his club. Mikel couldn't bring his thoughts to order as quickly as they had. Later, when he cast his mind back over what happened next, he was able to take it apart piece by piece in his memory.

The man slipped sideways around Zhon's sword with a motion as fluid and fast as a snake. In the same movement, he swung an arm in the second-in-command's direction. The impact of his arm against Zhon's body had made a sickening crunch and the guard had begun to yell. The intruder's face turned towards the others in the room. Everything was moving in slow motion. Mikel was floating in the water of his dream, drifting with the current.

Mikel was confused. This was a man he knew, behaving like no one he had ever seen. Lefi had been a keen man, a young recruit who would think nothing of running out into a storm when word came that help was needed, a man who might flinch but would still help lift a dead body out of the thick mud and marsh of the riverbank. Mikel had relied on Lefi's help only two days earlier. And now the boy was fighting him.

Lefi's face was turned towards him now, though it was hard to recognise the boy with his mouth twisted into a bestial scream and his eyelids pulled back, leaving his eyes huge and white in his face. Orange sparks from some light outside reflected deep in those eyes.

Zhosh swung his club towards that face as Zhon fell to the side. Mikel didn't think Zhon saw what happened next, as the man was grimacing and clutching his stomach on the floor, but it was a sight that Mikel would never forget. Lazily, casually, as though strolling through a field on a bright afternoon, Lefi leaned his body sideways to avoid the chunk of wood whistling by and then straightened up, extending his arm. At the end of his arm, his hand curled its fingers into hooks. Each of those hooks dug into the top of Zhosh's chest, where the flesh was visible around the neck of his shirt. The hooks dug into that flesh, ripping the skin and sliding deeper inside. Zhosh began to scream himself then, and Mikel realised that his throat was raw from the screams that were boiling from his own lungs.

Zhonhad barely hit the floor when Lefi caught hold of Zhosh's collarbone and yanked, lurching the young man towards him. Zhosh could not fight against the pull, not when the fingers tugging at him were inside his body and twisting his bones, and he stumbled towards the still yelling monster. Mikel watched in horror, his stomach cold as an ice storm, as Lefi heaved Zhosh off the edge of the stairs outside.

With time moving so slowly, Mikel was able to watch every expression that crossed the young man's face as he spun over the edge; the pain and shock that was still erupting from the wound in his chest, the intense terror as his eyes swung to the ground spinning towards him, and desperation as he reached out towards the bannister before vanishing from sight over the edge.

CHAPITRE XLVI

All sound had fled from Mikel's world as the door had opened and Lefi had been revealed. The only thing he heard were the yells and screams of the people in the room. There was no bang of boots on wood, no rustle of clothing as they moved. And then sound returned just in time to hear the sickening thud of Zhosh striking the ground in the alley below. There was a splintering snap, as though someone had broken a pile of sticks in a forest. Mikel drew in a shuddering breath. His sword was still held out in front of him, though he had stopped well short of the doorway.

"Who are you?" asked the lanky figure outside the doorway. Lefi glanced down the stairs to his side as he spoke. Mikel assumed he was checking in case someone had heard the commotion and was coming down the alley to investigate. Zhon moaned from the floor, where he was curled in a ball beside Mikel's feet. Zhosh's blood had sprayed across the Second in a spatter of ruby drops.

"I am the Commander of the Guard at Castle Sheerwall,

your commander! Did you kill the boy Filip or the Mercenary Akub?" Mikel was shocked at how calm his voice sounded. It was leaving his mouth loud and level, without a quaver to display the fear that curdled in the bottom of his stomach. He noticed that the point of his sword wasn't moving either. It sat solidly between Rasuco and himself, an ever-present deterrent to the possibility of attack.

Lefi blinked and frowned. With his blood-stained hand he ran his fingers through his hair. The blood left red marks on his forehead and streaked through his hair, slicking it against his skull. At Mikel's feet Zhon groaned again. But Mikel could see the man's fingers tightening on his sword.

"Who are they?" Lefi appeared genuinely confused. He glanced down the alleyway again and smiled. "You are lucky!" He turned his smile to Mikel. His teeth were disappointingly normal in the dim doorway. They were flat and dingy white, just like any other person's teeth. Mikel wished that they had been sharp and fanged like a snake, or jagged and red or perhaps yellow. A smile with terrible monstrous teeth like that would have suited the horrific sight that he had witnessed in this room. Instead, it was only a man who had caused such carnage.

Lefi reached up with one hand to the roof from where he stood on the landing. He began to lift himself on that arm alone, as though the weight of his body was no more than a feather. His feet left the landing outside the door just as Zhon swung out with his sword from where he lay, scoring a gash down Lefi's leg.

The man screeched, and now Mikel was rewarded with evidence that that the man was somehow inhuman. The commander flinched at the unearthly sound and dropped his sword from trembling fingers. He retched at the sound Lefi made. It was like a bird of prey being tortured.

However, the wound in his leg did not stop Lefi. He kept lifting himself to the roof and out of Mikel's sight. Mikel staggered backwards until he hit a wall in the small room and then slid down to sit on the floor. Soon he heard the pounding of feet on the stairs and the faces of three large men peered into the room.

"What's all this then?" bellowed one of the men and Mikel began to laugh. It began as a low chuckle in the back of his throat as his thoughts raced. *One of our guards is dead, a young man with plenty of promise in his future, and now he is dead with no warning. Zhon is wounded, and I don't know how badly yet. As for myself, I've nearly pissed myself without ever even taking a swing at... something that can't have been human! And these men think we are the ones causing trouble.*

Mikel sat slumped in the corner of the room, laughing and laughing, louder and louder, until someone recognised his clothes and sent for guards from the castle. As more men crowded into the room, muttering under their breath to one another about the foul surroundings, Mikel passed out.

In his semi-sleeping state, Mikel absorbed more about the men who had saved them than he would have thought possible. The large men were bodyguards of the craftsman in the rooms downstairs. They had been just locking up with him and leaving for the end of the day when they had heard shouting from the lodging room upstairs and decided to come and investigate. When they saw the crumpled body of a dead man at the bottom of the stairs, they had rushed up to intervene. And yet, somehow, they had not seen Lefi, or watched the way he escaped over the roof. Mikel had laughed again when he realised that. The Kirkman had been sent for as well.

By the time the Kirkman arrived, Mikel was sitting up by himself, and he had managed to slow his thoughts enough to start thinking for himself again, rather than reacting. He saw the Kirkman glance at him angrily, before taking a tour of the cramped rooms. When the old man returned to the front entrance, he looked shaken.

CHAPITRE XLVII

"I don't know what sort of beast you disturbed here commander," he said. He reached out to help Mikel off the floor and steadied him with one hand on his shoulder. "But it is something evil. I am glad you summoned me."

"Yes, although it was these men that called for you, not me" Mikel agreed, swallowing painfully as he gestured to the bodyguards. One of them nodded, but they were clearly intimidated by the presence of the Kirkman and stood quietly. Mikel continued "Thanks for your advice. We somewhat suspected that we were dealing with something evil when he threw our man off the stairs."

The Kirkman started and blinked but then shook his head and narrowed his eyes. "You say "He"? What do you mean?"

"It was a man. Actually," and here Mikel paused for a moment, unsure of how to continue. He wondered whether the Kirkman would believe him. He wasn't sure if he believed his own memories yet. "Actually, it was one of our own Castle

Guard. I don't know why he has decided to start killing people, but I think he may have killed two others already."

How had this evil man come to join the Castle Guard without ever having these aspects of his personality revealed, Mikel wondered. *And why did he kill Filip and Akub?* From all Mikel had managed to work out so far, there was no connection between the young man, the mercenary, and Lefi. Had he simply seen Filip waiting for Akub on the riverbank and taken an opportunity?

Standing beside the door with their hands clasped in front of them, the body guards glanced at each other with widening eyes. *Mercy's lack,* cursed Mikel to himself. *I didn't mean to let that slip. Rumours will fly now.*

"No, this not the work of a human." The Kirkman stood straighter, fussily arranging his pale robes around his shoulders as he declared what he thought he knew. "I have seen evidence of such evil before. The vermin flocked here," he indicated the rat corpses that blanketed the floor. "And whatever that thing was, it devoured them and discarded them. These are the actions of one of the gods, a god of darkness and death.' The Kirkman raised one finger into the air to emphasise his point. The bodyguards had begun to look nervous, peering into the corners of the room as though they expected a dark creature to appear right there and murder them. Mikel remembered the way Lefi had lifted himself effortlessly to the roof. Perhaps a dark creature really would appear before them.

"I don't think it is an evil spirit sir. My Second knew this man. I knew him. He was one of our guards," said Mikel, moving towards the door. He paused to consider the idea and then frowned. "How could we tell if he was actually a dangerous god?"

The bodyguards were following the Kirkman to the doorway also. Zhon was standing now, supported by a large man with a shock of red hair. The Second's arm was slung over the man's shoulder.

"It is late," answered the Kirkman, shaking his head. "There is much to clean up here, and I am sure you will need to make sure everyone in both town and castle are safe. Come and see me as soon as you can and I will explain as much as I know." He paused in the doorway as the others made their way out to the landing and staggered down the stairs. "Who will deal with this?" He gestured into the room and managed to include the body laying in the alley in his movement as well. At that moment five guards arrived from the castle, somewhat red-faced and puffing. Clearly they had run as fast as they could.

"These men will gather the rats outside and burn them." Mikel was still dizzy. The thought of the stench that would come from burning old rat bodies made his stomach turn again. He desperately wanted to eat or throw up. "And then they will take the body to the Kirk. Will you find the man's family and see to his burial?"

The Kirkman paused. Mikel's temper rose, wondering if the man would claim that the body could not be brought into the chapel. But then the Kirkman nodded slightly.

"Very well."

The new group of guards held their breath to avoid choking on the foul smell as they began moving tiny carcasses into the alley, but Mikel paid them no attention. He had to get home, and to sleep. By the morning there would be much to do.

Mikel blew warm air through his lips as he crossed the courtyards of Sheerwall in the black of night. His breath clouded in front of him and then swirled around his face as he strode on. A faint echo of laughter caught his attention and he paused, looking around to search out the origin of the sound. Two windows were lit high in a building next to the great hall.

"The heir's apartments," Mikel murmured to himself. He sniffed and glanced around, checking if anyone else was out so late. The castle grounds were thick with shadow and silence.

Mikel snorted and turned to continue making his way to his own bed. "So much for being exhausted by travel," he shook his head. *The boy is so exhausted he stays up with his friends carousing well into the night.* Still, it was Lord Uvaniah's problem to deal with.

Mikel slept deeply, which did his weary bones good. His chest hurt from his exertions in the evening, and his brain was muddled by too many terrifying visions. But sleep could not save him from the memories of what he had just seen, and his dreams would not let him sleep in peace. Over and over he saw the face of Zhosh, hanging in the air, waiting to plummet into the alley. That young man's eyes bore into him, burrowing deep into his brain. Sometimes it was no longer Zhosh's face pleading for Mikel to save him. Instead, sometimes the face in his dream, rising into the air and twisting upside down, was Tuomas'.

CHAPITRE XLVIII

The soft moustache on his son's face reminded Mikel of the boy's youth. Tuomas was so close to being a fully grown man, ready to take his part in the world, fully independent, but Mikel did not consider that he was there yet. Would Mikel be able to protect him from the horrors of the world long enough for him to become the man he should be? Mikel's arms and shoulders ached from where they had been clenched during the encounter with Lefi. He felt older than he did while waking, as though his muscles were shrinking and his skills were fading away.

Other horrors of the world intruded, and Mikel dreamed of Lefi silently slipping into his bedroom, stepping around the door with a broad smile and fiery eyes, a blade flashing as the moonlight caught its edge. Somehow Mata was asleep in bed with him still, though she was long buried, and Mikel dreamed that he lay next to her, with his eyes wide open, watching as Lefi reached down and crushed her head between his hands.

He dreamed of Lefi's face split in half by a grin as his arms stabbed through Zhosh and Zhon's chests as though made of steel. He dreamed of waves of red blood that filled his room and began to slide into his throat, leaving him choking and spluttering, a liquid cough that echoed the memories of his wife's final days. With every fresh dream of Lefi he could feel his heart pounding until his eyes rattled. Lefi's face would fill his vision, eyes wide and staring, tongue curling over his teeth like a snake. His hands would reach out and then Mikel would see nothing but blackness until the dreams began again.

Finally, eventually, there came a knock at the door and Mikel blinked his eyes into wakefulness. His body ached, though he felt more capable than his dreams might convince him of. He yawned and turned the movement into a groan.

"Who's there?" he called.

"Zhon." The man waited for Mikel to call him in before opening the door and entering. Mikel was surprised to see him up and walking around already. He had been sure that Lefi had caused some serious damage, and that the Second would be confined to rest and recovery for some time. To that end, Zhon's body was wrapped in thick bandaging like a roll of parchment. Mikel was surprised that there was no wax seal binding the bandages closed.

"How are you feeling?"' Mikel asked.

"Terrible."

Zhontook a seat on a small stool as Mikel got out of his bed and changed from his night robe into some clothes. Mikel's shoulder twinged when he bent over, but otherwise he was able to handle the movements satisfactorily.

Mikel's Second looked closely at him. "And how are you feeling yourself commander?"

"Better than you I'd wager," laughed Mikel in answer to Zhon's question. He thumped his chest with his fist and then coughed and winced. "Oooh, that was a silly thing to do." He straightened his shoulders. "But it would hurt you more. At least the bastard didn't manage to hit me." Mikel ignored feelings of cowardice that swam in his stomach as the memory of his encounter with Lefi raced through his mind. He lowered his face and frowned. "I should have stepped up. Maybe I could have done something more."

"I don't think so." Zhon pursed his lips. "You shouldn't be blaming yourself."

"What?"

"We all know that you've had some tough times this year. And that you've not exactly been handling them as easily as you might wish." Zhon had the grace to look away as he said that. "But there is nothing you could have done to save Zhosh."

"But if only I had moved faster-"

"With all respect sir, no. You couldn't have moved faster, you're not a young man anymore." Zhon's blue eyes shone. "And you didn't feel his strength. I don't know how he did it, but when he struck me it was like a horse had kicked me in the chest."

"Are you sure you should be up and about today in that case?" Mikel gestured at the bandages that were wrapped thickly around Zhon's chest.

"I've seen Marq and the healer, and neither man expects me to lay in bed right now. Actually, Zhuud told me that chest injuries such as this will heal just as well whether I am laying in my rooms or walking about." He chuckled. "I took that to mean that they don't heal well regardless of my actions, but at least it means I can get out and try to find that bastard."

Mikel shrugged. Zhuud was a good healer, although he had been unable to find a cure for Red Lung. He had warned Mikel that there was no known cure for the disease when they had first realised that Mata was ill, but Mikel had spent the next seven weeks hoping. It was difficult not to hold a grudge against the man, though sometimes he wanted to.

"Where was Mercy's Shield last night," he muttered softly.

Zhonsighed and nodded. "Things must be worse than we believed in Blackriver. Mercy's Shield must be stretched thin, its focus elsewhere. We must encourage everyone to support each other, so that the shield will keep Lefi from causing more harm."

"I'll remind people I see," groaned Mikel. He brushed a hand through his hair. "But what action can we take now? If we can stop Lefi, then Mercy can ensure dangers beyond Blackriver do not encroach on us."

"That's why I'm here. I want to know what you think we should do. Where do we start?"

The two men sat in Mikel's rooms and talked for a short time. Soon they had reached a plan together. They set out in opposite directions to set it up.

CHAPITRE XLIX

Zhon's part in the plan was to rouse the guards. They would set more watches than usual, and the guards would move in pairs whenever possible. Zhon would make sure to impress upon all the guards just how dangerous Lefi appeared to be. Mikel wondered if any of the guards knew what had happened with Lefi? Surely some of them must have joined up at the same time as he had. Mikel wracked his memories, trying to determine whether he had known the young man when he began his training, or whether he had been spending more time away from the office by then. He ignored the embarrassed warmth that leaked onto his cheeks, and the voice in the back of his head that told him he had been passing by his responsibilities.

While the alert was raised by Zhon, Mikel was going to speak to Lord Uvaniah, and find ways to keep him safe. Someone so violent and dangerous operating out of Blackriver meant that the safety of the lord was paramount. Then he would go into town and find the Kirkman. The old man said he had some ideas about Lefi being some sort of dark god. The idea was completely impossible to Mikel, but following up any thread was worthwhile. Any knowledge could prove helpful in stopping him. And after all, the man had pulled himself up and onto the roof with as much concern as a child picking up an acorn. Maybe the Kirkman was right.

Mikel tried to shrug off an unusual tension in his shoulders as he walked through the halls towards the Lord's personal rooms. They lay on the far side of the castle, in a huge building that housed many of the nobles' living quarters, and a massive kitchen. Between those rooms and the buildings that held Mikel's rooms and the Guard barracks there were clusters of other smaller buildings; stables and storehouses and a small well in case of siege. But the way was mostly a maze of narrow stone hallways, with tapestries hanging along them to brighten the stone, and small cold courtyards of grey cobble.

Mikel stepped through these spaces with trepidation. He wasn't sure if the constant feeling that he was being watched from behind came from his run in with Lefi, or whether it was years and years of Guard patrol that were finally taking their toll. His shoulders itched as though something was staring at them as he walked. Twice during the walk across the castle, he spun around, hoping to catch a glimpse of anything that was there. Each time he found himself facing a long, thin, straight, and very, very empty corridor. He shuddered and quickened his pace.

Lord Uvaniah's room wasn't under extra guard yet. The two standing at either side of the Lord's door saluted Mikel as he approached. Mikel hoped that nothing had happened overnight, and that the extra guards he and Zhon had agreed on would arrive soon. Normally there was at least one guard on bodyguard duty inside the rooms, so hopefully they would have at least had a chance to raise the alarm if anything untoward had happened in the night. Still, he would feel much better once the extra guards took their positions alongside the old man, and kept eye at all the entrances to the castle, as well as key doorways and passages. After seeing Lefi in action, at least four guards in the room would probably be prudent. Mikel knocked on the door.

"Who goes there?"

Mikel sighed a breath of relief that he didn't realise he had been holding. That voice could only have come from the guard who was on duty in Lord Uvaniah's anteroom. It certainly didn't belong to Lefi. Mikel wondered what he would have done if the terrifying former guard had turned up in these rooms. He called his name and station, waited for the guard inside to acknowledge him, then unlatched the door and entered.

Lord Uvaniah's anteroom was quite large, though not excessively so. A fire burned to his right and the guard on duty was standing to attention by it. She carried a short sword on her hip, though it wasn't drawn. Mikel frowned.

"Even if you think you know who is entering, you should really have your weapon ready to challenge them. What if I was being forced to provide entry for some assassin?"

The guard blushed and fumbled at her sword.

"No no, leave it now, there's no point. But I do encourage you to be much more careful. We have reason to believe that danger stalks this castle."

The young guard began questioning Mikel about this statement, but the commander brushed her comments aside with a wave. "Later, later. Master Zhon should let you know everything that you need to know later. For now, I must speak with our lord. Do you know if he is awake?"

"I believe so sir."

Mikel nodded and smiled at her to soften his rebukes. He moved to the door of the bedchamber and knocked again.

Shortly after he heard a sleepy call to enter. Again, he unlatched a door and stepped through.

The lord's bedroom was huge. As he entered, Mikel thought one again that he would never grow used to its enormity. The roof was a full three metres higher than any of the other rooms in the castle, except perhaps the great hall. Thick tapestries hung down each wall, depicting lands in full bloom and covered with happy embroidered farmers and crops. He supposed it was meant to be some form of good luck or positive aspiration. The detail in these tapestries was incredible. On previous occasions visiting the lord, Mikel had been given the opportunity to examine them closely, admiring the tiny stitches that gave a sparkle to this farmer's eyes or twisted the tail of a pig just so.

Tall thin windows lined the wall to the right as he entered, their shape filled with a spiderweb tracery of metal frames for each pane. From what Mikel understood, the metal frames were thick and strong enough to become protective bars in case an assault on the castle gained the grounds outside. He knew that the wall beyond the window overlooked the flat training grounds just inside the north walls. Out there would normally be the most recent batch of castle guard recruits, training with wooden swords and spears, yelling in pain and exhilaration. Mikel hoped they weren't there this morning, and that they were instead listening to Zhon deliver new instructions to the guards.

Of course, the glass wouldn't withstand much of an attack, but by that stage the room would no longer contain the lord. The room would be used for archers mainly, Mikel supposed. Or simply left empty and barricaded, keeping the invaders out but also stopping any defenders within from being wounded.

Opposite the door, on the far side of the vast floor, stood a massive four poster bed with thick drapes around it. The drapes were in the process of being slowly pulled aside by the occupant of the bed, the lord Uvaniah. Mikel wasn't alone in the room with his lord though. Two servants were carrying large pitchers of steaming water and pouring them into a shallow porcelain tub set up near the bed. Clearly the lord was about to have a bath this morning, before joining the residents of the castle in the great hall for a morning meal.

CHAPITRE L

"Good morning Mikel!" Uvaniah raised a hand in greeting and then pulled it to his mouth to cover a heavy cough. His face was long this morning, his cheeks falling beneath his eyes. "How fare you today?"

"Not well my lord." Mikel glanced over the servants. They looked harmless enough. Still, he watched them for a few heartbeats before moving his hand away from his sword. "I have some rather disturbing news."

"Oh?"

As the lord pointed out the clothes he wanted to wear for the day, and the servants moved amongst his dressers and wardrobes to collect the items he had selected, Mikel explained what had happened the night before. He quickly discussed the body of the young man that had been found in the riverbank, and how there was some sort of entanglement with the Guershan. He also explained that the Kirkman had declared that Lefi must be some sort of evil god.

"That sounds horrible," managed lord Uvaniah, stepping

out of his bed. He walked slowly towards the tub, his back bent and his legs shuffling like twigs. His limp made him clutch at his hip. "What are you going to do about it?"

"There isn't much we can do so far," admitted Mikel. He shifted his shoulders and the ache of old muscles shot down his arms. "But Zhon is doubling the watch and explaining what we have seen so far to the castle guards. Hopefully they will be more cautious than we were, spot this traitor before he can attack anyone else, and kill him."

"What makes you think they will find him here in my chambers? Why would he not simply continue to kill the people of my town like he has done so far?" Uvaniah's eyes were serious and hard above his soft cheeks. He coughed again.

"Because if he just wanted to kill the townsfolk at random, he would have already been doing that. He killed my man easily enough, and we had weapons ready to use against him. He could have been dragging people off the street by surprise for the last week. That's how long since the first man he killed went missing. And yet in that time he has only killed two."

"How long had he been hiding in our guards?" Uvaniah's voice turned hard as granite. Mikel swallowed and recalled that Iosef Uvaniah's father had taught him that strength was the key to securing his lands.

"He joined recently." Mikel's tongue felt thick in his mouth. "But I am sure he was not so depraved when he joined. Something must have happened. I am going to find out what that was."

"Yes, I suggest you do, and soon. Have you spoken to the Kirkman about his concerns?"

"I am going to see him immediately."

"Good. In such times it is vital to consider Mercy's protection as we find a course forward. Make sure Alaks is well guarded. I want to take him to meet with the Blackriver council today."

The conversation was at an end. Mikel bowed slightly from the waist and left the room as Uvaniah was derobed by his servants and then stepped into the hot water. Mikel couldn't help but notice how small the man looked now, with his narrow bony chest fuzzed by wiry white hair. *How much longer will he be with us, even if we protect him from this traitor? What will we do when he has gone?*

Mikel was glad to see a second guard had joined the first in the anteroom by the time he was leaving. The first guard's face was drained pale and Mikel assumed the newcomer had filled in his companion on everything that Zhon had been telling the guards. Both guards straightened their shoulders at the sight of the commander, but Mikel was pleased to see that they were both standing stalwart already. He saw their hands set on the hilts of their swords as he stepped through the doorway too, a good sign of readiness.

"Keep a close eye on our lord, guards. As you know, things are quite uncertain right now."

The two guards nodded as he left.

Mikel made his way towards the great hall, feeling his stomach twist in hunger. His forehead wrinkled as he considered what he had last eaten. It would have been some light meal with Zhon the previous afternoon, as they roamed Blackriver looking for off duty guards. After they had dealt with the room of dead rats and the horror of Zhosh's gruesome death at Lefi's hands, he had certainly had no stomach to look for a meal before dropping into sleep.

He turned a corner and found himself in a wider corridor, with large cross shaped windows cut into the left hand walls. Doors lined the wall to his right, and another guard was on duty here. This one nearly lunged at him with her drawn sword before she recognised him. Clearly Zhon had provided a very startling description of the threat that their foe presented. The guard relaxed as he approached.

"Good morning sir."

"Good morning. Is the heir awake?"

"I'm not sure sir." The doors in this hallway led to Alaks's rooms. Mikel hadn't been inside these since the boy was young enough to have a nanny living in the adjoining rooms.

Mikel had once escorted a new nanny to Alaks' rooms with Tuomas. Mikel had chatted to the young woman, asking her about her family and her upbringing, while Tuomas had clutched at the back of his father's pants. Then they had seen Alaks coming the other direction down the hall, stopping passersby to ask them questions about their jobs with that broad smile on his face. The heir had always been so personable and engaging, exactly the sort of thing that a future leader needed to be. Mikel reached behind himself to untangle Tuomas' arms. He had worried that his son would never grow confident enough to engage with his society.

Mikel imagined a few servants lived in those rooms now rather than a nanny, ensuring their master was clothed and fed at all times. But surely they should have begun to rouse him by now. He glanced through the narrow windows at the blue sky. The morning grew late.

"You should know sir, I had to turn your son away a short while ago." The guard shuffled on the spot, clearly not sure whether or not she should have acted as she had. Perhaps she feared that she had insulted her commander by implying that Tuomas may not be trustworthy? Mikel smiled to reassure her that she had performed her duties correctly.

"Good. Did Tuomas say why he was seeking the heir?"

"No, he looked like he wanted to argue with me for a moment, but he soon realised that he had not been summoned and was not expected." The guard shrugged. "He was quite upset."

"Thank you for letting me know." Mikel looked at the closed doors again. "Keep to your duties as you have, you are doing well. I do wonder when our boy will rouse himself to join the rest of us however."

CHAPITRE LI

Tuomas had had energy, if not charisma when he had been a small boy. Mikel remembered sitting next to the river Black as his little boy ran giggling through the reeds, chasing ducks. Their flustered quacks sounded clear in the warm bright summer air. Tuomas laughed and splashed through the mud while Mikel leaned on the stonework next to the drawbridge to the castle.

"Be careful boy," Mikel called when Tuomas began to splash towards the deeper water of the river.

"I'll be okay dad!"

"I'm sure you think so," laughed Mikel. "But nevertheless, be careful!" Tuomas was so young that he had not been swimming often. Mikel was not sure how well the boy would be able to carry himself if he was swept into the deep dark water.

The clomp of heavy feet sounded from the drawbridge and Mikel turned.

The young heir of Lord Uvaniah was racing across the wooden bridge with a broad smile beneath his fluffy blond hair. Two guards walked behind him, serious expressions on their faces. One kept his hand on the pommel of his sword and gazed around to take in the surroundings, while the other's eyes didn't waver from the heir himself.

"Good morning Salom. Good morning Zhameys."

The guards' faces softened but Mikel was pleased to see that they did not shift from their tasks as they took up spots near him.

"Good morning sir," said Salom, without glancing at the commander.

Alaks shrieked happily as he ran down to the mud and reeds, splashing heavily through the muck. Tuomas' head popped up from the reeds to watch the other boy. Alaks pulled off his shirt and then hunched over to pull his boots off as well. He bundled the muddy things together and threw them over his shoulder. Mikel grunted a laugh as the clothes splatted far short of dry land. He walked forward to retrieve their heir's belongings and moved them to a spot where they would not sink out of sight into the mud.

Zhameys groaned as Alaks began wading out into the river. He began unbuckling his mail and setting the armour aside as well.

"Don't you say a gods-cursed word, you," he snapped and glared at Salom. Salom appeared to still be watching their surroundings, without a glance for his companion, but Mikel could see how the corners of Salom's mouth were creeping up in amusement. Zhameys followed Alaks into the river.

The heir was as comfortable in the water as a fish. He dove and swam and splashed, turning in circles. It was a pleasure to watch. Zhameys did not swim. He strode into the water and clutched at his sodden shirt with hands on his shoulders, hugging himself.

"How's the water?" called Mikel.

"UnMercifully cold," was the curt reply.

"Can't I swim with Alaks?" asked Tuomas.

Mikel turned. He hadn't noticed his son walking up beside him. Tuomas looked up at his father with wide hopeful eyes, his hair spiky with mud, his clothes covered in a dark layer of grime.

"No my boy, you know that you can't. You're still learning to swim." He pointed at the heir. "Look at him! He's graceful and strong in the water. You're not the same as him." He put a hand on Tuomas' shoulder and squeezed it encouragingly. "Perhaps when you're older you'll figure it all out. Maybe then you can swim with Lord Alaks."

CHAPITRE LII

Standing in the hallway outside the grown Alaks's room, Mikel sniffed and scratched his chin as he pulled himself out of his memories. "Actually, do you happen to know when Alaks woke yesterday after the feast?" he asked the guard.

"I wasn't on duty yesterday sir, but I believe he wasn't up until the sun was already beginning to set."

Mikel was shocked, and had to stop himself from letting his mouth gape open. He had been prepared to hear that Alaks had slept in, especially after a large welcoming feast that may have gone on until the early hours of the morning, but until near sunset was far longer than should be allowed!

"That seems indulgent. Did our lord not say anything?"

Again, the guard shrugged, looking down to avoid eye contact with Mikel. The commander frowned and sighed.

"No matter. If no one has spoken to the heir today, then I think it is my duty to do so."

The guard nodded and let him open the door and enter the heir's chambers.

The rooms inside were still dark, drapery pulled across the windows. Mikel found his way through to the bedchamber. The air inside was heavy and quiet. He could hear Alaks's light snores from the bed.

Mikel strode to the drapes and pulled them aside, allowing strong sunlight to burst into room. He smiled as he heard Alaks grunt.

"Come on my boy, it's time to wake up and face the world!"

Alaks groaned and rolled over in the bed. He muttered something inaudible into his pillows.

"I'm not asking for much, but I do need your attention my lord."

Mikel walked over to stand beside the bed and held his hands behind his back. He stood waiting for a long time, and about to reach over to shake the heir when Alaks's bleary eyes rose over the blanket.

"Hrmph. Mikel? What do you want?"

Mikel waited a moment longer for Alaks to lift himself higher and rub his eyes. He wanted to be sure he had the heir's full attention.

"I am here to warn you that there is a traitor in Blackriver. We fear he may be in the castle, so we have increased the number of guards watching over you."

"What?" Alaks climbed out of the bed and twisted from one side to the other, stretching out his shoulders. "That sounds dreadful, I don't agree to it."

"Sir?" Mikel blinked and struggled to say anything. He didn't understand what the heir was saying."

"It's already difficult enough to do what I want to with the regular number of guards traipsing around me. I won't allow more guards to stifle me."

Mikel stood with his mouth open. Before he could summon up a response, a servant came into Alaks's room with the day's clothes hung over his arm. He walked up to the heir without speaking and stood with eyes slightly downcast, displaying the clothes.

"What is this?" said Alaks. He blinked and frowned. One hand reached out to finger the material and then quickly dropped it. The servant glanced up with wide eyes at the heir and then hurriedly lowered them again.

"No, really. I want to know. What is this and what were you thinking?"

"Sir?" the servant stammered. "I'm afraid that I don't-"

"How could you possibly think that this is a suitable shirt for me to wear today?"

"It's the pale cream with gold sir, which is what you asked-"

Alaks brushed the servant's answer aside and leaned closer.

"I can't wear something made of irritating fabric like this. I would spend the entire day scratching myself, my shoulders, my neck, my armpits. It would cause no end of gossip as the entire castle would think I was ill!" He flicked the clothing that hung over the servant's arm. "Get rid of this and bring me something suitable!"

"I'm sorry sir, I will just-" the servant didn't even finish speaking before he bowed and scampered out of the room.

Mikel waited patiently while Alaks saw to his dress. It was frustrating to be kept waiting for such a petty thing, and perhaps Alaks could have corrected the servant in a less irritated fashion, but it was important that people got things right. The world would come undone if everyone neglected their role and allowed their duties to be slipshod.

A spark of anger flashed at the back of his mind. If the inhabitants of Blackriver were better at maintaining the duties they owed to one another, perhaps Mercy would have protected his wife. Perhaps his guards would not need to work quite so hard to protect the town. Perhaps Mercy would have been able to drive Lefi out.

Finally Alaks was dressed.

"You're still here Mikel." It was a statement, not a question.

"Yes. I'm afraid that your father approved our plan, and so there will be more guards. I understand it may be an inconvenience, but we need to know you are safe, especially at the council meeting with your father today."

Alaks's eyes flashed. "Fine, your guards will just have to try not to get trodden under my feet. However, I don't expect to be at any boring council meetings today. I was thinking of going riding."

Alaks turned away from Mikel as though he were one of the servants who had brought clothes in.

"Is everything alright sir?" asked the guard on Alaks's door as Mikel left.

"It's nothing." Mikel waved his hand uncertainly. "Keep up the good work." He walked away down the hallway.

Mikel's brow wrinkled and he looked at the floor as he walked. How could the heir have wasted so much of a day? Uvaniah would not have been able to stay awake much longer than sunset yesterday and so he and his son must barely have had any time to speak. But Lord Uvaniah would need to know all the details of what had happened at Highfort in order to make further plans to marry off Alaks appropriately, surely? Would the connection to Highfort require some other maintenance now that Alaks and the daughter of that lord agreed to stay unwed?

It was simply not right for a man with as many important duties as the Heir of Sheerwall to stay in bed so long! He should have been out inspecting the town, letting the townspeople see he had returned safe and healthy, and that he was ready to begin the management of the winter season. Winter was usually a difficult time, with the lands frozen hard and no fresh food. Often the townsfolk began to grumble amongst themselves by the time spring began to warm the air. The heir should be out and making sure he took the people's complaints seriously, but also quelling any true unrest. And to hear him declare that he was to simply go riding! Mikel walked through the hallways with his eyes low and his thoughts troubled.

CHAPITRE LIII

Mikel ended up sitting by himself in the great hall as he ate a late morning meal. Clearly no one wanted to interrupt his deep thinking which ensured a clear space around his table. Occasionally he focused his eyes on one or another of the passersby and made sure to utter an appropriate morning greeting, but more often than not he simply stared up into the chandeleir's light. He chewed slowly on a thick wedge of pale yellow cheese.

When Tuomas entered the hall alongside Alaks Mikel nearly swallowed his cheese half-chewed. He coughed hurriedly to dislodge the hunk of cheese before he choked. The two youths laughed as they walked towards the table at the far end, each slapping the other on the back as they went. The piles of food on the tables had diminished since the initial crowd of the morning, but there were still rolls and cheeses enough for them.

Tuomas still hadn't shaved away the wispy moustache that he had returned with and Mikel wondered if Tuomas planned to keep the facial hair. *Perhaps it is his way of declaring himself a grown man.* The thought amused Mikel as he still thought of his son as a small child with puffy cheeks and hands, who would squeal with delight whenever anyone made a strange face.

Before and behind the heir came two of his personal guards, and Mikel was pleased at their diligence. He was sure their rough manner would earn a few complaints from the others in the hall, but he didn't mind that for now, so long as the heir was kept safe. He looked around the room. Sure enough, he recognised the face of at least one more guard walking through the room, far enough to seem unassociated with the heir. This guard wore a simple brown tunic instead of the usual guard uniform and mail and spoke sporadically with those he encountered. The secret guards were a suggestion of Zhon's that Mikel thoroughly endorsed. If Lefi did appear, hopefully he wouldn't realise that the man in the tunic was also a guard until a sword was sticking out of his back!

Tuomas and Alaks were making their way to a table, so Mikel waved them towards him. Tuomas saw him and then glanced at the heir carefully. His face stilled and the laughter in his cheeks rolled away. Alaks merely raised an eyebrow and then laughed again, waving for Tuomas to go. As Tuomas came over to join his father, his cheeks grew red. As the boy sat down, Mikel noticed that there were curly wisps of hair beginning to sprout along his son's jawline as well. *So, he's hoping for a beard indeed.*

"Good morning father." Tuomas didn't look at Mikel from the far side of the table.

"Good morning." Silence stretched as they both chewed a mouthful of bread. Mikel swallowed. "Have I done something wrong? Why are you so quiet now, though you were just laughing with Alaks?" Mikel looked around to see where the heir had ended up taking a seat.

The boy had settled himself between a gaggle of merchant's sons and wealthy daughters, all bubbling to be the most impressive conversationalist that Alaks had ever met. Technically of course, as they lived in Blackriver itself rather than the castle, they had no right to a meal in the great hall unless invited for a feast or celebration. But these youths were always keen to show their loyalty and impress the lord's family in the hope of earning patronage. Or marriage, in the case of the girls, Mikel realised, noticing for the first time how the girls were edging closer and closer to the lord's son. They must have heard that he has returned still unwed.

"He still seems happy enough at least." And indeed, Alaks chose that moment to tilt his head back and open his mouth like a bear trap, guffawing loud enough to be heard across the room. "You could have asked if he wanted to sit with us for a while."

"Oh father." Tuomas shook his head and placed his roll back onto the wooden plate before him. "Alaks is annoyed at you, just as I am." Now he turned to look at his father, a strange mix of accusation and guilt vying for position in his eyes.

"Annoyed at me?" Mikel couldn't keep the surprise from his voice. "Why on earth would you both be annoyed at me?"

"Isn't it obvious?" Tuomas' sharp gaze showed that he thought it was. When Mikel had no response, he continued. "You posted extra guards on his rooms. All the clattering about as they walked around in the hallway disturbed him this morning." And with that he picked up his roll again and occupied himself gnawing at it.

"What?" Mikel tried to speak but each word caught in his throat before he could shape it. Anything he said in response to such a bizarre statement would be too absurd to be real. "I posted extra guards for his protection. There's something dangerous in town."

"I'm sure you think that's true," shrugged Tuomas. "But you still upset him by it." The accusation in his voice grew stronger.

"So what? An heir to the lord's seat has plenty of duties himself that he should be out of his rooms attending to by this time of day." Mikel could feel anger growing in his chest, though he used all his will to stifle it. His eyes narrowed at his son.

"Father! How dare you try to tell the lord's own son how to spend his time!" Tuomas was staring at his father now.

"I'm not telling him what to do," Mikel began explaining. "But that doesn't remove the fact that he should-"

"You're doing it again! This is ridiculous father! By what right do you imagine you can say what the lord's heir 'should' be doing?" Now Tuomas' brow began to furrow in anger. His shoulders were shaking.

"Peace son, peace!" Mikel held up both hands to try and calm his son. "I meant nothing. But how have I annoyed you as well through this inconsiderate protection?"

"That's not as important I suppose," Tuomas admitted, turning aside slightly. "Your guards wouldn't let me through to see Alaks."

"I know," nodded Mikel. "They told me."

"And?"

"And what?"

"And I hope you told them off for it!"

"Why would I want to tell them off for performing their duties correctly?" Mikel was beginning to consider his role in this conversation completely upturned, as though he had ventured into a maze, such as the wheat farmers would grow in their fields some years, and that he had taken a wrong turning. Every time he thought he recognised a landmark, it turned out that he was facing in completely the wrong direction.

Tuomas was mortified. His mouth drooped into a gaping cavern and a sound half-sigh and half-groan slipped from his throat. "You just don't understand do you? You're a crazy old man, just like Alaks said."

"What? He said what about me?" Mikel thumped a fist onto the table and refused to look his son in the eyes as the boy continued to talk.

"He said that you were just a power hungry street urchin all grown up." Tuomas began to gather his bowl and food, standing from the bench that they shared. "And you are. You don't understand how proper people spend time with each other, you just want us to do as you think is best. But you don't even know what is best!" Tuomas' voice had been rising and he was shouting by the time he reached the end of his speech.

Mikel dared not look around. Already too much of a scene would have been caused, and he didn't want people to panic if they found out about Lefi. He could feel his cheeks glowing red and busied himself chewing on the last of his bread. He couldn't even explain himself to Tuomas, because the boy had risen as he finished his speech and now he was already halfway back to Alaks's table, sliding between the gathered children in their pretty clothes to sit near the heir himself. Alaks leaned over and touched Tuomas' elbow softly, a look of concern crossing his face. Then he shot his gaze in Mikel's direction, meeting the commander's eyes for an instant. As they saw each other, Alaks began to laugh. Not the huge shoulder-shaking guffaws that he had been letting loose earlier, but a gentle shiver alongside a patronising smile.

INTERMÈDE

The creature paced erratically backwards and forwards along the ridge of a roof, beneath a bright full moon. Terracotta tiles stretched away to either side and it limped and stumbled as it moved. At one end of the roof stood a short chimney. Each time the creature reached it, it would lean over the chimney, resting both hands on the bricks, and stare down at the figures far below.

It knew them now. It had learned the faces of the beings that had invaded its lair. Memories of the noise they made as they ravaged its nest drew grimaces and snarls across the ill-fitting face the creature wore, and it would turn back to its pacing along the roof.

Anger and hunger wound together in the creature's throat, fighting to be expressed. It moaned and whined like a trapped hound. The creature wants to launch itself off the roof and fall on top of the figures below, so that it could crush them beneath its body, rip them apart with its fingers. Vengeance swelled in the creature's chest.

But the one it sought hid itself now. It was always

surrounded by too many of the others, so many that the creature couldn't be sure that it would be able to kill them all. The wound in its leg throbbed, a reminder that these things could cause it pain, that they might even be able to end its existence. This was an unwelcome thought for the creature and a growl rattled in the base of its throat.

The creature picked fitfully at a seam of flesh behind its cheek as it stalked across the roof. The small flap of skin peeled a little looser every time. Another was beginning to appear around its wrists. Frustration hissed out of its nostrils and it shook down its length, like a dog drying itself after bathing. The wound in its leg stretched open and shut with every step and it paused to squeeze the flesh closed with both hands, as though it could heal the wound through pressure.

The creature was developing a strong desire to seek out those who had disturbed its nest and kill them, to punish them for the hurt and confusion they had inflicted upon it. But the smell of its prey remained tauntingly close yet inaccessible. Its quarry hid behind heavy doors, or in groups of beings that were too much for the creature, especially limping and peeling as it was now. Crouching on the roof, full of impotent and unfamiliar emotions, the creature howled out into the night.

CHAPITRE LIV

Mikel rose numbly and walked towards the doors leading out of the great hall. He could not help but notice the glances that turned his way, or how they looked between himself and the table where the heir sat. Lord Uvaniah had still not arrived for his morning meal and it was nearly time for lunch. Mikel was worried that something may have happened but for now he just needed to get out of the hall before he was struck by another surprise.

What was going on with Tuomas? He was being so hostile, and over something completely inconsequential. Mikel didn't understand where the anger had come from. Moreover, he was shocked at how unbalanced the encounter with his son had left him. He was physically shaken, and he found it difficult to walk comfortably as he left the hall.

As soon as he made it to the corridor he turned to his left, and ducked into an alcove by the stairs. The small space had been built to contain a statue, and the tall carved figure that now filled it left little room for Mikel to shelter. He shuffled behind it and lowered his forehead to the cool stone wall. His breath was too large for his chest. He was puffing, as though he had been chasing a thief through the halls.

What on earth was all that about? And what was the heir trying to say about him? He thought carefully about his actions, but reassured himself that there was no way he had ever been trying to increase his own power in the castle. He had always done his job loyally, and discussed all his plans with Lord Uvaniah.

In addition, the decisions he had made this morning were made in consultation with Zhon . The two of them had agreed on the plans they had made to ensure the Lord's protection. The extra guards and restrictions were not a manoeuvre to give himself leverage in the castle. And there was no way to underestimate the ability of someone like Lefi who would so casually throw a man from a building. Lefi was a threat that needed to be carefully considered and protected against. No, all his decisions had been perfectly reasonable. Mikel managed to get his breath back under control and straightened. He hoped no-one had looked too closely at the statue in this niche and seen him hiding behind it.

As he walked towards the courtyards, Mikel saw Lord Uvaniah on his way into the great hall. The old man's limp was heavy today, and he hunched and winced as he moved. A servant was bearing his arm on her shoulder to help him. Guards walked around him in a tight knot. Their faces betrayed the grim fear that had been instilled in them earlier this morning.

Lord Uvaniah saw Mikel walking in the opposite direction and motioned him to come over.

"Of course sir," Mikel called. He stepped in beside the lord, heading back towards the great hall.

"Have you noticed anything strange about Alaks since he returned?" asked the elderly man.

"Sir?"

"I can't deny that he has always been a difficult boy, inclined to take his own path. His rejection of this marriage is certainly a sign of that in itself! But now he is refusing to come to meetings with me, meetings that he should attend."

"Sir, I don't know what to tell you." Mikel wondered if he should tell the lord that his heir had complained this morning about being asked to attend a meeting with the Blackriver council. Presumably this attitude was what had prompted his father's question in the first place.

"That's why I'm asking Mikel, have you noticed anything unusual about Alaks's behaviour? Is something happening that I need to know about?"

Mikel considered what he had seen of the heir since he returned.

"You say he refuses to attend meetings with you?"

"Yes, you know the sort of thing, important people from Blackriver, wealthy nobles, all of that." He waved his hand about in the air in front of him. "He claims that the journey has taken its toll on him and he is exhausted."

"Travel can certainly wear down a person," Mikel allowed. "However, he has always preferred to enjoy himself if he can," he continued carefully. "Perhaps his journey gave him a taste of freedom from the duties of being the Lord's heir and he is now in too much of a habit?"

"You make a good point. He has been trying to get out of touring the lands around Blackriver as well, seeing some of the common folk. I think I will have to insist, to remind him of what he has to do. Thank you for this conversation Mikel, it has been helpful to me." Lord Uvaniah's face was pensive, but then he suddenly jerked and turned back to Mikel.

"Oh, your boy, Tuomas! I should ask how has he been since he returned?"

"Good my lord, Tuomas is good. The journey gave him courage and confidence." *At least, I think it did,* thought Mikel. *It certainly has made him feel stronger about arguing with me.*

One of the castle noble's interrupted their conversation. Madame Ovyonath, and her eldest daughter smiled warmly at Mikel but then their conversation washed over the top of him. Apparently the family income from their forests to the east was suffering due to a drought some years earlier that had left many trees stunted and they were not sure whether to fell the trees this year as had been planned, or to move on to other parts of the forest.

Mikel bowed aside and left Lord Uvaniah to the woman and her daughter. He didn't see any point in saying anything further about Alaks. Uvaniah was no longer as boisterous as he had been only weeks earlier and any more stress would not be good for him. Mikel decided that his concerns over the behaviour of the heir were not worthy of the lord even if he were in the best of health! It was his own issue, between the young man and himself, and he would find a way to resolve it alone.

CHAPITRE LV

The streets of Blackriver made him feel more vulnerable than Mikel had ever experienced before, even when he was young and hungry. He walked briskly down Long Road, keeping his eyes moving across the roofs and alley mouths that were potential avenues for Lefi to come upon him by surprise. He nervously fingered the leather that bound the handle of his sword, picking at a loose edge until he forced himself to still his hand by tucking it into his belt.

Passersby offered him pleasant greetings and a few street-sellers waved their fruit or cooked meats towards him in an attempt to gain his interest, but he moved along from them quickly. Although he had no way of knowing for sure, he was sure that stopping in one place while out in public would only attract Lefi to him. He imagined it was simply because in the Castle there were guards within calling distance at all times, whereas in the town he had no way to know whether anyone would come to his aid if he called out. He avoided thinking about what Lefi's hands would do to the people he passed by if they did try to intervene on his behalf. He quashed any thoughts of what had happened to Zhosh. His fingers strayed back to the loose leather. On the far side of Blackriver, Mikel eventually arrived outside the kirk.

Mikel hadn't returned to the kirk since he and Tuomas had been kicked out during one of the last sermons attended by Mata. Not long after that, she had succumbed to her disease, and Mikel had been forced to wait beside her in their rooms, while the Kirkman declared his sorrow and sympathy but refused to admit her to the kirk before her burial. Mikel knew then that the kirk was a bastion of pretend righteousness, a means for the kirkman to club down anyone who disagreed with his standards. It was unfair to deny honest people the chance to come in and hear stories of the inspiration that Mercy provided, to deny people the chance to learn how to live safely within Mercy. Not that Mercy had saved Mata.

Now the building wore a different light. The central tower that rose from the broad roof was a torch. The round stained glass windows at its sides were the sides of a lantern that stood above the town and shone out over it. Perhaps it was the sun, scattering through the windows. Though it rose high as the day neared noon, its light was still caught and reflected from the multi-coloured panes to pour out over Blackriver. The squat tower glowed from within. Mikel was more confident now that he stood beneath the broad building, with its solid walls. For some reason, he felt reassured that the Kirkman would be able to help him understand what was happening with Lefi.

Mikel entered through the chapel. As usual, the tall wooden doors that led into the largest space in the building were unlocked and slightly ajar. He pulled them closed after himself though it went against years and years of tradition. He was unwilling to leave an opportunity for Lefi to follow behind him unnoticed. He wondered if the Kirkman had considered that already. If so, the man must have decided to continue the tradition of welcome that the kirk maintained. Mikel was impressed, though he feared that the decision was foolish. The vicious man they had seen the night before would need no more invitation than the space between the frame and door.

The chapel stretched out before Mikel, lit by the windows in the tower above so that blue and red red light washed over the seats that lined the space. At the far end, directly beneath the empty space of the tower, was the lectern.

The lectern's dark wood was carved in the shape of a person carrying a heavy load upon their shoulders. Spread upon the figure's back, as it stood half-hunched, a massive book lay open. The edges of the page shone brightly from their gilt-edging. Mikel had always wondered what else lay inside the pages of the Biblos. The Kirkman, and his tutor before him, had always spent their sermons reading stories from it and explaining the meaning to the townsfolk, but Mikel had noticed during his infrequent visiting to the chapel that the stories were quite often repeated. The Ugly Godling tale was told each year at the time of its festival, and the story of the Discordant Wedding was popular too. The Kirkman was able to teach the townsfolk the virtues of sharing and listening to each other by comparing them to the selfish and violent wedding of the gods of Fire and Nature. The guests at the wedding of these gods had fought viciously with one another in their pasts, and even the gods being married had quarrelled throughout the ceremony. Mikel always enjoyed the end of the story, when each consumed the other and left nothing behind. The Kirkmen always explained that this ending showed that arguments amongst humans could only lead to trouble and that people should always find a way to resolve their problems. But there was a passion in the gods as they died that inspired

Mikel. He thought there might be some meaning to be found in the story other than the Kirkman's interpretation. Perhaps the story was supposed to teach people that conflict gave rise to life. Or something.

He chuckled at himself. Trust his thoughts to wander to the divine while in such surroundings. He called out to see if the Kirkman was nearby. His voice echoed in the stone chapel, ringing hollowly.

There was no answer.

CHAPITRE LVI

Mikel's heart started pounding. The meaty thump of his pulse rang in his ears. He walked cautiously past the lectern and inspected the space beyond it. In this small space he found a wicker screen that hid a low table, covered in various items used to perform the rituals of the Kirk, but no Kirkman. No signs of violence, either in damaged or moved inanimate objects or in tell-tale spatters of blood. Mikel found a very small door behind the screen as well, the entrance to the Kirkman's private area in the kirk, his living quarters. The door was closed tightly, unlike the implied invitation of the half opened doors to the chapel. Mikel lifted the latch.

Behind the door Mikel found a small series of low-ceilinged rooms. Damp pieces of cloth in a variety of shades of brown and red and orange hung from strings that stretched from wall to wall. The air was heavy with steam, and Mikel was sure that he could smell onions. He took a step forward into the rooms and heard a clattering from around a corner. He began to ease his sword from its scabbard when the white-bearded face of the Kirkman lurched around the corner, a wide smile on his face.

"Hello commander! I wasn't sure when to expect you!" He ducked back around the corner, out of sight. Mikel followed cautiously. He was not used to such an expression on the Kirkman's face. Presumably it implied that the Kirkman had experienced no problems through the night, no nightmarish memories of what he had seen. But then again, the Kirkman hadn't actually seen Lefi in action, only the fearsome remains that the former guard had left behind.

The banging noises had come from a kitchen, though it was the smallest, most cramped kitchen Mikel had ever been inside. That thought included his mother's dank hot kitchen beside the washroom in a tiny hovel of a house on Keyp Street. In these small rooms behind the chapel, pots were strewn across a narrow bench and had clearly overflowed to the floor. The Kirkman kicked a couple aside to make room for Mikel. The taller man had to bend over to stand up in his own kitchen and Mikel looked around in wonder.

"How on earth do you live like this?"

"Like what?" The Kirkman looked at the pots on the floor, and then back at Mikel. He smiled "Do you mean all these things? I suppose it's a little snug, but I'm very comfortable. Just smell my soup!" Mikel took a deep breath and appreciated the aroma that flooded the small space. The smell of onions and chives, a hint of beef, not to mention a variety of spices and vegetables that he couldn't quite identify slipped into his nose, making him feel warm through his stomach, and suddenly hungry, though he had eaten his morning meal less than an hour earlier.

"You must be hungry," winked the Kirkman. "Here." And he served up two bowls of soup, with a large wooden spoon for each of them.

The Kirkman led Mikel out of the kitchen into another tiny space. There were two benches in this one, benches that grew out of the walls in a way that resembled ridges or tree roots more than actual furniture. A rough-hewn wooden table squatted in the remaining space between them. Mikel's knees pressed up towards his chest and he had to twist in his seat to be able to place the soup on the table. However, he had to admit that the soup was delicious when he did manage to manoeuvre the spoon to his mouth. He said as much to the Kirkman.

"Excellent!" The old man smiled. "I'm glad it suits you Mikel. Now, to business. What exactly will you need to know about the creature you encountered last night?" His expression turned serious, as stern and harsh in its weathered age as Mikel remembered from being turned away. The feeling flustered him for a moment, making him feel as though he was still a young boy from the street sneaking extra bread and about to be switched for it. He pushed the thoughts aside and leaned forward, though he realised it put an ache between his shoulders to do so.

"What do you mean 'the creature'? I encountered no creature, I was up against a mad man, a former guard who has decided to become a murderer, though only the gods know why."

The Kirkman snorted in amusement and licked a drop of stew from his lip. "Why Commander, I am surprised! I always thought of you as a very clear headed man! You are known for thinking through your problems most capably."

"Thank you?" replied Mikel, slightly confused.

The Kirkman put his hands together and touched his lips with his index fingers together. He looked upwards for a second and then returned his gaze to Mikel. "I would have thought it was quite obvious that what you were faced with was not human. I have never heard of a man who could throw a person bodily from a doorway and then lift himself to safety with one arm in the moments it took three large men to run up a flight of stairs." He raised an eyebrow in question to Mikel.

"It is the case that he acted like no human I have heard of before," the commander had to admit.

"Therefore, it seems fair to conclude that the guard you fought last night was not human."

"Not human." Mikel paused with his spoon halfway to his mouth, a single drip slowly growing underneath it. "But then…" Mikel ate the mouthful of soup and returned the spoon to the bowl as he thought about the Kirkman's statement. "Wouldn't that mean that Lefi must be partly of the gods?"

The Kirkman smiled and lifted some of the soup into his own mouth before replying. "Indeed, as I said last night. I am not sure how fully of the gods this creature was, but he must have had some trace of them in his being."

"Do you have any idea what sort of god he is?" Mikel's mind was racing. There were so many different gods in the world. Some could be reasoned with, or driven away, if only one knew what drove them.

"No."

CHAPITRE LVII

Mikel's temper rose, so he coughed and took another spoonful of the warm, filling stew before continuing. The warmth filled his belly and helped him keep his calm.

"It sounded to me that you did know last night," he said through clenched teeth.

"No, I am sorry Mikel, I don't actually know." The Kirkman scraped the last of his soup out of his bowl and swallowed it with a satisfied slurp and then lay the bowl back on the narrow table between them. He leaned back as best he could in the small space and laced his fingers together over his stomach. "But we can try to find out. Tell me, have there been any strange happenings around Blackriver that you know of? Incidents that may involve this creature that appears to us in a man's body?"

"Of course, that is why we were in its Mercy-forsaken lair waiting for it to return!" Mikel forced his anger back behind gritted teeth. "We found a dead body in the riverbank.' Mikel realised that he had asked Marq to send the body to this man in order to be buried appropriately. Suddenly he wondered how the Kirkman would feel when he made the connection. Mikel had been about to explain just how disfigured and damaged the body had been, and the Kirkman had been the one who performed the final rituals over it. Mercy knew the Kirkman was strict with those rituals. How would he react to this information? He scooped up more soup before it could be thrown at him. "It seems that the body belonged to a young man who was meeting with some of the mercenaries in town."

"A young man meeting with the Guershan?"

Mikel nodded. "Yes. However, the man he was meeting with went missing a short while ago also. And that mercenary may have been meeting with Lefi for about a week before we found his room. And Lefi was one of our guards." It pained Mikel to say that out loud.

The Kirkman hummed loudly as he considered all the connections that Mikel was laying out. "It seems to me, from what you have said, that you have only actually found one body?"

"That's right."

The older man lifted the far edge of his bowl so that he could investigate it for any final dregs of stew. "Was there anything unusual about this body?"

"Yes." Mikel sniffed and then pressed his lips together as he considered his next words carefully, dreading the response that he knew must be coming. He tensed his muscles, ready to leap from the room. "It had been partially flayed. The skin had been taken off its hands and face. And it had no eyes."

"Mercy protect us." The Kirkman's face fell as he took in what Mikel had said. "How horrible for the boy's family. Hold on." The Kirkman sat straighter, though the ceiling kept him bent mostly in half. "From the way this has all happened quite recently, I assume the body was the one your alchemist at the castle sent to me a day or two past?"

There it is. Mikel clenched his jaw, trying not to bite his lip. "Yes."

"Mikel!" Now the Kirkman looked more like the stern man who had barred Mikel from his wife's Resting Day. His white hair bristled like gorse prickles and his eyes flashed. "That was extremely unfair! You don't know what rituals must be followed when interring the dead, and such a disfigurement as that requires different steps."

"You would not have accepted the poor boy then?" Mikel could not help but challenge the older man angrily.

"Of course I would not have refused him!" The Kirkmman spread his arms in dismay. "The kirk could never do such a thing to a suffering family. But the rituals to ensure his soul is taken into Mercy's protection should have been very different, to keep unsavoury gods from leading it astray after death. Perhaps it is not too late. I shall contact his poor family and arrange for them to come and perform some of the farewells and cleansings again. Yes, I'm sure it will be okay." His eyes swung their focus back to the commander and bore into his like augers. "But had this not slipped out of you now, I imagine his soul may have been left wandering the crossroads for years before finding his way to Mercy. You tell that man Marq that he should be ashamed of himself!"

Mikel pursed his lips and looked down. He held anger against the Kirkman for how he had been treated after Mata passed on. Those traditionally open doors had slammed shut in his face. But he remembered how Mata had never wavered in her peaceful devotion to the kirk.

"Sweetheart," she had said in her soft voice. Mikel had been already walking to the door, ready to leave their rooms, and he nearly missed it.

"What? Mata, are you alright?" Mikel rushed back to the bedside and knelt down so that he could take her hands in his own. His wife smiled weakly. Her skin was pale.

"I'm fine. I feel better than usual. I would like to go to sermon today."

"Sermon? But, you're so weak, I don't think that you should be getting out of bed." Mikel rubbed his thumbs over her hands. "Maybe we can plan ahead and go next week. Yes, we can make sure that one of the servants is able to help you walk, and we can see how strong you are feeling and-"

"Mikel." The softness of her voice cut her off more effectively than any shout could have. She lifted a hand and pressed one finger to his lips. "Hush sweetheart. I am as strong as I am going to be, and I wish to go to sermon. Help me up."

Mikel's shoulders fell slightly, but he nodded and stood. He held onto Mata's hands and helped her sit up on the bed and then move so that she could put her feet to the floor. Even that small task left her breathing heavily

"No no, I can do it," she insisted before he could say anything. She slowed her breathing until she was calmer and then stood up. She clutched onto Mikel's arm and wavered for a second, but then she leaned on him and together they walked over to their wardrobe. Mikel helped his wife select a gown and then she held onto the large wooden cabinet while he undressed her and then helped her into it.

She sat on the bedroom chair as he fastened her shoes onto her feet. Once he finished, Mikel looked up at his wife. She was looking back down at him, her face still pale, a soft smile still lifting the corners of her lips.

"Are you sure that you're up to this," he asked, his hands holding each of her ankles. "I'm worried that this might be too much exertion."

She shook her head. "It's important that I make sure Mercy will recognise me when my time comes."

"I don't know if Mercy will save you now, even if it recognises you finally," said Mikel. He was beginning to think that Mercy was not going to be of any use to Mata at all. They had prayed that Mercy's Shield protect her for so long, and still she grew sicker.

She chuckled and then winced. "Oh you silly man. Come on."

Mata struggled upright and together the two of them walked slowly out of their rooms.

CHAPITRE LVIII

Blinking as the memories passed out of his mind, Mikel wanted to protest or explain further, but the Kirkman shook his head as though he was shaking his outrage off his physical body, patting at his arms and shoulders as he did. It was like the anger was a physical covering on him that he was pushing aside.

"Clearly things are different in the alchemist's country. Perhaps he meant well," the older man muttered."Well, at least we can take solace in one thing. I have an idea about what we may have on our hands here."

He stood, gathering the bowls as he went, motioning for Mikel to follow him.

They quickly passed through the kitchen again, where the Kirkman left the bowls in a pile on one bench alongside knives and old dishes that still sat with scraps of long past meals stuck to them. The Kirkman went from the kitchen into the small hallway Mikel had entered through but then passed through a different door than the one that led back to the chapel. He gathered a candle holder with a short stubby white candle in it as he went through the kitchen, cupping his hand around the flame after he lit it. When Mikel followed, he found himself amazed by what lay beyond. The reason for the cramped low ceilings and cramped living quarters became clear.

Behind the door lay a steep stone staircase that led up to a broad room full of parchments and books. The roof stretched off into the dusty black distance above them both, and ladders reached towards it, leaning precariously against hundreds of shelves. The ladders and shelves were both in a multitude of states of repair or disrepair. Some were barely held together by thin strands of strings and twine, while others were solidly connected via metal brackets.

The books were good matches for their surroundings, some covered with thick drifts of dust and joined to their neighbours by wispy conglomerations of spider web, while others were clearly referred to often and were clean, even reflecting the light gently from their leather covers where fingers had polished them smooth.

The sunlight came in through the windows, but barely managed to leach into the shadows between the shelves that filled the space. Between that meagre light and the Kirkman's candle there was still not enough light enough to read by, especially any older or faded texts, but it was enough to find one's way between the shelves and select something before returning to the chapel or living quarters. Mikel followed the Kirkman through the narrow canyons between the shelves. The older man apparently knew exactly where he was going.

"I always thought that the kirk was all about the Biblos," said the commander as he stood near the entrance to the dim space. He was unsure whether he was asking a question or not.

The Kirkman laughed. "Many would agree with you, including many other Kirkmen. But the gods do not restrict themselves to the stories bound in the book of the Kirk. They have been amongst us for hundreds of years, and many peoples have their own stories. Some of us, myself included, feel that we can learn something about the gods from anyone. I am sure there are gods and stories beyond Mercy's reach that we have never even heard of!"

It made sense, although Mikel had never really considered the possibility before. The gods existed alongside and within just about everything that he saw and experienced, so it only made sense that there were so many stories about them.

"And some of these are stories about humans, our tales and the histories of our kingdoms."

"Why do you have those?"

"Because it helps us in the kirk advise those who come to us for help." The tall old man turned his head to glance at Mikel. His eyes peeked from above his beard. "Did you perhaps think that you were the only one who had ever had cause to ask for my assistance?" His eyes twinkled as they watched Mikel. Then the Kirkman faced forward again, turning left into a darker set of shelves.

"I think this is what I'm looking for." The Kirkman stepped forward and began rummaging through a set of books on a shelf at shoulder height. Most of them were quite small, bound in covers of thick board but bearing no decoration other than a simple title. One or two were larger, with metal edges used to bind them together, though the metal had long since lost its sheen. The Kirkman closed his hands around one of the larger books on the shelf and drew it from between the others. It was not as dusty and unused as most of the others, though the tattered edges of the leather cover implied that it was not being as well taken care of as some of the cleaner editions they had already passed. Mikel could not read the lettering on the front cover, twisted and angular as it was. He presumed it must be written in some other language.

"Yes, this is the one." The Kirkman held the book up for Mikel to see, although it made no difference to the commander. "This is a catalogue of gods, a list of many different types of gods that people have encountered over the years. Hopefully we can find something about your Lefi in here."

As they returned the way they had come, heading towards the stairs that led down to the small, yet well lit, living quarters, Mikel asked the Kirkman a question. "You looked like you knew exactly what to look for after I had described the body we found. Do you have an idea already?"

"Not specifically." The Kirkman steadied himself against the wall as they descended the short flight of stairs. "But I do recall seeing something about dangerous gods and godlings in this catalogue once before, when I was trying to find out about the gods of the fields."

CHAPITRE LIX

"Are the gods of the fields dangerous?" Mikel was surprised. He would have thought the gods that helped the crops and farmers would be generally sedate and helpful creatures.

"Oh my yes!" The Kirkman chuckled. "Field gods are the same gods who delve into the deepest darkest parts of the forests, to tend wild plants and wild growth! They are jealous of their territory and skills. If you cause problems in their patch of land or to their chosen plants, they will not hesitate to visit painful suffering on you and often your whole family! That's why farmers seek to keep them on side, to protect their crops and land. But I don't think that Lefi is involved with those gods."

Mikel thought about the gods of the fields abandoning a farmer who had not given a worthy offering to them, or decided to change his methods, or planted new crops without consulting the gods. He would find himself with a field of dry dead wheat most likely, or tending to a diseased flock with greasy wool that no-one would want to buy. It made a certain amount of sense.

Soon the two men were back in the strange little dining room, with its odd benches and low table. The Kirkman laid the catalogue on the table and opened it. Mikel winced as the pages creaked, feeling sure that they would crack or split instead of turning. They were ancient.

Although Mikel asked him questions about what was written on those pages, the Kirkman simply motioned for quiet as he turned them one by one, or occasionally three or four at a time. Mikel had to make do with sitting in silence, shifting uncomfortably on the narrow surface of the bench. He noted the shadows cast by the window sill creeping slowly towards the Kirkman before the older man suddenly stabbed a finger into the book with a cry of success.

"Here we are!"

"You found something?" Mikel craned his neck around in order to read the writing on the page, but found that it was too small and splotchy to read even if he could twist his head around far enough. It looked as though a mouse had drunkenly crawled through a puddle of ink and draped itself across the page.

"Yes, it's not a lot but it seems relevant. Here, I'll read it to you." The Kirkman began to read, tracing a finger along the lines as he did.

"The gods of forest decay gather in the piled leaves and undergrowth of the woods. They grow in the cold and the dark, and dwell within caves and isolated springs. It is their voices that call back to you when you shout in an enclosed space, the voices of the echoes. They are the faces that peer back from the clear icy cool ponds that lie still beneath a canopy of trees, seemingly identical to you but somehow different.

In form, these gods bring that same mimicry to life,

echoing the shape and form of humans that they choose. Like leeches that drift in stagnant water deep beneath the canopy, these gods draw essence from the living and twist it to something else. Although it is not recorded first hand, it is believed that these beings are capricious and violent creatures. Stories are told of victims who were killed before the god stole their face and began living their lives.

These godlings can be identified in a few ways. They do not eat human food, preferring to take sustenance from the decay that falls around them. They consume things that grow in the quiet and darkness of deep woods and caves, such as mushrooms or vermin and insects. They are paranoid creatures. Someone who has been mimicked by one of them may appear to become jumpy and easily shocked, twitching and spasming uncontrollably."

The Kirkman leaned back and closed the book with a soft thump. "And that's pretty much all the book says."

Mikel took a deep breath through his nose and considered what they had learned. "So, Lefi is a forest god of decay?"

"It would appear that way."

"And he probably isn't Lefi. At least, he may have once been, but now he is being mimicked by one of these things."

"Again, that seems likely."

"But why?"

"Unfortunately, that's all the information we have on these gods that I can think of. Of course, now I can try and look for more in our library, but I couldn't guarantee you that I would find anything of use, especially not in a hurry."

Mikel considered this new information. A god of decay. Some sort of malevolent spirit that would take on the face of a person and then instigate calamity. *That explains all the half-chewed rats we found in that room,* he realised. *It truly must be one of these gods we are dealing with here.* But he still couldn't figure out why it was here, or what it wanted.

"You're the expert on the gods. Do you have any ideas why it is in Blackriver?"

"I could make some guesses." The Kirkman shrugged. "Of course, they would be no more than guesses. Possibly someone in the town has committed some offence against one of the gods and they have sent it to perform some sort of retribution. Maybe it was passing through these lands, and we are simply unfortunate to suffer its brutal nature as it does. Or perhaps someone has discovered a ritual that binds the creature and has sent it with some task in mind."

"Is that even possible?"

"Oh yes, the gods are usually quite willing to respond to our requests, so long as we use the proper forms. That is why we perform our blessings during the Resting Day ceremony. We exhort the gods around us to rest and submit to Mercy's guidance and protection, just as we do ourselves, which should allow all of us to rest also. It is a form of control, though it requires careful forethought and consideration.

It is the same for funeral rites, I must ensure that the gods leave the souls of our loved ones at peace as they approach Mercy's crossroads." The Kirkman glanced intently at Mikel, but then sniffed and looked back down at the book.

"If someone has found the forms that appeal to this god, perhaps they have given it some purpose against us."

A small fire flared in his chest. The warmth gave him hope and even the room they sat in looked brighter. It spread through him, encouraging him. "Could we do the same then?"

"I don't understand what you mean." The Kirkman's brows furrowed.

"With our local gods we ask them for peace and rest and to help us with our tasks. Farmers beseech the field gods to help their crops grow strong and healthy. Families taking their children to swim in the river murmur quiet requests to water gods to help their children swim safely. If someone else gave this thing instructions, perhaps we could do the same, but better somehow. Could we perform a ritual that would force this god to leave the town, permanently hopefully?"

The Kirkman ran a hand over his white beard, pulling the tangled hair into some order. "I suppose that is theoretically possible, though I imagine it would be quite difficult."

"How difficult?" Mikel had to fight not to break into a grin. There was no reason to think that this idea would come together yet.

"It might require some study in the library in order to figure out some particular nuances, but all of these rituals follow similar structures. I suppose I could possibly be ready to attempt something in a day or two. Yes, give me some time to investigate these books and I will attempt some form of ritual. We will see what happens."

"You get working on that." Mikel began to stand, though he needed to remain hunched over in these low quarters. He held out one hand to the Kirkman. "I'll keep my guards on duty to protect those we can. Thank you for your help!" They clasped hands together and shook firmly.

CHAPITRE IX

A clatter of noise burst from the chapel, followed by a strange cry and the rhythmic slap of feet on stone. Mikel spun, grabbing at his sword.

"By the gods, what was that!?"

The short hairs on the back of his neck began to rise as he jogged towards the door back into the chapel. He could feel the Kirkman close behind him, one hand on his shoulder. He wondered if he should tell the older man to stay back but then realised that he was too old to deal with Lefi himself, if the sound was indeed the missing guard. Mikel's body still ached from his efforts the day before.

Mikel drew his sword and held it out before him as he walked back into the wide open space of the chapel. He moved cautiously around the low wicker screen, wary of being taken by surprise. Beside him he was aware of the Kirkman grabbing a large ritual goblet from amongst the items stored in this area, gripping it like a stout club. Mikel nodded to himself. At least he would have some sort of assistance. The other man's face had gone nearly as pale as his beard.

The front door to the chapel was still closed, exactly where Mikel had left it after he came in. However, one of the windows on the side of the chapel overlooking the narrow wooden pews was open, which he hadn't noticed before. *Was it always open,* he asked himself. Three birds were pecking at the stone floor beneath the window. They cooed and hopped along the floor, seeking crumbs under the pews. A tall candelabra standing on the floor had toppled over.

Mikel carefully investigated every corner of the chapel, between the pews and up into the high vaulted stone ceiling. Eventually he was satisfied that the noise he had heard must have been the birds, lured in through the window by the various shiny objects in the chapel. He caught one of the birds by surprise as he rounded a pew and it emitted a call that echoed between the solid walls and grew in volume, until it sounded very similar to the cry they had heard from the Kirkman's quarters. *They must have knocked over the candelabra and scared themselves,* he decided. The Kirkman shuddered a sigh and returned his goblet to the table behind the screen.

Mikel was surprised at his own reaction to the noise. His first thought, leaping to the front of his mind without any logical thought process preceding it, had been that Lefi had followed him and was in the chapel. Then, instead of looking for another way out of the cramped space that the Kirkman lived in, he had drawn his weapon and moved to confront this god of decay that looked like one of his guards. In some ways, he was proud of himself. It was as though he was still young, still ready to step up and be the guard that protected the weak from harm. But he also realised that by seeking out the creature he was putting himself in harm's way unnecessarily. He was too old to deal with a monster like this now. He didn't have the reflexes or strength to put up a fight. After all, Zhosh had been young and he had been killed as casually as a person might swat a fly that was annoying them. This thing would make short work of Mikel.

The Kirkman reiterated that he would need time to search through his books and to prepare so that they could attempt a ritual that might rebind the god to their own ends. Mikel agreed to come back in two days, praying that Mercy would shield the castle and townsfolk from Lefi until then. Once their plans were set, Mikel headed off through Blackriver to return to the castle. He longed to feel himself within the comforting heights of its massive stone walls. He wanted to know that men were watching his back and were prepared to step forward should the thing that was pretending to be Lefi reappear.

As he walked he wondered when it was that the god had taken over Lefi. Had he been a man when he joined up with the guard? In that case, how had the god come across him? Had it found a way to sneak up on the man during a watch, managing to slip past the other guards? That thought made a cool sweat rise on Mikel's back.

Or had Lefi always been this being? Had he used his position to find people to kill, such as Filip and Akub? That thought was no better, because it implied that this god was killing utterly randomly. No-one could claim to be safe.

It was quiet in the castle when Mikel returned. The afternoon sun was quite warm, although in the shade the breeze had a sharpness that stuck in his nostrils like a slick thin dagger. Mikel noticed the stablehands were keeping their heads low as they shifted hay into the stalls. Mikel assumed that they were quiet because the day had been boring for them. Although a warm clear day in the autumn would often be a perfect day for various nobles to go riding, it was impossible not to notice that there were more guards patrolling through the halls than usual. Each of the guards wore a grim expression, whether their face was smooth and young or grizzled and worn with age. Clearly, something dangerous was happening in the castle. And therefore many nobles would be confining themselves to the comfortable familiarity of their rooms, rather than going riding in the wide and potentially dangerous unknown.

But then Mikel saw one of the stalls was empty. On either side of it, horses stood quietly in the other stalls, some being groomed by thin young boys and girls who would normally be cracking jokes with one another but worked silently now.

This stall is empty, thought Mikel again. He stood beside the stall and stared at it, trying to will his brain into revealing why this fact was ensnaring him so thoroughly. He looked around to the left and right, spotting one or two other stalls that were also empty. A boy who looked to be about eleven years old was walking by with a bucket of water for the trough alongside the stalls. Mikel grabbed his shoulder.

"Who went out riding today?"

CHAPITRE LXI

T he boy's eyes were huge and white and he stammered as he answered.

"Why, the heir went for a ride today sir. He took some few of his friends this morning, but I had nothing to do with it. It doesn't matter does it?"

Mikel shushed the boy, who was clearly overcome by the heavy feeling in the air coupled with the intense questioning of a scary older man. Mikel stepped back and gave the boy room. The stablehand's eyes were skittering backwards and forwards like a cornered rat.

"Hush boy, it's alright. I just thought that most people would have wanted to stay inside on a day like this."

Slowly the stablehand turned his gaze out the stable doors to the bright blue sky that hung over Blackriver. Mikel smiled as the boy looked back at him.

"I'm not talking about the weather." He crossed his arms and looked out through the doors again. "He was supposed to be at a council meeting with his father," Mikel mused. "I suppose he must be out surveying the farms instead, as Lord

Uvaniah instructed him to. It will be good for the people to see him out amongst them, readying them for the winter."

"What?" The boy's face scrunched up in confusion.

"Isn't he surveying the homesteads?"

"I'm not sure what you mean by that sir. But he's out hunting. I think..." The boy licked his lips and took a deep breath, scanning the stables before leaning in closely and whispering to Mikel. "I think that he may have been drinking!"

Drinking and hunting? In the morning, after having wasted a whole day due to his carousing. Something was wrong with Alaks, he wasn't behaving in the way that Mikel had seen of him as he grew up. But Tuomas had spoken so well of him and his behaviour in Highfort.

"Thank you for your help lad." Mikel patted him on the shoulder. Taking advantage of the opportunity given to him, the stablehand dashed from the stables and knocked over a bucket of water as he went. It spoke to how unsettled the boy had been by Mikel's presence that he didn't return to pick it up.

Mikel looked at the horse in the stall nearest him. The animal was a tall, strong, dark wood-coloured beast with huge wet eyes. It chewed slowly and watched Mikel. Alaks was insisting on doing as he pleased, with no regard to the responsibilities of his position.

The heir returned just before the evening meal was due to be served in the great hall. He rode through the gates and in towards the stable as the last warmth of the sun finished leaking away from the sky. He was followed by his companions: a group of lean hunting dogs that pounced and scampered around his horse's hooves as he moved, the tall son of a wealthy miller's family who rode with a heavy crossbow resting on the saddle in front of him. And, to Mikel's surprise, Tuomas was with them as well.

Alaks was covered in a thin film of dirt and sweat, and wore a smile that spread from ear to ear. The other boys were just as grimy and happy. All of them were carrying bundles of grouse and wood pigeon tied by the ankles across their saddles.

Mikel attempted to catch Tuomas' attention as they rode in, but his son didn't look in his direction at all. Mikel stopped walking across the courtyard towards the great hall and stood, watching the new arrivals. The riders and their horses trotted around a corner into the stable building.

A weight was forming behind his ribs. He caught his breath and puffed out with difficulty, lifting a hand to press against his chest. It was hard to imagine what the strange sensation was. Panic was solidifying in his body. But he had set up guards around the castle. They were watching over the inhabitants of the castle, keeping everyone safe from the thing that had taken Lefi's place. Across the river the town was quiet for now. The Kirkman had created a plan. It may be uncertain, but it was something. Soon life would return to normal. Even as he said this to himself, Mikel knew he was lying.

Dinner passed without incident. Tuomas continued walking past his father without a second glance. When the boy sat at a higher table with Alaks, Mikel did manage to catch his son's eye. Mikel had just about finished his own meal, wiping the grease from a roast chicken off his fingertips and onto his jerkin. He sighed happily to himself then looked up and saw his son looking at him from that far table, next to Alaks. Alaks was talking loudly to the others at the table, gesturing with large windmill movements and throwing his head back in laughter.

Everything's just a joke to that boy, Mikel realised. *Any time he has done something laudable, it has only been because he didn't feel like doing whatever would have been the other option. He never took the right course of action because it was the right thing to do, or because he felt it was his responsibility.* Mikel considered what had happened in Highfort. Alaks had decided he didn't want to marry the daughter of the lord in that town. While Mikel had initially thought that was a reasonable decision, now he wondered about it. Had Alaks even ever really considered the option? Had he really considered what it might mean beyond himself? Or had he just decided that he didn't think she was pretty enough and so there would be no marriage? Mikel was beginning to see that Alaks was more spoiled and selfish than he had thought. What would that mean for the future of Blackriver, for Sheerwall? *And more importantly, what does that mean for my son?*

Tuomas was good friends with the heir to Lord Uvaniah now, for whatever that might mean in the future. Would Tuomas be trapped joining in with Alaks's whims? It looked that way so far. After all, he had set out hunting for the day, when Lord Uvaniah had given him other duties. A day out hunting might seem a relatively harmless activity, but Alaks had responsibilities that should have come first.

What if a grown Alaks, in his power as lord of the Castle, decided one morning to cancel a trade alliance with a distant lord in a fit of pique? Perhaps he would dislike his morning meal, and destroy years of carefully maintained relationships? In such a future, would Tuomas be forced to support the measure? Mikel wondered if his son's friendship with the heir might mean that Tuomas would be given a position of responsibility, and whether Alaks might decide to take away the position just as easily, especially if Tuomas was unable to follow the heir's future whims as easily as he had gone hunting today. Mikel worried for his son. The tight feeling in his chest grew, weighing him down.

INTERMÈDE

The god of decay was uncomfortable. Its latest skin was decaying and peeling away. It was hungry; so hungry. It needed to find a new face to wear, a new way to move through the crowds of beings that smelled so tasty. But it could not feed on these creatures, not even to sustain itself for the hunt before it. They were too many, and the god knew that if it let its hunger take control then they would manage to kill it.

The scent of its true prey was all through the air, swamping its mind as it kept moving, seeking the one being that it knew it must devour. The feeling was like a hook in the back of its skull, pulling it forward at all times. Its muscles itched beneath its skin, and nausea swam in its stomach.

The prey was proving more and more difficult to track each day. Even more beings surrounded it now than before. Their eyes were wide and seeking, and they carried weapons. So instead the god had decided it must take the face of a new being yet again, one of those who could move closer to its prey. It wasn't used to having to change faces so often to achieve its ends, and it grew tired and angry at the delays. Each new face drew some of its will from it, and it was weakening.

However, it had found one such being, one who moved alone. One who could move amongst the beings in this place whenever it wished. The god had followed this singular creature all day, sniffing for their scent in the air and listening for the sounds of their voice. Now it waited, feeling the warmth of its prey's blood through the wall that separated them. Soon, it would wear a new face. Soon it would be revitalised. Soon, it would kill.

CHAPITRE LXII

As Mikel's worries had flashed through his mind, Tuomas had been looking at him with a sorrowful look in his eyes. He looked away as Mikel met his eyes, and then slowly, bashfully raised them again. Just as Mikel was about to venture a smile for his son, Alaks's hand came clapping down on Tuomas' shoulder. Instantly Tuomas turned to the heir with a smile, clearly forgetting the shared moment with his father.

Mikel quietly ate some fruit, slicing bites off the small red orb with his pocket knife, before standing. Around him the usual conversation buzzed, though it was broken by a few sharper laughs than usual, a harsher tone. He moved through it all without a word, and decided to head for bed.

One of the castle guards woke Mikel in the morning and he sat up and rubbed at his eyes, trying to scour the sleep from them.

"What? Yes?" he called from where he was twisted in his sheets. His heart raced as he considered what disaster may have fallen that prompted the guard to wake him. He shoved his legs into his pants and sought his swordbelt.

"Sir?" The guard looked puzzled. "Are you alright?"

"Who has died?" rasped Mikel.

"No one!" The guard stepped back in shock. "Lord Uvaniah sent me to fetch you."

"No one has died?" Mikel shook his head. He must be mishearing this young man.

"No sir. No one is dead. Lord Uvaniah is taking the heir to visit some local farms and has asked for you to be a part of the guard that is to travel with them."

But I am more useful here, seeking out Lefi, whatever he may truly be. Mikel didn't bother muttering his disapproval. This guard would only find it awkward to be exposed to a disagreement with the castle's lord. Instead he straightened his clothes and then joined the guard in a quick walk to the lord's quarters.

"Thank you for joining us Mikel," smiled the lord.

"Sir, I am honoured to join you, of course, but may I raise a small concern?" Mikel stepped closer to the lord. The guards with Lord Uvaniah watched him closely and Mikel was pleased with their stern gaze. *That's it, suspect even me,* he thought. Lord Uvnaiah nodded at him with a frown, indicating that he should speak.

"This Lefi could be anywhere. I am needed here in order to track him down."

"Did you not claim that the man was a possible threat to me?"

Mikel nodded. "Exactly, so I should-"

"You should accompany me in case this traitor should attack while we are travelling to these farms." Iosef Uvaniah tilted his head and smiled ruefully. "Mikel, would you really be of any use here?" He gestured towards Mikel.

At first the commander of the guard didn't know what his old friend meant by the movement. Then he became aware of the aches and pains that twinged across his body, from where his muscles had recently been pushed further than they could cope with. He noticed the way his breath was raw in his throat.

The lord put an arm across Mikel's shoulder and led him towards a tall narrow window overlooking a courtyard. In the cobbled space a collection of horses was being prepared. Mikel could see Alaks sitting on one already, with a stiff back and a face that stared steadfastly ahead, as though he was trying to pretend that the other travellers in the courtyard did not exist.

"You are old Mikel, as am I. We must begin looking to the future, instead of holding onto our pasts."

Mikel could not shake the feeling that something terrible would happen in the castle if he was not there. As the group rode their horses out of the castle and through Blackriver he looked back over his shoulder. Was that Zhon standing over the drawbridge, watching them leave? Would his second be skilled enough to manage the guards and deal with any unexpected attacks from Lefi. For a moment Mikel considered turning around and riding back into the castle, but then he saw Lord Uvaniah's eyes resting on him. Mikel swallowed and cleared his throat and then flicked his reins. He would do as his lord commanded.

The procession made their way out of Blackriver and across the fields towards the first farm they would visit. Mikel watched his guards with pride. They kept close to Lord Uvaniah and the heir, with three others riding at a distance to ensure no surprises could catch them unawares. He had less admiration for Alaks, who snapped instructions at the guards beside him while they rode. He treated the guards as though they were his servants, sending them to fetch fresh water or fruit as his whims dictated. He even ordered them to stop and adjust his saddle for him before they reached the first farm.

Mikel rode closer after this, and began talking softly.

"Sir, I hope that you understand why I have ordered these guards to watch you so closely."

Alaks snorted, his eyes barely flickering towards Mikel.

"There is a very dangerous threat that may be in the castle, and we only want you to be safe."

"You are treating me like a small child, exactly as you treat your son. You have no idea what anyone else is capable of because you judge them when you meet them and then never consider adjusting your expectations of them." Now he turned to Mikel. His eyes travelled up and down the commander, a sneer demonstrating his disappointment. "You seem to think that you are the only person who understands the world, or has the ability to lead us forward into the future. Mercy save me, but you are so blind."

Mikel's cheeks flushed with anger and embarrassment. He rode beside Alaks for a while longer, in an attempt to maintain his pride instead of fleeing from the unwarranted accusations of a selfish child, but his breath was shallow and his stomach tense until he slowed down and let the heir move ahead.

CHAPITRE LXIII

The first visit went as well as Mikel had anticipated. Lord Uvaniah was gracious and friendly to the farmer and his family, and they were given a tour of the livestock and some of the nearer buildings. Iosef nodded and asked questions about how well the farmer was prepared for the winter and what troubles the lord might be able to help with.

At the same time, Alaks made himself at home in the man's home and gestured to their daughter to bring wine. Mikel saw a flash of anger in the farmer's wife's eyes, but she motioned for her daughter to obey. Mikel pursed his lips and then left the home. He had no desire to watch the heir act so disrespectfully.

Mikel made his way outside and looked around the fields that surrounded this farmhouse. By the fences in the distance he could see one of the guards, keeping a lookout. He decided to join the young man. The guard's eyes moved constantly along the treeline and the dusty trails that led towards the farm.

"How goes it, young man?"

"Well sir."

"I'm glad to hear it. It's not going as well inside." Mikel nodded towards the farmer's house. "Alaks is taking advantage of his position somewhat."

The guard nodded slightly.

"Yes, it's probably not the best way to build a positive relationship with the people on his father's lands. But at least he is here this time. Apparently he decided to just go hunting yesterday, despite his father's instructions!"

The guard pursed his lips and nodded again.

Mikel found it frustrating. He used to have such a good relationship with his guards, but this one didn't seem to be willing to speak at all. He decided to try a different angle. He took a breath, widened his smile, and asked "So, how long have you been with the guards?"

"Six years."

Did he say six years? But that was well before I stepped aside. Mikel blinked rapidly and his smile faltered. He caught himself, coughed, and then continued.

"Excellent! Excellent! You must remember, ah-"

"Sir, it's alright, you don't need to start having conversations with me now." The young man's brow was furrowed. He glanced about and then licked his lips. "Look, I'm here to do my job and, if anything, having you here chatting will only make it harder for me. Do you mind?"

He motioned his head back towards the house.

"Yes, of course, sorry. I just wanted to- I'm sorry, you keep watch," Mikel muttered in a fading voice as he headed back to the house.

He stopped outside the door, his thoughts whirling around him. He didn't even remember this guard's name. And that wasn't very surprising, because he hadn't managed to speak with most of the recruits who had arrived in the last year, nor go over their papers. But this guard said he had been here six years, and Mikel made sure he knew all the guards who had joined while he was commander, at least until recently. How had he missed this one?

Did Tuomas and Alaks have a point? Was he blind to what was happening in the world around him?

He swallowed and his throat felt thick. No. There must be a mistake. He knew all his guards, this one must have just been having some sort of joke. Well, it wasn't funny. And he would have to speak to Zhon about it too. New recruits such as that boy should not have been chosen for such an important task as this, guarding Lord Uvaniah and his heir from the godling that hunted in their lands! He grimaced and opened the door to duck back inside.

The tour stretched on for hours, and Mikel found that his attention wandered often. At first he told himself that he was ignoring the conversation of his old friend and the landholders because he was too intent on keeping watch for Lefi. Then he had to admit that he was tired and shaken by the way he had been spoken to. When the party returned to the Castle, Mikel ate dinner and retreated to his rooms as soon as he could.

Sleep hid from Mikel, despite the exhaustion that lay like heavy iron on his limbs. He stared at the ceiling above his bed. Outside, the light of the autumn moon briefly rose and fell as clouds shifted across its face. Mikel wondered if he was doing the right thing. But even as he wondered this, he could think of no other action that he should be taking.

A shout echoed across the castle grounds and in through his window, hanging in Mikel's ears long after the sound had faded. He sat up and stared at the window. Was that an alarm? It would need to be followed by another call, to make sure that more men came to help, but what if the alarm had been raised because some guard had seen Lefi and then the godling had moved too quickly? Mikel remembered the way it had lifted itself up to the roof after killing Zhosh. A creature like that must have strength and speed that would totally overwhelm a single man caught by surprise. He swung his legs over the side of the bed and reached for his shirt and leggings, still lying in a muddled heap in the corner of the room where he had thrown them.

The second cry carried anger and fear with it. It was sharper, lifting higher in the quiet still evening, and it carried on and on. Now Mikel hurried, pulling at his clothes and cursing as he had to pull them half off in order to straighten them before shoving his limbs through them again. He grabbed his sword from beside the door as he swung it open and raced out into the hall.

CHAPITRE LXIV

He shook his head as he jogged through the hallways, imaging himself as he must appear to others. A tired old man, half-dressed, carrying his sword held before him like a man with a torch rushing through a cavern. He knew he would be little to no help against the godling, and yet he found himself running to face it again. He was a fool.

He rounded a corner and found himself nearly colliding with another guard. It was Surman, the man who had helped comfort Saara after the discovery of her brother's body in the muddy rushes alongside the river Black. Surman's face was white, all the blood having fled from it, which made his lips look thin, and when he spoke the redness of his mouth and tongue were shocking.

"Sir! Thank the patient gods that it's you. I heard footsteps and wondered if I should swing my sword, or if I should wait and-"

"I'm glad you chose to wait!" Mikel hoped his voice sounded more confident to the guard than it did to himself. He understood why the boy had considered swinging first. Knowing that the creature was out in the night somewhere made his heart race, and fear made his skin cold.

"Where did the alarm come from?" The younger man was looking past Mikel and around the hallway now, his hands trembling a little.

"I don't know. We should head out into the courtyard so that we can decide which way to go easier, and see if there is anyone else around who knows where it was."

As they moved along the hallway, Mikel ventured a question. "You look quite shocked Surman. Are you alright?"

"Yes, I'll be okay." The guard swallowed heavily. Their footsteps echoed down the shadowed hallway, ringing like kirk bells. "It's just that..." He swallowed again. "As you know, I saw what had been done to that body in the riverbank. The poor man. It did not look pleasant. And from what Master Zhon told us yesterday morning about the culprit still being here... I'm a little frightened, I don't mind saying."

Mikel slapped Surman on the shoulder. "Me too lad."

The two of them walked cautiously out into the courtyard at the centre of the castle. Behind them the huge bulk of the gatehouse and the low guards barracks blocked out part of the night sky. Clouds swirled across the moon and glowed silver from its light. Stars broke free and winked briefly before being covered again by the shining wisps. Mikel shivered. The night air was cold and he wasn't wearing any thick clothing, having rushed out of his room so quickly. The walls of the castle reminded Mikel too much of the high fences that were used to keep cattle in their holding pens, leaving him feeling trapped. He hoped that the godling would feel the same way.

"I haven't heard anything else in a while," muttered Surman. "Do you think it was a false alarm?"

"No," Mikel shifted his shoulders and adjusted his grip on

his sword. "I'm sure that the thing is here somewhere. I just don't know where to go next if we are to stand a chance of tracking it down."

They stood still, searching through the darkness around them.

On the far side of the courtyard a few lights still burned in a massive dark structure. Mikel recognised that the lights must be coming from the narrow windows of the great hall. *Alaks must still be drinking and feasting with his friends.* He wondered if the heir had forced many of the servants and cooks to stay awake in order that he and his friends could eat and drink to their heart's content, or whether he had allowed them to get their rest. The servants would be expected to rise at dawn, regardless of their work in the night, so every hour spent awake tending to his whims was an hour's rest they would be missing during their duties the next day.

"I can't believe the heir has been acting this way since he returned," growled Mikel out loud.

"I'm sorry sir?" Surman sounded confused.

"It's nothing. I just wish the boy would cease his silly feasting and start tending to his duties, just the same as everyone else under Mercy's Shield.

"The heir doesn't really have many duties though, does he?" Surman spoke slowly, clearly trying to avoid causing offence to his commander.

"No, not in so many words. But we all have duties to one another that allow Mercy to keep us safe. Which is all the more reason that he should have tended to them already. And he should consider the needs of his servants as well." Mikel gestured at the light glowing through the great hall windows. "Even now he wastes their sleep."

"Oh." Surman looked at the hall. "I suppose he only just returned from his journey. Perhaps he will settle down soon."

"I had thought so myself. But since his return he has acted like a different boy to the one I saw growing up." Mikel paused and lowered his sword slightly. A bubble of bile reached up his throat as a horrible consideration began to stir in his mind. "An interesting thing to think of. Tell me, did Zhon explain to you what manner of creature we are facing here?"

"Not in detail. Just that it looked like Lefi and had killed Zhosh as easily as a bear would kill a streetcat."

"Indeed it did."

"It shook me to the core, to be honest, the idea that this thing would look like Lefi. I joined at nearly the same time as him. Lefi and I used to get drinks in Blackriver together!"

"You have?" Mikel tore his gaze away from the hall. "Did he seem to have changed recently to you? Was he acting unusual?"

"No, not really..." They began to walk cautiously out further from the buildings. Not a movement could be seen in the open space around them, but the corners and crevices were thick with shadow at this hour of night. No further calls pierced the air. Were they too late to help?

CHAPITRE LXV

"I mean, I didn't see him often in the guards rooms or on patrol, but I knew him. He started keeping more to himself over the last week perhaps," continued Surman as the pair crept across the courtyard.

"Do you know why he would have been meeting with a member of the Guershan in a room on Long Road?"

"No. Perhaps they met at one of the taverns nearby and wanted to conclude some business in private?"

Mikel frowned. "Yes, probably something like that. I think I am more wondering what sort of business he might-"

A yell burst from the far side of the courtyard. Black figures came rushing from the doorways that led to the hall, a string of about five of them, though it was hard to be certain in the shadows that surrounded the building. Mikel and Surman both began running towards the figures. Mikel's heart was thundering in his chest as he ran, and his mind floated away from his body. It was as though he was behind himself, watching his body run forward across the gravel. He winced as he watched his old body stumble but then righted himself and kept running. He thought of both nothing, and of everything he had seen and experienced over the last few days. He wanted to laugh and cry all at once.

The figure nearest them, racing away in front of the group that had burst from the confines of the great hall, was Lefi.

He looked more savage than the last time Mikel had seen him. In a flash the commander observed that Lefi's clothes were threadbare, exposing much of his flesh beneath. The flesh was hard and knotted with muscles, but shifted and stretched in a way that was not human. Lefi's left leg moved quickly but unsteadily, like a spider's. He was clearly having trouble holding his weight on it, though it wasn't slowing him down enough that his pursuers could catch him. Mikel could see flesh flapping open around the wound Zhon had inflicted on the creature's leg. The wound was bloodless and empty.

As Lefi closed on them, Mikel saw the godling's face harden. His lips pulled back from his teeth in an animalistic snarl and hair clung damply to his sweaty skull. His eyes bulged horrifyingly from his face, as if they were about to explode. Then, just before Mikel and Surman could swing their swords, he screeched and lurched sideways.

Mikel and Surman stumbled as they spun to try and follow the creature, joining the group in pursuit. The guards pounding past them were red-faced and puffing, but they ran as hard as they could. They knew that the thing they were chasing was one of the most dangerous creatures that had ever threatened the castle and the town, and they would uphold their sworn duty to protect the people sleeping all around them no matter the cost.

Lefi ran fast enough to stay out of their reach, despite the massive wound in his leg. Mikel was sure the wound was wider now, gaping more than humanly possible. He could see flesh dangling from Lefi's calf through the tattered remains of his leggings. He watched as the split in the skin tore further up, oozing a thick red liquid from inside. For some reason, Mikel doubted it was blood.

They were gaining on the thing.

Mikel and the others gained on Lefi faster than the commander expected. He wondered whether he should try to leap forward, in order to grab the godling, and at that moment it whipped around, swinging its arm back at them with curled fingers like claws. He had thought that they were still at a safe distance, but somehow its arm stretched far enough for the hand to connect with the face of one pursuer. The tip of one finger caught the man's nose, ripping it off as though it was a fluffy dandelion struck by a strong breeze.

The guard spun from the impact and collapsed to the ground, shrieking in pain. For a moment Mikel saw blood spurt onto the stones beneath the man, leaving a black puddle in the moonlight. Then the commander jumped aside, as did the other guards, to avoid the creature's arm swinging back again.

It snarled at the group facing it and then launched itself towards the nearest wall, scrambling along the courtyard on all fours like a wounded dog. Mikel lifted his sword and was about to yell for the others to follow when the creature reached the wall.

The godling barely looked up at the wall it had found, an expanse of heavy stone with only a single row of windows far overhead, before leaping onto the rough surface and climbing. The sound of bones cracking echoed across the courtyard as the thing slammed its hands and feet into small cracks between the stones, breaking into the mortar and creating its own holds. Like a spider up a wall to its web, the creature swarmed up the wall faster than Mikel would have believed possible. Far above them, a light shone out from one lonely window. All the others were as black and dark as a dead man's eyes.

"He's going for that window," called out one of the guards from the hall. He was sucking huge lungfuls of air into his red cheeked face.

"Does anyone know who's room that is?" asked Surman.

"No," answered Mikel. The darkness of the night, coupled with the shock of the creature's actions, meant that he was still a little out of sorts. "But if we're going to catch him we need to get inside and find out."

CHAPITRE LXVI

The group ran across the courtyard, searching for a doorway that would let them into the building, but soon slowed to a jog, then a determined walk. It was late, the night was cold, and the adrenalin that had kept them moving was already beginning to ebb. The shadow of the creature moving up the wall kept their attention as sharp as a knife despite the ache in their limbs.

"Here," called one of the guards, motioning to a door. Moving quicker now, they slipped inside and began stalking through the corridors.

"That window was at least four storeys up," said Surman. "We should find the nearest stairs and get climbing."

The others agreed, and began to fan out, searching for the stairs. *Clearly none of them are used to coming through these passages,* Mikel thought. If they were familiar with this part of the castle then they would know where to go to find a stairwell. It only took a hurried glance down the first hallway for him to recognise where they were, and his memory quickly supplied directions for him. He was about to tell the group where the next stairwell was, when the full realisation of exactly where they were blossomed in his mind, driving out everything else.

"These are the Lord's family apartments," he whispered, horrified.

"I'm sorry sir?" Surman moved back towards him while the other pushed open heavy wooden doors gingerly and peered around corners. The hallway was very dark, with only one or two torches still burning in their sconces.

"These rooms. These belong to Lord Uvaniah and his family." Mikel had walked through here two days ago, to explain to the lord how much danger the thing that looked like Lefi could be. All he had had to do was keep the lord and his family safe until The Kirkman was able to perform his ritual and things would have worked out! And now here he was, tracking the beast through the hallways of the most important people in the castle!

He banged his fist against the wall in anger. "Lord Uvaniah's rooms are not far above us, and that's the direction that thing was headed. Let's hope that we're not too late."

"Are you sure that is where-" began Surman, but Mikel stormed off without listening to the end of the sentence. Where else would the beast go?

With the other guards following in his wake like a cluster of puppies rolling after their mother, Mikel bounded up the stairs as fast as his legs could carry him. They dashed past entrances to the other floors until they finally reached the highest landing. Here they walked through a large door into the halls where Lord Uvaniah would be slumbering in his bedchambers. At least, Mikel hoped the lord was still slumbering. As he ran, he offered a prayer to the silent shadow gods of the night, for speed and silence so that he could come upon the creature by surprise.

The hallways outside Uvaniah's chambers were dark and silent. Mikel saw a single figure standing by the chamber doors, silhouetted by moonlight slipping through a tall thin window. Mikel paused and stared at the figure as his thoughts raced. Was it the creature, standing in the hallway, plotting a way inside the lord's chambers? Or perhaps it was a survivor. Someone who had withstood the violent passage of the thing they chased and now needed assistance? Frustrated tears welled in the corners of his eyes as he rushed forwards, to discover which was true.

A sword and a spear slid as smoothly and quickly out of the darkness around him as a pike hunting in the river. The metal blades levelled themselves to stab dangerously towards his stomach and his neck. Guards stepped forward from the deep shadows that they had been using to conceal themselves, their faces set and grim. Before Mikel could explain, they recognised him and lowered their weapons slightly. Their faces didn't lessen in their intensity however.

Mikel realised that they had not offered the traditional challenge of "Who goes there." Clearly they expected to either recognise anyone in the hallway at this hour or have to kill them. He was glad they realised the severity of the threat.

"I'm very glad to see you both," said Mikel as the rest of his group caught up. They made sure to lower the weapons they carried. "We have been chasing it and we thought it was heading for our lord's quarters. Have you seen anything, heard anything?"

The guards from the shadows exchanged a look of confusion.

"No, nothing sir," offered one. "It's been quiet as a graveyard up here." She blushed as she realised how inappropriate the comparison was.

"Can we check in his rooms?"

"Certainly."

Together both groups of guards approached the entrance to Lord Uvaniah's rooms. The guard who had spoken to Mikel rapped on the door, a pattern of short rapid knocks followed by longer spaced out knocks.

"This way they know it's us coming in," she explained. "We wouldn't want them to loose a crossbow bolt at your gut if they don't recognise you soon enough."

Mikel nodded. Nevertheless, he was glad when one of the other guards offered to go through the doorway first. After explaining the situation to the guards in the anteroom beyond the doorway, they all carefully and quietly worked their way through the quarters, examining any hiding places thoroughly.

The anteroom held solid and well cushion chairs for the lord to entertain guests, and low tables to hold their food and drink, but few places to hide. Some of the guards pushed open to door to the lord's toilet slowly, check the cupboard of perfumes, the baskets of clothes to be laundered, behind the folding dressing screen.

Another door led to a room that was barely more than a cupboard, where two young servants slept in case Lord Uvaniah had a sudden need for anything in the night. They woke quickly and their eyes widened as they saw the group of guards prowling through the rooms. Mikel saw that they were spoken to and that they knew enough to lay back down and rely upon the guards.

Mikel was the only one to check the lord's bed chamber itself. He moved through the space as quietly as he could, his sword held out in front of him as he twitched tapestries aside, and sought the smallest nooks to check. A bead of sweat formed at the back of his neck and slipped down his spine. It comforted him to know one of the guards stood in the doorway with a crossbow pointed into the room. If the godling was in here, he hoped it would not catch him by surprise.

CHAPITRE LXVII

It was clear that the creature was not in these luxurious surroundings. The group moved slowly out of the rooms so as not to wake the slumbering old lord. His snores rumbled out of his bed chamber with a shuddering irregularity and Mikel found he was sad at the thought of the man dying. Iosef Uvaniah had always treated his people well. Alaks, his son, did not seem to be the sort who would continue in that mould.

Once the large group had returned to the dark hallway, Mikel scratched his chin, rubbing his fingertips against the sharp short bristles of his beard. "Where could it have gone?"

"Shall we check the other rooms in the apartments sir?" Mikel didn't recognise the guard who spoke. That made him pause in his response, studying the guard closer. *Am I so out of touch,* he asked himself. *Or is this the creature, sneaking close enough to kill us all at once?*

"Yes, it seems the only way," he muttered after a moment. He cursed to himself. *I only pray that we haven't lost the beast.* Now, with so many guards around him, he was confident that they could face it and kill it. But there was no time to waste, if it had found some other victim.

They left behind the guards from the lord's rooms and moved down the stairs to the next level. Instantly Mikel could tell that something was wrong. It took him a moment to realise where he was. The small candles burning in their curved metal holders on the walls flickered as they burned low, and the shadows in the hallway danced. The sight was strange and made Mikel feel as though he were entering someone else's dream.

But then he found his bearings. This was Alaks's hallway. His rooms were at the far end, hidden in darkness. Mikel had come to those doors from the other direction yesterday morning. Now the emptiness of this hall was somehow threatening.

As the group moved quietly closer to the doors, it became clear that there was no one standing watch outside the room. Mikel wondered in a whisper where Alaks's guards were.

"I believe Alaks ordered most of them away," answered Surman. "He said that they only made it harder for his wine to be served. Apparently the guards kept stopping the servants at the door." Surman's face remained carefully neutral as he spoke. Mikel frowned.

"Surely there were some who remained? He is the lord's heir, he can't be left completely unguarded. Zhon would not have allowed it." *And neither would I, if I had been paying close enough attention.*

"Of course, I think there were one or two who convinced him to let them remain, though I think he required them to join him in a drink or two tonight at dinner."

Only allowing one or two guards to stay in your presence, and getting them drunk at the same time? Mikel couldn't understand how Alaks expected to get by in the world if that is how he dealt with the men whose job it was to protect him. A memory flashed through his mind.

"The lights in the hall. Perhaps there is no one here because they are still feasting?"

"It is possible," murmured Surman doubtfully.

They reached the end of the hall, which finished in a junction. To the left the hall stretched away into blackness, a heavy tapestry on the wall soaking up the light and leaving only a thick shadow on the wall. To the right was the entrance to Alaks's bedchambers. The guards with Mikel walked over to investigate. The door was hanging slightly ajar.

"Be ready with your weapons," Mikel whispered. *The boy's door should be shut tight. If they have returned, then one of the guards assigned to him should be in this hallway. Perhaps they decided to move into the next room and guard him from inside?* Try as he might to justify the situation, Mikel doubted his own thoughts tonight.

The air was silent and still. The footsteps of the guards beside him rang louder than normal. Mikel fought the urge to hiss at the men to step lighter. He knew that his own footsteps would sound just as loud to them. The hinges on the door creaked softly as they pushed it open. The room beyond was empty also. The door that led from this small anteroom into the actual bed chamber of Alaks hung open as well. A light from the bed chamber glimmered dully against its wood.

When they entered the bed chamber, their swords outstretched and each guard's muscles tensed hard as stone through fear, they found Alaks standing between his bed and a window, smiling at them.

Mikel was puzzled, and somehow not as pleased as he should have been at the sight of the heir standing alive and well in his own room. He knew that it was a great relief to find that the heir to the castle was safe, but he realised that he had been completely convinced that Alaks was dead already. The shock he felt to find the young man looking back at him could have knocked him over.

The window behind Alaks was fully open, its pane tilted out as far as its frame would allow. Moonlight and a cool breeze drifted in through the opening. The breeze made a tall candelabra beside Alaks twinkle and the flames at the end of its candles danced in spasming repetitive movements. Alaks himself wore a nightgown, his chest slightly stained with sweat, and a light sheen of moisture glistened on his forehead.

On the floor by his feet were the bodies of two guards.

CHAPITRE LXVIII

The heir's smiling face as still as a mask. He stared towards the open window in his wall. Mikel's stomach clenched as he stepped closer so that he could investigate the bodies further.

They lay strewn across the floor, clearly having been struck as they lunged forward, leaving them face down on the thick rug that still soaked up their dark red blood. On the ground beside each figure's out flung arm lay a sword that must have tumbled from their grasp.

The first man had been viciously attacked in the face. Mikel prodded the body gingerly with his boot, turning him over to try and identify who he was. The sight revealed by the movement nearly made him vomit. The man's nose, upper mouth and eyes had all caved into his head, like a rotten melon that had been gripped in a firm hand and collapsed between the fingers. The second man had deep tears through the flesh of his face and chest. Blood pooled across the floor in a thick puddle that was slowly congealing.

Mikel stepped closer to Alaks. The boy was breathing heavily, but a smile stayed fixed on his face. Glassy eyes stared straight ahead. He showed no sign that he had seen Mikel.

"Are you alright lad?" asked the commander.

Alaks nodded.

"What happened here?" Mikel gestured with his sword, pointing at the bodies and the window.

"I'm not sure I can really explain sir," began the heir, bobbing his head slightly as he spoke. He moved over to his bed and sat down on the edge as he continued. "I woke to the most horrendous noise, like rocks being smashed against each other. I sat up and saw something come in through the window, and so I yelled out. I jumped out of bed to try and get away from it and the guards you had assigned to me came in. Unfortunately they turned out to be no match for it.

It turned and ran at me, but thankfully I was standing next to the window by then. Just as it reached me I dodged aside and it tumbled through the window. If you take a look outside you'll see it seems to be dead. It must have hit the stones quite hard!"

Mikel did take a look, stepping to the window and carefully waiting for one of the other guards to step up as well. He felt uneasy in this room and didn't want to leave his back to it as he leaned out the window over such a height. He was also nervous that the creature might be lurking just outside the window, ready and waiting for some fool to stick their head out far enough that it could be torn off.

Despite these misgivings, he was relieved to see that Alaks was right. Visible on the cobblestones far below, barely illuminated by the moonlight, a body lay, broken and bent.

"You, stay here and guard the heir," said Mikel, pointing to two of the guards who had come in with him. "The rest of you, come and follow me. Call for others to come and secure the rooms." As he left he heard the guards in Alaks's room call out from the window, followed by the faint reply of guards on their patrols. He hoped that it was enough.

The thing on the cobbles was barely able to be recognised as human anymore. It looked as though it once had four limbs and a head, but the impact had smeared the body across the stones. Red flesh lay in torn pieces around the head and hands, while the rest of the body had been surprisingly well contained by the threadbare clothes the creature had been wearing when it fell. Mikel bent closer for a moment. The clothes looked familiar, old and ragged and torn in the same places as those worn by the creature as it fled from him across this same courtyard less than half an hour earlier.

As he studied the remains closely, Mikel wondered when he would feel the rush of nausea that had come with such inspections in the past. Somehow, it never arrived. At first he was glad to not feel the sickening wave, but then he realised that it was because he had seen so many ravaged corpses in the last week that he was beginning to get used to them.

"Gather it up. See if Marq is awake. If he will let us, I would like to have these remains kept in his workroom overnight." He straightened up and stood over the corpse as the two guards who had come with him ran off. Slowly, he slid his sword back into its scabbard. He lifted his head to the sky. Even with the body of the creature lying ruined at his feet, Mikel did not feel safe yet. The events of the night did not feel as though they had finished anything.

As the guards returned and dealt with the body, lights appeared in the windows of the Lord's rooms overhead. The noise had finally woken up Uvaniah, and candles and torches were providing him with light to dress. Mikel imagined the lord's servants would be illuminating him with gossip from the excitement as well. He drew a long slow breath. His chest ached and wheezed as he exhaled, and his legs throbbed from the exertion they had endured. After twisting and stretching his old body as much as he could, Mikel made his way back to his own rooms. Dawn would not be far off. He would not get much sleep anyway, so it was best if he could steal as much as possible.

CHAPITRE LXIX

Mikel stretched in his bed as he woke, feeling his twisted shoulder muscles groan as he moved them. His neck and spine made sounds like splintering twigs as the bones jostled each other back into place and he turned his head back and forth to try and make himself comfortable. Light billowed through the window. He rose and dressed, each movement reminding him of his age, before heading to the great hall for his morning meal.

He was late, which meant the room was nearly empty. He scrounged some leftover cheese and bread and then left, eating it as he walked. Before long he had finished the meagre breakfast and was knocking on the door to Marq's workroom. It was flung open immediately, and he was hurried through.

"How are you doing Mikel?" asked the alchemist. He was busily stirring a clear liquid in a flask with a long thin stick of glass, then occasionally spooning in small amounts of green powder from a jar on the counter before him. At least three apprentices stood by his shoulder, their eyes intensely watching.

"Not as well as I'd hoped," replied Mikle honestly. "My body can't handle this sort of thing anymore. I'm aching all over."

"You do look like you're limping a little," agreed Marq. He passed the flask over to one the apprentice alchemists, who squealed and nearly dropped the glass container in their excitement. Marq turned away immediately, leading Mikel to the back of the workroom.

"I was surprised to come in this morning and find you had left me another little surprise. You're beginning to make a habit of this Mikel. I'm going to have to find something as a present for you in return or you might think me rude."

Mikel snorted in response to the alchemist's humour. "We chased it through the lord's apartments and found it in the heir's room. It fell out of the window by mistake."

Marq raised an eyebrow. "The heir's room you say? Surely you didn't allow it to get so close to our precious boy, Mikel?"

"It was no matter of allowing the creature to do anything Marq. Even with extra patrols on watch, it killed two more of my guards on its way there." Mikel's anger and shame built in his throat like bile. He coughed to try and clear his throat of the scratchy sensation, but found it had no effect.

"Oh." Marq made no further comment about the situation. Mikel wondered if the other man was judging him for his failure to protect the guards, or sympathetic to the horrors he had experienced. He didn't want to find out.

The two reached the back of the workroom where Mikel's guards had left the corpse of the creature on a wooden bench. They had wrapped it in some old sheets, which were now stained darkly with blood. Mikel hoped the blood hadn't caused too deep a stain in Marq's bench. The alchemist might get quite upset about such a thing. Mikel was surprised to find

Zhon was already standing by the bench, examining the remains of the creature.

The second-in-command of the castle guard had peeled the sheet away from the body. Pieces of flesh and skin had stuck to the old cloth and lifted up with it. Zhon looked pensive as he peered at the exposed broken body before him. Occasionally he used a small knife to prod or shift some flap of skin or clothing.

"Good morning Zhon," said the commander.

"Good morning sir," replied the man without looking aside.

"Have you discovered anything new or useful?" Mikel glanced down at the body and then up again. He had seen more than enough of that thing last night.

"No." Zhon shrugged and sighed, his face falling. "I had hoped that I would be able to discover what it was doing here, especially in the heir's rooms, but there's nothing. I am amazed that it was able to keep running on this leg though."

"What do you mean?"

"Here, you can see where I wounded it in that room above Long Road." Zhon used his knife to push the thing's leg over until a massive split in the calf was visible. A blackened crust of dried blood covered its edges and the flesh inside looked putrid and red, like a half melted candle. He was right, a wound that deep and vicious should have left the godling unable to crawl, and yet it had been faster than any of the guards following it.

Mikel felt unsure, a tight feeling across his ribs that left him feeling slightly unwell.

"This really is the creature then? This was Lefi. And it's dead now, the castle is safe." Mikel's questions were half directed at Zhon, and half his own concerns bubbling to the surface.

Zhon looked at the commander now. His forehead was creased in concern.

"It is obviously the same creature."

Mikel nodded. His second was clearly correct. This body bore the exact wound Zhon had inflicted on the creature, and that Mikel had seen hindering its movement as it ran across the courtyard only a few metres in front of him. There was no way to deny that this was the same figure he had pursued.

"This is a very strange man," muttered Marq as he examined the body closely. He leaned until his face was within centimetres of its strange looking flesh, holding a hand over his mouth and nose as he did. Mikel could tell from the way the alchemist moved that he did not do it to stop the fumes or smells from affecting him, but in order to stop himself from disturbing the body in any way. "Will anyone mind if we take some samples?" asked the alchemist.

"No, you feel free to chop it into as many small pieces as you like." Mikel turned to leave.

"Did anyone see where the skin from its head went?" asked the alchemist as Mikel walked away. Instantly Mikel turned back to him.

"What do you mean?"

"Well it's clear that there's no skin left on the head, but I would not have expected a blunt impact, such as hitting the ground, to cause such a wound." The round-faced man pointed at the horrifying mulch that remained of the godling's head.

"Then where did the skin go," whispered Mikel to himself.

"Not to worry," Zhon insisted. "I've seen all sorts of bizarre injuries while chasing scoundrels across this town. I'm sure his face has battered against the wall on the way down. That'll be where his skin has gone. We could probably send someone to check."

"Perhaps," murmured the alchemist doubtfully. He glanced at Mikel. "I'd suggest you check that wall soon."

CHAPITRE LXX

Mikel walked through the hallways of Sheerwall, thoughts buzzing through his head like a swarm of agitated bees. The body of the creature that was lying on the bench in the alchemist's chambers did not appear to have a face left. Mikel found himself thinking back to the body of the poor young man, stuck in the thick mud of the riverbank outside the castle. That unfortunate body had had no face left either. Neither Mikel nor any of the others he had spoken to had really considered the matter any further, or wondered what such a strange situation might mean.

Had the creature done this on purpose? Had it skinned the heads of its victims? Mikel could think of no reason for the godling to do such an horrific thing. But, if that was true, then did that not imply that the body they had recovered, smashed on the stones below Alaks's window, was another victim of the creature?

The thought made Mikel blood run cold. Was the creature still roaming the castle, after a full night in which it could find a place to hide? But no, there was no denying the gash in the body's calf. The decay of the wound, the nauseating way it had not quite healed, all combined to suggest that this body was indeed that of the creature they had fought while surrounded by dead rats, in the small second story room in Blackriver.

Mikel found himself walking across the courtyard, heading towards the gate to the town. He realised that he was intending on going to the Kirk. As he walked, he wondered if the Kirkman's ritual was still needed. On the one hand, the creature was dead now, surely. On the other, perhaps it would not hurt to ensure the creature was driven away, in case his paranoia was correct. As he walked, he passed by the stables. He noticed a pair of guards walking towards him, each directing a frustrated glare at the world that had dared disappoint them.

"Good morning," said Mikel as they approached.

"Aye sir, it was," growled the first, an older man whose beard was beginning to show signs of grey.

"Yeah," agreed the other, only slightly younger than the first but carrying much more weight around his shaven jowls. "We began the day quite pleased to hear that that bastard Lefi had been cornered."

"Yup." The first man's face brightened and he nearly smiled. "When I heard that the lanky sod had fallen out of a window..."He bowed his head and chuckled. "You'll have to forgive me sir, but it was certainly a fine way to greet the dawn."

"Indeed," Mikel's smile was as weak as a baby bird. He wanted to match their level of glee at the fate of Leif so that they would continue speaking, but the visions in his memory were strong. "But then why are you so unhappy now?"

"It's that damned heir." The second man blushed slightly and lifted a hand in a gesture of defence. "Meaning no disrespect sir. It's just that he suddenly decided to go for a ride and declared that we weren't to go with him."

"What do you mean, you weren't to go with him? Were you his bodyguards for the day?"

"Aye, we took over from those lads who had watched him since the hubbub last night." The elder guard sucked on his teeth. "Would have been fine 'til he jumped up at breakfast and went pelting out of the room."

"Where did he go in such a hurry?" Mikel's heart was pounding. His mind was growing too large for his head, as though the world was shrinking and fleeing from him.

"No idea. I think he said something about hunting?" The younger guard looked at the older for confirmation. The bearded guard gave it, nodding his head firmly.

"Aye, hunting. Annoying child. He barely gave us the dignity of explaining that any threat had been dealt with last night, before he mounted his horse and went galloping out of the castle!"

Mikel didn't spend any time saying farewells to the two guards. Instead, he turned and walked briskly to the gate and across the drawbridge towards Blackriver. He wanted to run, but he knew that the kirk was too far away to run the whole way. Better to step lively and retain some of his strength. Sweat soaked into his shirt and the damp material stuck to his shoulders, chafing under his arms as he strode through the streets. He considered what to do when he arrived at the Kirk. He contemplated what was happening.

Was Alaks the creature? That was the thought that was hurtling around his head over and over like a horse racing around a field. The words clattered against the sides of his skull until his temples were pounding painfully. What would he do if the creature had somehow managed to take over the heir to the lord of the castle? The blood in his veins was ice pumping through his body.

How could it even be true? What of the wound in the calf? And Alaks had smiled at him, spoken to him, and let him leave the room unharmed. The godling had shown no sign of such duplicity before now as far as Mikel could tell.

Sooner than he had expected, Mikel arrived at the Kirk. It looked just as it had the last time he had seen it, the great tower lifting high over the houses that surrounded the building, wide coloured windows reflecting the glorious patterns of Mercy back towards him. He knew that, inside, those windows would have the kirk ablaze with every colour imaginable crisscrossing the pews and walls. As usual, the door to the chapel sat slightly open to show that anyone who wished to enter would be welcome. The wind blew, making the door swing a few centimetres further open, before it settled on its hinges and swung back to its initial position. Mikel strained his ears, but could hear nothing.

CHAPITRE LXXI

Mikel thought about how cold the streets in Blackriver got during the winter. When he was small he would trudge his way through the streets in the middle of the night, hoping to find a pile of rags that might give him a warm spot to curl up in while he slept. He never imagined going to his own home, a tiny wooden shack with gaps in the boards so large that it was colder inside than out.

One year, the coldest that he could remember, he had been walking for hours as the winds rose and clouds hid the comforting light of the stars that twinkled overhead. The windows of the buildings along each street were black and closed. Doors were bolted against the storm that was rising. The young Mikel clutched at his shoulders and shivered, forcing himself to take another step over and over again.

Then he saw it. A line of orange light outlining the edge of a door, beckoning him closer. The door was half open, propped against a long heavy wooden pew inside to stop the wind banging it open further. The kirk traditionally kept the chapel door ajar, because anyone and everyone was always welcome to come in and find Mercy. He stepped through.

Beyond the door he found himself in the kirk, with candles lit along the walls, leading him to the front of the room where the old Kirkman stood reading at the lectern. He glanced up and smiled when he saw the small soaking boy nervously approaching between the pews.

"It's alright my boy. The kirk is always here for any who need to come in. Here's let's find you some warm dry blankets and hot soup."

"What will I owe you?"

"Nothing lad. It's my duty to do Mercy so that it is free to shield others from worse than this storm."

Mikel took the blanket gratefully, and as soon as he had filled his belly with hot simple soup his eyelids crashed shut. He had curled up among a pile of cushions that the Kirkman provided and disappeared into a dreamless sleep.

With memories of the warm safety of the kirk chapel in his mind, Mikel crept inside as slowly as a hedgehog, caught during its night wandering. He squeezed past the door, moving it as little as he could. He was hoping to avoid the squeaking hinges that would let someone inside know that he was entering the building. Try as he might, his belt caught on the edge of the door, dragging it halfway open with a deep metallic creak before he could disentangle himself. He walked up between the pews, trying to see past the colours that cracked across everything in his vision.

Something had definitely happened here. A table had been moved to the front of the chapel beside the carved lectern with its massive copy of the Biblos. A variety of items were clustered on top of that table, including a collection of candles, each in their own candlestick. One still burned, already nearing the bottom of its candle, while the others were either snuffed out or toppled over. Mikel's eyes widened as he realised that the chapel had nearly been set on fire by the tumbled candles.

A large hand-mirror lay in the middle of the table, with ashes smeared across its surface. Looking at the finely carved detail of the ivory frame and handle, Mikel assumed that the mirror was worth a great deal. Why would it be covered with dirt and left askew on the table, untended? He stepped up to the table and took a closer look at the mirror. The ashes on the polished bronze surface formed patterns. A semi-circular series of symbols that Mikel didn't recognise. He put the mirror back down where he had found it and looked around the front of the chapel.

Behind the screen, furniture had been knocked aside. Chairs lay on their sides and one spare table was broken nearly completely in two. The doorway to the Kirkman's apartments was hanging slightly open as well. While the chapel door was traditionally kept open, the kirkman's quarters were not. Mikel pulled his sword free of its scabbard and tested his grip before he stepped through the doorway.

The apartments looked as though a herd of pigs had been rummaging through them in search of food. Everything was knocked to the floor. Nothing was the right way up. Books, clothes and broken dishes mixed in a jumble across the small floors.

Mikel's throat tightened as he noticed blood mixed with the broken objects that littered the floor. Clearly, the Kirkman had found trouble. The commander thought carefully as he picked his way through the detritus. The objects he had discovered on the table in the chapel implied that the Kirkman had begun his ritual, hoping to drive away the creature. That would make sense. Mikel had forgotten to send any word of the events last night, so as far as the old man knew the ritual would still be required.

Mikel wondered if the ritual had been successful. If, as he was beginning to fear more and more strongly, the heir Alaks had been taken as some sort of puppet by the creature, then perhaps his sudden flight from the great hall was a sign of that change. Perhaps the ritual had begun to have an effect, and he had been forced to move. Even now he could be racing away across the countryside, being driven far from Blackriver and the castle. Mikel's shoulders straightened and he wondered if perhaps the people he watched over would now be safe.

Then he grimaced and his shoulders pulled with tension once more. Perhaps the ritual had begun to have an effect on the heir, sitting in the great hall, eating his morning meal. But instead of forcing him away from Blackriver, what if the ritual had merely driven the creature to respond? Mikel looked at the blood that pooled beneath broken clay plates on the floor beside his boots. Perhaps the creature had simply decided to deal with something that was annoying it.

But what if Alaks had just been indulging the foolish whims of a young man who had always been given whatever he wanted, yet again? What if the petulant young man had suddenly decided that he absolutely had to go hunting, and may Mercy retreat from anyone who thinks that they could stop him? What if Mikel was wrong in his paranoid concerns? After all, Alaks had been so angry that he could not do what he wished without guards because of the threat, but the threat was gone now.

Why could Mikel not simply accept the world as it had been presented to him, a world where the creature had fallen from a high window and killed itself on impact, a world where the heir was dazed from an encounter with a nightmarish thing, but had recovered some of his normal spoiled attitude by the morning? However, if Alaks wasn't the creature, then something else must have caused the carnage in these apartments. And what on earth could have done such a thing except that creature?

Rounding the corner, Mikel found the Kirkman.

CHAPITRE LXXII

The old man had been torn apart. Each of his limbs had been ripped off. The stumps ended in ragged ends that dripped with tendons and thin veins. The torso, bereft as it was, lay chest down on the floor. Mikel could see the gaping holes where arms and legs had once been connected to the remains of the man. He dropped to his knees and lost his grip on his sword. Tears filled his vision, thankfully blurring the sight of the mutilation that sat before him. He cried deep racking sobs from the pits of his chest. What had gone so wrong?

After some time Mikel was able to bring his breathing back under control. He stood, like a newborn calf, legs shaking and wobbling beneath him. With a supreme effort he managed to pick up his sword. Swallowing and choking as he struggled to regain his composure, Mikel looked around the room. The Kirkman's head was nowhere to be seen. His torso ended in a stump of a neck, with bones peeking out of it. Mikel realised that the man's blood was still oozing from the body, bright red and warm. That meant that whoever had done this was not far away. He found it hard to imagine that the perpetrator could be anything but the godling, using Alaks's body. Anger and a desire for revenge flooded him, making his skin prickle and his muscles twitch.

Mikel moved through the rest of the chamber looking for the Kirkman's head. He was fairly sure that the creature must have left the chapel already, or it would have attacked him while he was overcome by the sight of the dead Kirkman, but he kept his sword drawn just in case. He whispered quiet prayers to Mercy as he searched the apartments, prayers of attention and safety and deliverance.

Every creak of wood shifting as he walked, every clink of pottery clattering against the floor, made Mikel think the creature had returned and was about to strike. He jumped constantly, his heart pounding in his ears and the hairs on the back of his neck standing up until he thought he must look like a frightened cat. He determined that the living rooms were empty and then looked with trepidation at the stairs that led higher. The massive library that he had seen last time he was here was the only place left to search. The Kirkman's missing head had been nowhere so far. The library waited overhead, calling him. Moaning softly to himself, Mikel began to climb the stairs.

The roof of the kirk library reached up and into the narrow confines of the tower, broken by shafts of coloured light that stabbed from decorated glass windows in its sides. The coloured rays bore down on a steep angle, driven by the noonday sun overhead, and the library shelves were dimmer than they had when Mikel had last walked by them. The paths between the shelves were black and silent. Glowing geometric shapes in red and yellow and blue and green lit the higher shelves, and shattered crazily across the objects that were stored there. If Mikel had needed to look through the dusty labyrinth for any length of time he would have struggled, as he had no light source to bring with him.

However, Mikel did not need to find a solution to travelling the darkness between the library shelves. Lying in the middle of a small circular clearing positioned directly beneath the tower, at a crossroads near the stairs, covered in a triangle of orange light, sat the Kirkman's head. Tears welled up in the corners of Mikel's eyes afresh. His nose became blocked and he had to breath in large gulps through his mouth. The old man's face looked calm as it sat on the wooden floor. Blood spread around the stump of his neck like a collar. His hair was as wild as ever, the beard curling up where it sat on the floor, with long thin hairs wisping down across his face. His eyes were closed.

Mikel crouched in front of the head and looked at it closely. It was an internal battle to investigate the discovery effectively, pushing aside the wail that was building in his chest and instead force his eyes to search over the horrific sight. *His face,* he thought to himself eventually. *It's all here.*

Mikel remembered that the face and hands of Filip had been torn off before his body had been dumped in the riverbank. The face and hands of the body they had found smashed on the courtyard had been sliced away also. Clearly the creature they had been chasing found some purpose in taking the face and hands of its victims. But in this case it hadn't done that. It had behaved differently, ripping apart a poor defenceless old man. None of the other victims had been so abused.

But how defenceless had this old man really been? Mikel noticed a strange mound underneath the head, camouflaged by the blood that ran over the top of it. He reached out and then paused, hands only a few centimetres away from the pale skin of the man he once knew. He bit his lip. *I can't just manhandle this head,* he thought. After chewing on his lip for a minute longer he decided that there was no other way. *Mercy forgive me.*

Carefully, slowly, Mikel reached out and placed his hands on either side of the Kirkman's jaw. He lifted slowly, shuddering as the flesh moved beneath his fingers. When Mikel had ever touched someone's face before, he had touched someone who was alive. Their muscles worked to hold their face in position, and he could feel that strength beneath his fingertips. But here the muscles simply gave way like the soft raw meat in an uncooked sausage.

The Kirkman's jaw swung open as Mikel lifted his head into the air. Mikel carefully put the head down on the floor to his right, far away from the pool of blood and the object covered by it. Not wanting to go so far as to touch the thick blood, Mikel used the tip of his sword to push at the object. It dragged noisily over the wooden floor as he moved it further from the red pool and then he slid his sword underneath it and lifted, flipping it over.

CHAPITRE LXXIII

It was the catalogue of gods that the Kirkman had showed him. Mikel had a flash of inspiration, and imagined he knew exactly what had happened. The Kirkman must have been referring to the book during his ritual to force the creature away when the beast had burst into the chapel, chased him into the living rooms and killed him. Perhaps the thing had left this head here as some sort of warning for the next man who might trust in the books that the kirk had collected.

Mikel remembered the comments the guards had made that morning. According to them, Alaks had burst from the hall in the midst of breakfast, barely explaining himself as he ordered his guards to remain behind. Mikel's stomach was hollow as he realised what must have happened. The parasite godling had taken over Alaks's body somehow, and his panic this morning was the creature's reaction to the ritual.

Mikel felt exposed and vulnerable as he crouched on the floor in the dark space. No sound echoed through the empty library. The dust drifting on the air smelt musty and thick. It stuck to his cheeks on the wet trails left by his tears. Wiping his face roughly with the sleeve of his shirt, he rose and jogged quickly down the stairs, passing through the door to the chapel and rushing through it so that he was outside. Here he paused, breathing in deep lungfuls of fresh air. The sun beat down from above and he could see people at the end of the street haggling over the price of a knife. He sucked down the clean air, wishing that it and the sun could burn away the feelings he carried from within the kirk, that they could cleanse him of the things he had seen.

Then he turned and faced Sheerwall, at the far end of Blackriver. He could see its grey stone bulk rising higher than the roofs around him, like some giant slumbering in the midst of children, and a chill raced down his back. *Alaks was clearly taken over by the creature,* he told himself. The thought crackled in his skull like lightning. *And by now the thing that was once the heir would have returned to the castle. What guard would deny entrance to the heir, especially if they had been told that the threat had been uncovered and defeated? Their suspicions will be down and the creature will be able to take advantage of that!*

Mikel began running down the street, panic giving him a small burst of strength. However, soon his chest was aching and his knees groaning, and he slowed to a jog. He would have to conserve his energy or he would be no use when he arrived. His frustrations manifested as a knot of pain at the base of his neck. Was he never able to get anywhere in time?

The sun had begun its slow journey towards the horizon as Mikel eventually passed through the strong gates that led into the castle. He glanced up as he walked through, admiring the height and thickness of the stone walls that housed the gate. The gate itself was made of strong black iron, with sharp spikes lining the lower edge. Above it, holes peeked down from the battlements, allowing defenders to pour boiling liquids or rocks or flights of arrows down on anyone attempting to break through the gate. It was such a well-designed defendable piece of the building. And yet it had been bypassed by a single creature that mimicked the people who passed through it every day. Suddenly everything felt futile to Mikel.

What was the point in trying to capture or kill this creature? No matter how successful he might manage to be, and he was not certain of the likelihood that he could stop this thing, would that just mean that the inhabitants of the Castle and Blackriver were only safe until the next time danger came? Some other creature would find them, and though it may not steal the faces of its victims, perhaps it would stalk them in their dreams? Perhaps it would appear as a child, laughing and innocent even as it killed those Mikel was sworn to protect? What good was Mercy if its sanctuary was so easily pushed aside?

Even if he should find a way to stop this creature now, four people were already dead. Did Mercy not extend to them? The Kirkman had used his knowledge of the gods and Mercy to drive this thing away, and yet that had only ensured his own death.

Why had the thing come here, to his Castle, now? What had drawn it to them? Why had it killed the people it had killed, and yet passed over the other townspeople? Had it been sent to them as a punishment, or an act of war? Mikel wondered who Alaks might have insulted at Highfort, who might have taken such offence that they unleashed this thing on Blackriver. Was his refusal to marry the lord's daughter such an insult that they called this thing down upon Blackriver and Lord Uvaniah? How long ago had the offence occurred, because this thing had been in Blackriver for weeks, if he was right about what it had done to Filip.

Or was the godling just another force of nature as unpredictable and murderous as a drought?

Was there any point in trying to halt it now?

Mikel left the shade of the gatehouse and began walking across the courtyard. He wasn't sure where to go. He knew he had to figure out where the creature might be lurking, but had no idea where to start. Finally, he decided to head towards the stables. If Alaks had come back from his morning outing, then Mikel wanted to know about it. He also needed to see if he could find some more guards to back him up. He had no intention of facing down the creature alone.

The stables were almost empty, though each stall contained a horse slowly chewing from a sack of oats. After walking past at least twenty such stalls, Mikel turned a corner to find an older stablehand pitching fresh hay across the floor of an empty stall.

CHAPITRE LXXIV

"Afternoon sir," said the stableman, not pausing in his work.
"Good afternoon. Would you mind if I asked you a question?" said Mikel.

"Sure wouldn't, you feel free sir."

"Do you know if Heir Alaks has returned from his hunting this morning."

"I surely do. Heir Alaks made his way back into the stables just after midday I believe, just in time to go rushing off and calling for wine. He acted pretty happy, which was a bit peculiar."

"Oh?" Mikel was running his fingers across the handle of his sword. The creature was indeed back within the walls.

"Yup," the stablehand said, then paused to spit into the dirt floor. He continued spearing hay on his fork as he finished his statement. "The heir was cheerful as any summer's day, but he didn't have any quarry to pass off with him. Seems to me that coming home without any catch at all would be a bad morning's hunting and worthy of a frown or two." Mikel watched the man shucking hay. *He really has no idea how important all this gossip is,* he thought.

"Thank you for that." Mikel left the stables and headed towards the great hall. There should be more guards in the corridors around the hall that he could call upon, and it sounded as though the creature may have headed there as Alaks anyway.

Clearly the thing had been pleased to have dealt with the problem of the Kirkman so easily and quickly. *I wonder how he cleaned himself up,* Mikel thought. *There should have been blood all over him after what I saw in that Kirk.* But still, that was where Alaks's happiness had come from, Mikel was sure. Now he just needed to gather those guards and figure out where Alaks had gone.

The great hall had yet to gather its evening crowd. It was a comfortable place for those who were eating to spend their time. The high stone walls made it cool to sit in during the middle of the day, out of the sun. Mikel walked through the tables, looking at the people who sat at each of them. None were guards. As he turned to leave, he noticed someone walking in who he recognised. Tuomas.

His son was rubbing at red-rimmed eyes and muttering under his breath. Mikel walked towards him, but as soon as Tuomas saw Mikel coming he glared at his father and turned to leave. Mikel jogged to catch up with the boy and clapped a hand onto his shoulder. "Tuomas my boy!"

"What do you want now? You've already ruined everything!" Tuomas spoke in a low snarl, barely glancing over his shoulder at Mikel.

Mikel chased his son out of the hall, and caught up to him in the hallways outside. He placed both hands on the young man's shoulders. Tuomas turned towards him, but his son glared at the floor instead of meeting his father's eyes.

"What do you mean? What have I ruined?"

"You are so utterly disconnected, aren't you?" Tuomas rolled his eyes and then allowed them to pierce directly into Mikel's. "You have ruined my chances with the heir."

"How? He looked very happy to have you join him the other night. I would have thought that the heir had ruined your chances of getting along with your father, if anything."

Tuomas made a frustrated noise and turned to walk away.

"No stop!" Mikel called out. "I'm sorry. Please, explain to me. I want to understand."

Together they walked back into the hall and sat at the first empty table they found, just a few metres inside the door.

"It's simple," Tuomas began. "You've offended Alaks so much that he can't bear to have me around anymore."

"Did he say this to you?" Mikel asked.

"He didn't have to. He made it quite clear."

"How?"

Tuomas pursed his lips and looked from side to side. He was obviously finding it difficult to meet his father's gaze. "He... He treated me differently."

"In what way."

Tuomas sighed. "When I saw him today, he ignored me. He was sweaty and heading towards his rooms to get bathed and into new clothes, and I tried to talk to him as he walked. He was short with me, almost annoyed, and even glared at me when I wanted to enter his chambers with him."

"Were there any guards with him?"

"Father!" Tuomas turned his eyes to the ceiling, the corners of his mouth drawn down as if by hooks. Mikel had never seen his son look so upset. "The heir to the castle is a wonderful man. I don't understand how you have upset him so much in such a short period of time."

"He's not that wonderful Tuomas, he was neglecting the

people on his return. He really should have made some sort of effort to-"

"Like Uvaniah is any better! He does whatever he thinks is best for him. If it turns out well for the rest of us, that's simply luck."

"Tuomas!" Mikel was shocked to hear his own son say such things about Lord Uvaniah. "Our lord has never treated us poorly, and all his actions have been to help the-"

"He doesn't understand the world!" Tuomas managed to keep his voice low. The anger in his voice turned it into a growl. "He thought he could marry off Alaks to some stupid woman in Highfort, he insists on all these tours and visits when Alaks should be allowed to simply enjoy the income from the farms. That wretched old man is just like you." Tuomas stabbed a finger at Mikel so hard that Mikel flinched from it. "Neither of you want us to enjoy ourselves. Well too bad!"

CHAPITRE LXXV

"You can't expect someone in Alaks's position to be allowed to simply loaf around all day! The lords of the castle have responsibilities, duties. They must visit the people in their lands so that they can find out what decisions will be most helpful for those people."

"You just can't let it go can you? You aren't the lord of this castle! Alaks will be, and you aren't going to control him when he is!" Tuomas sneered down his nose at his father. "He was right. You simply can't handle it when others are able to make decisions for themselves or to run their own lives. You can't wait to get them back under your thumb."

"Tuomas, I-"

"You were so pleased to declare that there was a threat that required your guards to escort everyone around and tell them what they could do. You got to tell Zhon what to do again. You didn't leave anything to anyone else. But now the threat has passed and you still won't stop!"

"I don't know if the threat truly has passed."

Tuomas scoffed. "Of course you don't. Be sensible and just

send those stupid guards away. What good are they anyway, no one's going to try and harm Alaks."

"It's our job to protect him-" began Mikel.

Tuomas shook his head.

"No, it is!" continued Mikel. "Mercy watches over us all and keeps danger and discord at bay. But it is my job to deal with all the little problems that arise, so that Mercy can keep its shield raised high against those larger threats. When we all work together to care for one another, then Mercy is at its strongest. If everyone falls into arguments like this, then Mercy falters and its shield weakens as it tries to protect us from one another instead. Who knows how difficult our lives would become then."

The anger in Tuomas' eyes faded into a pitying sadness. "Aren't you lucky that Mercy needs everyone to do what you want all the time. That must be so comforting to you."

"It's not just what I want. You've been to sermon often enough. You know that it is what the biblos tells us about Mercy and the gods around us."

"So you became commander of the guard just because you are such a dutiful and pious man. You simply did it to help Mercy protect us all."

"Well. Yes." Mikel blinked in confusion. Of course he was trying to protect the people of Sheerwall and Blackriver.

"Ma knew that you joined up so that you could impress Safi."

Mikel coughed and his mouth hung open.

"She told me all about it. But you had left that life behind long before she met you, so she wasn't upset by it." Tuomas tilted his head slightly as he looked at Mikel. "But I think you should stop pretending that you being in charge is some sort of sacrifice on behalf of everyone else. I'm going to Alaks to apologise on your behalf, and to let him know that I want nothing to do with you!"

With that final outburst, Tuomas spun on his heel and marched out of the great hall. Mikel scrambled to his feet so that he might pursue his son. Instead, his legs caught on the bench as he stood and he nearly tripped. As he righted himself he had to pause to allow a matronly woman with her hair bundled under a scarf to come through the doorway first, carrying a basket full of eggs. By the time he reached the hallway, his son was gone. *If he's going to see Alaks, he'll probably start at the heir's rooms,* Mikel told himself. He began striding in that direction.

As he moved through the stone hallways, passing servants and finely dressed aristocrats alike, Mikel fought not to stare into each one's eyes, searching for some sign that they truly were human. The remains of the creature that had been killed by its fall to the cobblestones still filled Mikel's memory. It was evidence that he was mistaken and paranoid. But the nightmare he had found in the kirk made him sure that somehow the godling was still hunting through his castle.

Mikel frowned as he recalled what he could of the guards schedule; which guards were watching over these corridors, and where they would be positioned. He gestured from windows and down long cross corridors, hoping that some of the hidden guards would understand his message and follow him. He knew it was taking a chance. Many of the guards would be unwilling to leave their post on such a vague command. Some of the posts would be unoccupied during the middle of the day anyway, now that the threat appeared to have been dealt with. The thought reminded him that he no longer knew which posts were considered unnecessary during the day and which were vital. He didn't know which were only watched on some occasions, and which were swapped at random to ensure the most eyes on the castle at all times.

Thankfully, two young men did leave their posts and join him. The first was a lanky figure named Shorn. He was slightly built, though enormously tall. His armour was noticeably small for him, leaving wide patches of cloth and leather in between the good solid plates that had been sewn to his jerkin. His sword appeared as small as a knife in his wide hands. Mikel wasn't sure how much use the boy would be if they found the creature, despite his stretched out size.

The second man was a little older, and had a sturdier frame. He bore a shirt of mail on broad shoulders and his strong jaw was covered in specks of stubble. His eyes were harder than Shorn's and he said his name was Willam. Mikel reminded himself to spend more time getting to know the guards as they joined up, for he did not know either of these men. He explained that he was worried about the heir, and the men nodded their support. Together they continued towards Alaks's rooms.

CHAPITRE LXXVI

The corridor outside those rooms was empty. At first Mikel was horrified at the sight of the empty hallway, and the thought that the castle guards were abandoning their responsibilities towards the lord's heir. But then he wondered whether it was unusual or not. Alaks had only recently returned from his wild dash beyond the castle walls, and the guards who had been set to accompany him today had been abandoned before he left. Perhaps they didn't know he had returned. With luck they would be rushing to regain their posts even now.

When Alaks had returned, he had clearly been brusque with Tuomas. But Tuomas had implied that Alaks had not allowed him to go into the heir's rooms. Had that meant that the guards had questioned Tuomas' presence? Or did that mean the creature that had taken over Alaks had shut his door on Tuomas and left the corridor empty?

The distinction mattered. If the guards had been there then, what had happened to them now? And if they had not, would that mean that Mikel might find Tuomas inside? What would he do if the thing that had been the heir now had a hostage?

It would do no good to consider this further. He would find out beyond the wooden door. There was no time for pleasantries. If Mikel was right, and he was sure that he was, there was no time to knock on the door and warn the thing that might be inside. Nodding at Willam and Shorn, Mikel lifted the latch and shoved the door open hard.

The anteroom to the heir's chambers was empty. Mikel caught the door just before it crashed into the wall, and then stepped through, hoping that one of the other guards would defend his back should an ambush unfold. The commander breathed more easily when the trio were not suddenly attacked as they moved further into the room. Mikel hoped their boots didn't echo too loudly. There was still a chance that they might catch the thing unawares. *Is it in here,* he asked himself as he approached the door to the next room.

The door swung open with the slow inevitability of an avalanche. Mikel watched everything unfold as though in a dream, slow and impossible to stop. Beyond the door Alaks stood in the middle of his bedchamber with fury twisting his brow. His eyes bore across the room like drills, powered by anger. Mikel allowed Willam and Shorn to step up beside him as he took in the rest of the scene. Standing before Alaks, the subject of his temper, was Tuomas, Mikel's son.

Tuomas had his hands up, one of them outstretched somewhat towards Alaks. He was clearly in the middle of some form of explanation, and his words trailed off as the pair of them noticed the guards that had burst into the room. Alaks's anger lessened not one bit, but the flash in his eyes as he looked up appeared to be recognition to Mikel. *It knows that I have identified it, it knows I have come to destroy it!*

Tuomas' face grew angry too, his cheeks flushing with a

red glow. He turned towards the newcomers, closing his hand to point at Mikel. Before he could say anything though, Alaks stepped forward and swung his arm to push Tuomas aside. The young man lifted bodily off his feet and Mikel had just enough time to register the surprise that crossed his son's face before he was hurled across the room. He crashed to the ground beside the tall candelabra that had lit the room last night. Tuomas bounced on the hard stone floor and Mikel heard a sickening crunch. The last dying candle on the candelabra flickered, and cast its meagre light on the boy. Mikel had no time to see if his son was alright, because the creature wearing Alaks's face had begun to walk towards the guards at the door.

"What are you doing here?" it demanded. The voice sounded similar to Alaks's but there was an extra depth to the tone. It spoke with an emphasis that made the voice coming from that familiar throat sound subtly different.

"You killed my men. I'm here to stop you."

"What?" Willam spun to stare at the commander. The sword in his hands lowered. "The Heir killed the guards? What about Lefi?"

"You told us that the Heir was in danger!" Shorn's forehead wrinkled in confusion. "What's going on?"

Mikel gestured frantically for them to turn around and face the creature again. "You have to trust me! This isn't the heir to the castle anymore! It's a type of evil god."

"Are you mad?" Shorn shook his head in disbelief. Behind him Alaks smiled, it's eyes glinting orange in the light of the candles. Mikel was sure that the corners of that mouth pulled just a little bit further than was natural.

"I'll explain later, just defend yourself," roared Mikel, but it was too late for Shorn. The creature reached forward with both hands and placed them on either side of Shorn's head. The tall youth blinked in surprise and then gasped as his head was wrenched firmly to one side. The crack of Shorn's neck snapping sounded like someone breaking the icy surface of a winter pond. Willam cursed and sprang sideways, spinning to bring his sword around between himself and the thing. He spoke from the side of his mouth as he addressed Mikel.

"When we come in this room I thought you was a hard man out to stop his own son. But now our own lord is trying to kill us?"

The creature wiped its hands on its leggings. It sniffed and then clucked its tongue as it looked down at the slumped pile that had been a tall thin guard. Then it looked back at the two remaining guards from beneath a darkening brow.

"It's not our heir. It's an evil god that has taken over his form. I fear that Alaks may already be dead, though I don't know enough about this horror to know for sure."

CHAPITRE LXXVII

The creature giggled. The sound was horrifying, as sweet and innocent as water rushing over a small waterfall in a forest, yet as threatening as a whitewater rapid.

"You say such nice things about me, that's so kind! Maybe I could have come to like you." It smiled again, revealing a row of gleaming white teeth. "But you are stopping me from finding my prey." The smile turned into a snarl and the creature leapt forward.

Mikel and Willam dove in opposite directions. There was a crash as the creature slammed into the open wooden door behind them. It growled and spun around, smashing the door closed as it did. It faced the two, body crouched low and arms spread wide. With long feline steps it walked between the two guards, circling around so that it was facing them with every stride.

Willam kept his sword out, pointed at the creature's chest. Mikel was glad of the other man's distraction. It allowed him to sneak glances beyond the creature to where his son lay on the floor. Tuomas hadn't moved, though Mikel saw no sign of blood. He prayed that some god of bone or breath had shielded his son from the worst harm.

The creature caught his gaze and began to turn. The fire reflected in those eyes burned like hate and hunger. Before it could investigate Tuomas closer, Mikel began to taunt the thing. He would keep it from his son as long as he could.

"Hey, where are you going? Too tired to attack an old man? Too weak to take me down? Come on then, show me what you've got!"

The creature's face twisted with anger at Mikel's words. A cold wash of fear flowed over his skin as the monster turned its full attention onto him. Behind it, Willam continued to circle sideways around it, looking for an opening that would allow him to advance and thrust his long metal blade into it. Mikel moved carefully as the thing approached him, each step slipping gently across the floor as he sought to keep a safe distance from it. He dared not risk tripping on some dropped object while he was facing down this thing. Willam must have seen a chance, for he dashed forward, but the creature kicked out backwards, knocking his sword away with its foot. Mikel would have sworn that it could not have seen Willam make the move. Perhaps it could hear him?

Willam recovered his weapon and balance quickly, shifting further away from the creature. It still stared its wide eyes at Mikel. Between himself and Willam, Mikel hoped to lead the creature towards the far side of the huge bed that dominated the room, wordlessly agreeing to keep the dangerous beast as far from Tuomas's prone body as possible.

Mikel kept studying the room as he taunted the creature, keeping well out of its reach and holding his sword high to dissuade it from rushing him. He could feel the muscles in his shoulder burning with the strain and his legs were beginning to feel too tired to keep him standing. When had he last rested properly? His head felt hot and thoughts were moving slowly. There had to be something in this room that he could use to finally end the killings.

Willam was backed up against the huge bed. It had four thick wooden posts in the corners, tall, with drapes and curtains hanging down from their lofty height. The mattress was wide and looked very soft. The servants had made it up well, fitting the blankets tightly across it.

Mikel took a deep breath, letting the air fill his ribs, stretching him until he was about to burst. He dared to let his eyes stray from the creature for a second, looking into Willam's brown eyes and trying to convey his thoughts to the other guard. He worried that the creature would also read his thoughts, and avoid the plan Mikel was beginning to form.

Willam nodded once, and then transferred his gaze back to the creature between them. He began to walk backwards, lifting himself onto the bed as he went, using his spare arm to pull himself up one of the posts and always keeping the point of his sword lowered towards their foe. Mikel's skin flushed with a cold sweat as he anticipated what would have to follow.

He swallowed and began to move towards the creature. Would it back away, or meet him with a furious rage? As he came he endeavoured to show anger in his eyes, instead of the fear that swam through his veins. He remembered all the people who had been horribly killed by this thing. He remembered the sight of the Kirkman, torn apart within the supposed safety of his own home, his own kirk. He thought of his son, lying on the far side of this very room. His throat clenched as he wondered whether Tuomas was alive or dead. He remembered the sight of Zhosh, tumbling through the air to his death outside a foul-smelling room in Blackriver. He gritted his teeth, relishing the feeling of them grinding slowly against each other. Heat built behind his eyes, filling his skull and spreading down his neck, shoulders and arms. New reserves of strength pushed him towards the creature in fits and random bursts, and he was relieved to see that it lurched away from his erratic movements, forcing it to step away with narrowed eyes. Mikel realised that the anger driving him forward was real.

CHAPITRE LXXVIII

William had reached the other side of the bed now. The creature screeched like a captured bird when the mattress pushed at the back of its legs. Watching that unnatural sound erupt from the face of Alaks, his lord's son, was unsettling for Mikel, but he roared a wordless threat and lunged at the thing anyway. His sword whistled by its throat as it leaned backwards to avoid the swing, toppling onto the bed.

Willam began thrusting his sword towards the creature, which rolled around on the blankets to avoid the blade. A few lucky cuts were scored along the thing's shoulders, but it was fast, managing to avoid most of the blows. Mikel leapt as soon as the creature fell, reaching up with hands and blade to strike at the drapes that covered the bed. He tore them from their places, ripping the fastenings through the fine fabrics. As the drapes fell and covered the creature, he bent to try and pull the blankets up and around its form as well.

While this happened, Willam was leaning in to drive his sword through the blankets and drapes, stabbing at where he thought the creature was. Again and again he plunged his blade through the thick embroidered fabric. Then, just as Mikel began to dash away from the bed towards his son, an arm thrust up from the pile of material that wrapped confusingly across the mattress. The hand shot with unerring accuracy at Willam, grabbing the guardsman's wrist. Mikel heard bones splinter in that fearsome grip as he continued to run, but he held his breath and kept going. Willam's best chance was for Mikel to finish what he had started.

Willam's voice rose in an anguished scream. Mikel risked a glance over his shoulder and saw that the creature had managed to untangle its head, and was pulling Willam down towards its white white teeth. Mikel grabbed the candelabra that stood by Tuomas and spun, just in time to see the creature lunge forward to bite through Willam's ear, spilling blood down its chin and across the drapes that still entangled its body. He hefted the candelabra in his grip, shocked at how heavy the thin metal was, and hurled it towards the bed. The stubby remains of its candles spilled across the bed, spatters of wax flicking forward.

The creature twisted its head around to stare at the candelabra that had clattered against the posts and thumped onto the mattress, then raised a shocked expression to stare at Mikel. Willam was still screaming in its grip, pulling away but unable to escape. Mikel moved closer to the bed as flames started licking out along its embroidery, lifting his sword to try and free Willam, but he was too late. The creature moved like a hunting cat, releasing Willam's shattered wrist and punching forward into his chest. Its fingers stabbed straight through the guard's armour and ribs as though they were twigs.

Willam was flung back through the air and slammed into the floor, panting and gasping for air, fingers clutching at the ragged hole in his chest. As flames grew thick and strong on the mattress, Mikel heard Willam's breathing falter and stop.

The creature rolled off the bed, still gathered in burning drapery, and Mikel swung his sword, trying to keep the beast in the centre of the room. If the thing rolled around too much, there was a chance it may put out the flames before they could destroy it. He sliced off pieces of flaming material from the blankets, spreading them across the room haphazardly. In the back of his mind he could hear a voice of panic telling him that the fire would consume the entire room quickly, and he should escape before he was trapped, but his anger drove him to see the creature finally dead. From inside the ball of flames that staggered across the room, an ear-splitting whistle rose, like steam rushing from a boiling kettle. Mikel stabbed into the flames again, ignoring the heat on his hands.

There was a clattering of feet behind him and he spun around, ready for anything. Four new guards were standing in the doorway, looks of shock and terror covering their faces.

CHAPITRE LXXIX

"Mercy's shield, what is going on?" yelled the first. One of the others shot back out to the hallways of the castle.

"Where's he going?" asked Mikel. His voice sounded strange to his ears. The sound of fire crackling and the strange whistling filled them. But his voice left his mouth sounding still and calm and level. He wondered why he wasn't shrieking to these guards. He turned back to the creature and saw the pile of burning drapery had stopped moving in the centre of the room.

"To get water of course!" The man who had spoken looked at Mikel as though the commander had sprouted a tree in his forehead. "Are you okay sir?" He looked at the blankets again. "Mercy, is someone in there?"

"Not anymore." A smile drifted across his face like a single white cloud on a summer's day. His sword clattered to the floor as the tightness in his muscles relaxed. He stood, swaying slightly, next to the doorway and watched in bemusement as the three guards grabbed some tapestries off the walls and began trying to beat out the flames, smothering the smaller fires wherever possible. Soon the fourth guard returned, with a few others following him. They all carried wooden buckets of water, which quickly helped douse the flames. Mikel kept smiling though. The blanket hadn't moved since they started.

One of the guards noticed Tuomas' form sprawled across the floor. She called over another guard and, as a team, they managed to lift Mikel's son up so that he was supported between them, with his arms slung over their shoulders. As they carried him past, Mikel reached out to trail his fingers through his son's hair. There was blood on the boy's scalp, but the wound didn't look too deep.

"Is he alive?"

"He's breathing sir," managed one of the guards carrying Tuomas. "But we'd better take him to find some help fast."

Mikel nodded, but the guards didn't see the movement. They were focused on managing Tuomas out of the room as quickly as they could. Mikel wondered if he should leave the room as well. He tried to take a step but his legs were watery and weak. He didn't think his legs would keep supporting him if he started walking anywhere. He knew that he would tumble to the ground the instant he began to take a step. So instead he decided to just stay where he was.

The first guard Mikel had seen was now trying to unwrap the scorched and blackened material from the body on the floor. Of course, he didn't know it was a body yet. The thought made Mikel blink and giggle softly. Soon he'd find out.

The figure revealed beneath the material was horrifically burnt, but still recognisable. Its flesh had run like wax, and much of the skin was a blistered red mess, but the shape of the face and the build of the body were clear enough.

"Sir..." The guard was stunned, his voice low. "Do you know who this is?"

"I know who it looks like. It looks like Alaks, the heir to Lord Uvaniah. But it's not him, not anymore." Mikel's throat was raw, and he had to cough and clear it after he spoke.

"And you simply stood by as the lord's heir burned to death?" The guard's voice was beginning to rise.

"No. I wasn't just standing here. I had to make sure he didn't get out. He killed our people." Mikel gestured towards the ruined body of Willam on one side of the room and Shorn's body at their feet.

"What?!" Within seconds the guards had drawn their swords and held them pointed at Mikel. The speaker kicked aside Mikel's sword from where it lay on the ground.

"Do you speak the truth? You intended for this man to burn to death?" His forehead creased as he spoke, as though the idea was crushing him.

"I intended for that thing to burn to death. It's not a man anymore." Mikel did intend to explain further but before he could the guards stepped in and grabbed his arms, twisting them painfully behind his back. The speaker sheathed his sword and spoke over the top of Mikel's words.

"You will be taken before Lord Uvaniah to answer for this treason. But for now, not a word."

"Treason? No, I was doing my-"

The guard stepped forward and grabbed Mikel's jaw, forcing his mouth to stop moving.

"I said, not a word."

Exhaustion washed through Mikel and the world slipped away from him as he passed out.

CHAPITRE LXXX

Mikel awoke laying on the stone floor of the cells deep below the castle. Weak light from candles on low tables beyond his bars outlined the space he found himself in. He had no idea how long he had been lying here, in the damp and cold, untended. He shivered and clutched his hands around his shoulders.

There was no way to track time as he lay there. He fell asleep more than once, but could not tell if he slept for minutes or hours each time. Mikel leaned in one corner against the rough stone walls of the room and thought about how he had ended up here. He had never really spent much time down in these cells before. He had always preferred to hand off any prisoners that he had caught to someone else, even when he was a new recruit to the Castle Guards. As he listened to a single infrequent drip somewhere in the shadows beyond his cell, he wondered how many people he had sent down here in the same position as he was now. How many people had justified reasons for the actions he had judged so harshly? How many had waited, shivering as he did now, wondering whether they would receive a fair hearing or be judged before they could defend themselves?

The candlelight was not enough to illuminate the space properly, and shadows swelled all around him. Sometimes Mikel heard things moving somewhere in the blackness that engulfed him. He grew hungry and thirsty by turns, but eventually his body realised that food and water were not coming and those feelings faded. In their place, a dull ache settled into his bones.

His body throbbed with the weariness of what he had been through. His shoulder ached, as did his thighs. There were stinging scrapes along the backs of his knuckles, and much of his face. Even with those reminders of his actual body, it was hard to separate the waking world in these dungeons from the dreamworld that waited behind his eyes. Visions of Alaks flailing while wrapped in burning blankets filled his mind. Were they dreams, or the reaction of his waking but exhausted mind? He could not tell. Mikel had to remind himself that the figure had not been Alaks any more. The smell of burned fabric and flesh filled his nostrils, no matter how he scrubbed his hands across his face.

When the guards came for him and dragged him out of the cells Mikel was interested to find that it was evening. He managed to catch a glimpse of a dark blue sky deepening to black through a window in one of the hallways. A single star shone back at him. *What day is it,* he wondered silently. *How long have they kept me down there?*

They shoved him through the halls of the castle, thick grimy chains fastened to manacles around his wrists and ankles. He stumbled through corridors, past servants and extended members of the various families who made Sheerwall their home. Mikel struggled not to look aside from their shocked faces, forcing himself to meet their curious stares with what he hoped was a calm expression. He wanted to keep his head up so that these casual observers might realise that he was not as traitorous as they had no doubt been told. From the scowls that met his gaze, he assumed that most of the castle's inhabitants had already made up their minds about him. His mouth was dry and his breath burned in his throat.

Whispers echoed from the stone walls around him. At first he wanted to block them out, so that he would not have to hear voices that he knew tearing him down. But then some words began to make themselves known and he realised that he was not the only gossip to be had in Sheerwall.

Snatches of conversation about Highfort reached his ears. Some said that Lord Uvaniah would offer to adopt a child from the Lord of Highfort's family, now that his heir was dead. Others spoke of a new marriage proposal, though it was unclear who in Sheerwall would take up that offer. Mikel even heard some say that Alaks had brought bad luck back from Highfort, after declining the hand of the lord's daughter. Mikel wondered if he would ever be free enough to discuss these matters with anyone.

Soon he stood before the doors to the great hall, guards on either side, their heavy hands on his shoulders. He didn't recognise either of these guards. How long had he put aside his duties as their commander? The huge wooden doors to the hall were closed firmly, though a murmur leaked through them anyway. He was very familiar with what would await him beyond these doors. The tables that usually lined the hall, providing a place to feed the everyone who lived inside the castle walls, would have been shoved to the side of the hall. Lord Uvaniah would be seated upon his high-backed ornate chair, which would have been placed on a dais that would have been erected opposite the great doors. The raised chair was never used in day to day affairs, but a hearing and judgement like this would require its formality. Mikel wondered how many people would be standing within the hall to witness this meeting.

The doors opened.

CHAPITRE LXXXI

Mikel swallowed. Row upon row of people stood, staring silently at him through the doorway. At the same time, Mikel was able to see Lord Uvaniah approach his chair. He must have entered the hall only a short time earlier, and he strode with purpose. He reached the chair and lowered himself into it, with a tall straight back and his gaze on Mikel at the doors to the hall. Mikel began hobbling forward, accompanied by the noisy clanking of his manacles, a sound that echoed back at him in the stifling silence of the hall.

When he was halfway to the lord on his dais, Mikel began to hear soft muttering from the crowd that now surrounded him. He kept his gaze forward, on the old man who waited for him, and ignored the sounds rising from the crowd. He was sure some people were spitting at their feet as he walked past, but he held his awareness away from them.

When he reached the dais, Mikel lowered himself to his knees. His joints ached from his time in the cells and the chains pulled heavily at his shoulders. He felt as old as he ever had. With an effort he raised his eyes to Lord Uvaniah.

Lord Uvaniah's face looked down at Mikel. Pain and confusion deepened the wrinkles in his aged skin. He leaned back in his chair, as though he wanted to keep as much space as he could between himself and Mikel. A stab of pain entered Mikel's heart at the thought that his friend had been so badly hurt by his actions. He wondered whether he would be able to convince the lord that he had acted properly.

"Commander Ofeli," said a woman standing next to the lord's chair. Her collar rose tall and stiff beneath her jaw and her eyes were dark and angry as she looked down at Mikel. He blinked under that glare. He didn't recognise her. Was she a new clerk for the lord? Mikel blinked and refocused on on her words as she continued speaking. This encounter was going to determine the rest of his life.

"You have been accused of treason. You were found in the heir's bedchamber, with the burned corpse of the heir wrapped in cloth. Two guards agree on this account."

Mikel lifted his head a little and opened his mouth, but was cuffed on the side of the head by one of the guards standing beside him. He closed his mouth again.

"When they asked what happened, both of these guards claim that you told them that you had killed the heir. It is very important that you think carefully before you reply to my next question."

The woman leaned forward slightly, her wide eyes bringing to mind an owl perched on the rafter of a barn, searching for mice scurrying along the floor beneath it.

"Did you kill the heir?"

Mikel heard a rush of air as everyone in the hall drew their breath and held it at once. His heart thudded behind his ribs and wondered whether that thumping noise was loud enough that even the crowd could hear his fear. He swallowed thickly. He drew a shuddering breath and then consciously slowed his breathing. Finally, he was calm enough to speak his answer.

"No."

Shouts and angry calls rang out immediately. One of the guards next to him grabbed his shoulder roughly, but the clerk standing next to Lord Uvaniah held up an arm and silence was soon restored.

"Are you saying that these guards have lied?" The clerk looked out to the hall. Mikel was sure that she was looking for the guards who had found him, ready to shift the blame to them if he was able to provide enough evidence for her.

Mikel shook his head. "No. They truly told you what they believed. But I did not kill the heir." Mikel looked up at Lord Uvaniah, trying to meet the old man's eyes. *He has to understand,* thought the commander. *I couldn't live with myself if he thinks I killed his son.* "The heir was already dead-" he began to explain.

"Yes, the guards told us this," interrupted the clerk, but Mikel continued on over the top of her.

"He was already dead when I wrapped that creature in blankets and set fire to it."

The anger that burst from the crowd behind him was a physical force that knocked Mikel forward, and he caught himself on his elbows, kneeling down before the dais. He pushed himself upright again, desperate to continue explaining himself to Lord Uvaniah.

"The castle had been infiltrated by one of the gods of the forest," he called out, unsure whether his words were being heeded. He caught the old man's eye again, addressing the lord as directly as he could. "It killed the Kirkman, and so many others, and it had found its way into our halls! It killed the heir and took over his body. I am so sorry my lord, I tried to defend this town, this castle, your son. But I failed."

"Ah yes, we are aware of this thing. Your second in command spread word amongst the castle guard to keep watch for it. He himself fought it in Blackriver, by your side."

Mikel's head lifted. With Zhon's actions to support his own, perhaps he had a chance to convince Lord Uvaniah of what had happened.

"As well as this, the guards on duty that night all attest to having chased after this thing. Is that not so guards?" The clerk's voice cut through the tumult in the hall.

A chorus of agreement rose in from the guards in attendance.

"However, you already caught that creature, did you not?" The clerk's face bore down on Mikel like the weight of Mercy's shield. Her eyes were wide, one eyebrow lifted quizzically.

"We thought we had, but-"

"Marq, was the creature caught?" She spoke without shifting her piercing eyes away from Mikel's face.

CHAPITRE LXXXII

Mikel turned his head and saw the alchemist step forward from the crowd until he stood level with Mikel. The man sighed and glanced apologetically at Mikel before lifting his eyes to the clerk.

"We still have its body in my rooms, my lady."

"Are you certain of this?"

"We are absolutely certain that the body I have is the one that was pursued three nights ago. That was one night before the commander was found over the heir's body." He stressed the word "before".

"Then why would the commander claim that the creature was still on the loose?"

Marq's jaw opened as he struggled to think of an answer to the question, his hands lifting as though they might be able to draw an answer from the air around him, but then they fell to his sides and he shook his head. "I do not know." Again, he glanced over at the commander. Mikel could see that the alchemist was sorry that he couldn't do more, but that he would not lie for Mikel either. Mikel smiled tightly and nodded at his old friend. Marq nodded back and then turned to disappear back into the angry crowd that filled the hall.

"Guards!" The clerk lifted her voice. *Her's is certainly a voice I have not heard before,* thought Mikel to himself. *Where has this woman come from?* "Did any of you see another figure causing the mayhem as suggested by the commander?"

Mikel did not look around this time. The only guards who had actually seen the creature that night had been the ones who came with him. The ones who had died in that bedroom. Silence spread in the wake of the clerk's question.

"Zhon, please step forward."

Mikel turned his head and saw his second step forward from the crowd. He had dressed in his finest clothes and he held his head tall as he looked towards the dais. Mikel wanted to smile at his friend, but Zhon never looked in his direction.

"You ordered the castle guard to be prepared for an attack by this creature, a creature that you personally fought at one time, this is correct?" asked the clerk.

"It is."

"We have heard that he claimed the creature looked like the heir, and that he was chasing it. We have also heard from the alchemist that the body of the creature you saw killed remains in his rooms."

"I have."

"Do you have anything further to add, to help us clarify what may have happened?"

Zhon's shoulders slumped briefly and he drew a slow breath before blowing it out sharply. He swallowed.

"I regret to inform my lord that the commander has shown signs of confusion recently."

"What?" Mikel yelled. The guards beside him grabbed his shoulders. "No, what are you talking about Zhon, I-"

"Be quiet." The clerk's quiet voice cut through his protestations like an arrow through a haystack. "Please continue Zhon."

"Unfortunately the commander was deeply affected by the death of his wife last year. He has not undertaken his duties as commander for most of that time. In conversations with him recently, he has been unclear on the identity of many of our guards. He has expressed anger towards Mercy. He has told me that his son did not seem to be himself anymore, and..." Zhon trailed off and finally glanced towards Mikel, not meeting his eyes. "And he thought that Alaks had something to do with the change in Tuomas."

Mikel's mouth hung open and his throat was tight. He didn't know how to begin to explain himself. Zhon was his second, they had worked together for so long. He had not thought that expressing his fears and grief could be held against him this way.

"Then you believe the commander may be confused about this as well?"

Zhon nodded.

"Thank you, you may step back."

"My lord, please," Mikel addressed Iosef Uvnaiah directly. "You know me, I would not lie about this. We have been friends for so long." Mikel wished that he could reach up to the old man and take his hands in his own. He wanted his friend to understand.

Lord Uvaniah stood. The clerk moved to step closer to him, but he waved her away and she stepped back instead, her face still. The lord strode forward and took one step down the dais but no further. His jaw was set and his shoulders firm. Tall braziers burned at either side of the dais, illuminated him before his people. He looked down along his nose to where Mikel knelt on the cobbled floor of the great hall. Mikel saw a muscle flicker at the corner of the lord's jaw, and a flash of orange light reflected from his eye. The commander's heart turned cold.

"You have been a good and loyal friend of my family and I, for many years," began the figure that Mikel had thought was Lord Uvaniah. That voice was loud and clear. "And it is those years of friendship that keep you from immediate execution at the swords of the very guards you trained to defend this castle." The man on the steps looked up to take in the guards as it spoke about them. Then it looked back down to Mikel.

"He is to be locked within the dungeons once more, but this time he is not to be brought out again. Pass him food and water through the portal of the door, and rinse his cell when the smell grows too loathsome for the guards to endure."

What looked like the lord lifted its gaze to the assembled crowd. It raised its hands in a gesture of pleading and sorrow, tilting its head. Mikel wondered if tears were rolling down those old cheeks.

CHAPITRE LXXXIII

"Forgive me for my mercy friends, but my heart is already torn in half at the loss of my son. To know that my oldest friend had died by my order is too much for a frail old man to bear. But this treachery will not go unpunished."

The crowd gathered in the hall murmured their assent. Mikel lowered his head to his hands where they lay on the floor, focusing on the feeling of the heavy iron manacles that bound them. He would have to grow used to those metal cuffs.

Mikel paid no attention to what anyone said after that. The formalities of his punishment were drawn out, and various people with a high view of themselves made speeches in sympathy and support of the man they thought was Lord Uvaniah. Then Mikel was lifted to his feet and led back to the darkness of the dungeons.

"That was not our lord," Mikel muttered to the guards beside him as they walked.

"Be quiet sir," answered a young man on his left. Mikel

risked a glance at the young man and saw a pale face with sad eyes watching him.

"You must listen to me. The thing got away from the fire somehow, and took over our Lord. We must do something about it."

Mikel yelped as a fist struck the back of his head, nearly clamping his teeth down around his tongue. The woman on the other side of him spoke angrily.

"Don't talk to the traitor Somin! He will only try to twist your mind to him!"

"I know," nodded the sad-eyed boy, looking past Mikel to the other guard.

"No, it is true! I could see in his eyes that he was no longer our Lord!" insisted the commander.

The boy sighed and his eyebrows drooped. "But you said that you killed the monster, while it was wrapped in a blanket and set ablaze. There is no way it could have escaped."

Was that true? The thought flashed through Mikel's brain like lightning, leaving a scorching pain in its wake. *Could I have been wrong about what happened with the heir? But he had not been the heir anymore, he had attacked me!*

"Unless you were lying about that part, and you did kill the heir," snarled the woman behind him. "Which means you would have killed a young man and let a monster go roaming the castle at its pleasure."

"No, I didn't, I..." Mikel could hear the confusion in his own voice as he strained to explain himself, and so he let his mouth close. Had he so endangered the castle? Could he have been so wrong?

"Best stay quiet now sir," encouraged the boy, and so Mikel walked where he was bidden, without another word.

The pair directed him through the halls and back down to the black cells under the castle. He was shackled to a wall he could not see and then the door behind him was locked with a heavy thunk. *Is this the same room I was in before,* Mikel asked himself. *But it doesn't matter which room they have put me in. I will never leave this room now.*

He leaned against the door's bars, listening to the soft sound of the guards' footsteps leaving him alone in the darkness.

What did I do, he thought as the silence spread around him. *Did I kill my friend's son? Did I get it wrong?* The memory of Lord Uvaniah's face, crumpled in pain, was the last thing that hovered before Mikel's eyes.

THE END

Keep informed of any new writing by Aaron, by signing up for his Mailing List at: bit.ly/3kLKaaG

ACKNOWLEDGMENTS

On the internet there is a sort of competition called Nanowrimo, which is short for National Novel Writing Month. It is an international event now, but the name stuck after the first few years. Basically it asks participants to spend all of November writing a novel. A novel for this purpose is defined as 50,000 words, no questions asked. A good friend of mine and I gave it a go many many years ago and I managed to successfully type out 50,000 words in 30 days! Of course, a lot of those words were notes and ideas, and mostly they read awfully, but that was the first draft of this story.

That draft sat on my computer for probably about a decade before I pulled it out and had a look at it recently. I thought that there were some interesting ideas in there that I still wanted to visit, and so I spent a long time polishing this all up and getting it ready to present to you. I also ended up pretty much doubling that initial draft. I really hope you enjoyed it!

There are a lot of people to thank for their help and inspiration in completing this novel.

This novel was edited by my mother, which was a particularly heart stopping thing for me to do! My mum has always been a huge support to me, in every part of my life. But she is also not afraid to point out the things that I do wrong! So letting her go through this manuscript and find all the flaws and mistakes was a big step to take. I am so grateful for her help with this book.

Always a huge thanks to Steff for her help and inspiration and chats about books. You can check out her books at www.steffanieholmes.com

My regular editor Kat, I want to say that I hope this wasn't as depressing as you feared it might be, but also I hope it had an emotional impact anyway!

I'm always grateful to anyone who read one of my books or stories and then decided to come along with me and read some more. Thank you.

And lastly, all the love in the world to my wife Andy who fights my inherent desire to relax in order to push me through to the end of a big project like this!

ABOUT THE AUTHOR

Aaron Dick is a teacher living north of Auckland in New Zealand with his wife, their two daughters, and a small menagerie of household animals. They all love when his eldest daughter visits too.

He grew up as a voracious reader of science-fiction and fantasy, often to the annoyance of his unheeded family. Becoming an author was a childhood dream, alongside being a palaeontologist, or a rock star.

His stories have featured in a collection of New Zealand short stories inspired by Grimms' Fairy Tales, the gothic art and lifestyle magazine Nocturne and the online literary journal Headland.

You can keep informed of any new writing by Aaron, by signing up for his Mailing List at: bit.ly/3kLKaaG

You can also find him on Facebook at: fb.me/AaronDickNZ